Cha

Sofa time!

I pressed down on the .... p of women with designer-label .... ;antly raised in the air in an attempt to ...... he repeated pings on my phone that were supposed to alert me to would-be customers. I'd made enough today to pay my bills so I was on my way home to put my feet up. The joys of being self-employed. I can clock off when I want and, darn it, that's exactly what I was going to do.

I turned up the music and grinned happily to myself. If I took the right roads I could be home in fifteen minutes. Then I slammed on the brakes, almost giving myself whiplash in the process.

A red-robed witch was standing at the corner up ahead. Hello... I pulled up alongside her and rolled down the window. 'Where to?'

'I thought you weren't going to stop,' she said with surprise. 'I'm heading to the Order headquarters.' She looked at me nervously as if she were expecting me to decline politely. She obviously didn't recognise me, but I wasn't anti-witch. Far from it: I used to avoid the Order like the plague but things are different these days.

'Excellent!' I beamed. 'Hop in.'

She clambered awkwardly into the back, the flaps of her robe almost getting caught in the door. She tugged at them, finally managed to pull them inside with her and we took off.

'It's a bit late, isn't it?' I enquired.

She gazed at me blankly in the rear-view window. 'Huh?'

'For work,' I said helpfully. 'It's a bit late for work.'

She scratched at her arm. 'I'm on call.' There was a pause. 'It's a confidential matter.'

I almost snorted. I didn't give two hoots why she was on her way to work at this hour. Nonsensically, the Order still keeps its machinations to itself as much as it possibly can; if they want to hide away from the real world, that's up to them. I was just trying to make conversation. Frankly, I prefer the more taciturn customer. Sometimes, making the effort to discuss the weather or politics or whatever is just a pain in the arse.

I took the back roads, avoiding the rush-hour traffic, and dropped her off right in front of Runic Magic. Another witch was waiting outside and ambled over to get in my taxi. I pretended not to see him and took off down the campus road before he could open the door, keeping my eyes peeled as I went.

I knew I was being silly; perhaps I was even verging towards the obsessive. I wasn't stalking Winter though, I reasoned. I just happened to have had a customer who wanted to go this way. It was just coincidence.

Perhaps if I told myself that often enough it would become true.

I stopped again, this time outside the squat grey building of Arcane Branch. Due to the late hour, there weren't many lights on inside and I wasn't going to wait for long. But if Adeptus Exemptus Raphael Winter, with his lapis-lazuli eyes which could stop a herd of stampeding women in their tracks, happened to be finishing work around this hour...

I drummed my fingers on the steering wheel. He had his own car. He didn't need a taxi. But if he came out, it would be impolite not to say hello to him. After all, we had worked together very closely last month. *Very* closely.

Now that the binding that magically tied us together had been removed, I was no longer required to stay near him. I no longer had to work with him. But the man had an irritating way of sneaking unbidden into my thoughts, which had nothing to do with magic and everything to do with the hot, zippy kick of sheer lust. And maybe something more, which I was trying not to think about too much.

STAR WITCH

THE LAZY GIRL'S GUIDE TO MAGIC

Book Two

BY

HELEN HARPER

For Audra, Sonny, Jo and David -
my fellow Friday night Survivor mates

Hallowed Order of Magical Enlightenment Hierarchy
First Level

- Neophyte
- Zelator
- Theoricus
- Practicus
- Philosophus

Second Level

- Adeptus Minor
- Adeptus Major
- Adeptus Exemptus

Third Level

- Magister Templi
- Magus
- Ipsissimus

I'd not seen or heard from Winter since he'd abandoned my bed at great speed after our rather inebriated visit to the karaoke bar. I shouldn't have cared about that. But I did.

Another light flicked off inside the building and I held my breath. A minute or two later, an older witch with a heavy gait shuffled out of the main doors, followed by three younger ones. All of them looked tired. The Hallowed Order of Magical Enlightenment certainly demands its pound of flesh.

I couldn't help wondering what they were working on. It wasn't really my business, not any longer. I didn't want to end my working days feeling like those witches obviously did. I just wasn't that kind of person. All the same, there was no denying my flicker of curiosity.

Five minutes went by. Then ten. I sighed. This was ridiculous; either Winter was inside and still working – and would be for some time yet – or he had already left. Waiting out here was pointless. In any case, if he didn't want to see me then I could hardly force the matter.

I shook my head at my own idiocy just as another witch emerged from the building. This one I recognised. I jumped out of the car and waved. 'Eve!'

My long-limbed neighbour blinked in surprise but she smiled and wandered over. 'Good to see you, Ivy. What brings you to this part of town?'

I twiddled with a loose blonde curl. 'Oh,' I said in an overly casual tone, 'I had a customer headed this way. I thought I'd come by in case you were around and needed a lift home.'

Eve's smooth brow furrowed. 'I have a car. I thought you knew that.'

I did. Of course I did. 'Er...'

'But if you're looking for some company, I can come with you.' She peered at me anxiously, as if worried. 'It'll save on petrol and then I can take the bus in tomorrow morning.'

I winced internally. Eve was such a nice person that she'd actually do that but it was hardly fair. Waving my hand dismissively, I smiled. 'Oh no, there's no need for that. It's only because I'm in the area that I dropped by.'

Given how little I'd seen of her lately, I reckoned she was keeping very long hours. I didn't think that the buses were even running when she left for work these days and I certainly wasn't filled with urgent desire to get up at that time to drive her back here. I couldn't understand how anyone who wasn't short of a million brain cells would want to get up so early. Each to their own, though.

For her part, Eve seemed relieved. 'I have to make a quick house call on my way home anyway,' she confided. 'It's for this new assignment I'm on.'

I pasted on a disinterested look. 'Oh yes?'

'There's a group of non-Order witches who've been causing a few waves. My mentor wants me to have a chat to one of them and try to get them to cool things.'

Eve's mentor was originally supposed to be Winter but instead she'd been assigned to someone else. I nibbled on my bottom lip. 'How are things going with your mentor?'

'She's great.' Eve smiled. 'I'm learning so much, Ivy, and it's so much fun.'

Fun? We clearly had different definitions for that word. Vegging out on the sofa is fun; fourteen-hour days with a bunch of Order geeks are not. 'And are there other new witches with you?' I asked. 'New to Arcane Branch?'

Eve pressed her lips together as if to avoid giggling. Darn it. She knew exactly why I was here. 'Adeptus Exemptus Winter still hasn't taken on a new partner.'

'I wasn't ... I mean, I didn't...' Arse. I sighed and yielded to the truth. 'How's he doing?'

'I could give you his phone number and you could ask him your-self,' she suggested with the serene maturity of someone who didn't have an almost soul-destroying crush to deal with. 'Or I could tell him you were here and...'

'No!' The last thing I wanted was for Winter to think I'd been hanging around in the vain hope of seeing him – whether it was true or not. And if I called him and he didn't want to speak to me I'd feel even worse. He had told me we should forget our night together had ever happened. Anyway, we didn't have anything in common. I had to stop mooning after him and get on with my life. I wasn't a lovesick teenager, even if I felt that way.

'I better get going,' I said hastily. 'Brutus will be wonder-ing where I am.'

Eve grinned. 'Sure, Ivy. If you change your mind, let me know.'

I nodded distractedly. 'I'll see you around.'

I waited as Eve headed off towards the car park then turned back to my taxi. I was going home to order a curry, crack open a bottle of wine and not think about Raphael Winter. Not once.

I turned on the engine, forgetting that my For Hire light was still on. Before I'd even put the taxi into gear, someone had opened the door and got into the back. 'I'm off the clock,' I grunted.

'It's good to see you too, Ivy,' Tarquin's smooth voice murmured.

I gritted my teeth. This was why I should have stuck to my in-stincts and stayed as far away from the Order as possible. If I'd had anything to do with it, my floppy-haired foe would have been hung, drawn and quartered for his machinations to get rid of Eve. She'd let his meddling pass, however, believing he deserved a second chance.

'Get out, Tarquin.'

'Your light is on.'

I switched it off. 'No, it's not.' I turned my head and gave him a hard look. Unlike the other witches I'd seen tonight, he appeared as rested and unruffled as it was possible to be. 'Piss off.'

In response, Tarquin clicked his seatbelt into place. I rolled my eyes. Why me? I flicked my fingers into a simple rune and the seatbelt immediately undid itself.

Tarquin tutted. 'Now, now. The law is very clear, Ivy. I'm a paying customer and you have to take me to where I want to go. Otherwise,' he shook his head in dismay, 'I'll be forced to make a formal complaint against you.'

Seriously? 'Tarquin, don't be a complete plonker. Just get out of my taxi.'

He folded his arms. 'No.' He met my eyes. 'I'm not lying, Ivy. Either you take me to where I want to go or I will complain.' He smirked. 'In writing.'

I wondered whether he really thought that was supposed to scare me. 'I think I'll cope,' I said drily. 'I'm going home.'

'Perfect.' His smile grew, revealing whiter-than-white teeth that must have cost a pretty penny. 'So am I.' He leaned forward. 'And now we live in the same building so you have no reason not to drive me there.'

I stared at him. 'Pardon?'

'I've moved.'

'To my building?'

'Yes.'

'You're lying.'

He gestured towards me with open palms. 'Why would I do that? I'm on the fourth floor. Flat C.'

The family who'd been living there had indeed moved out last month. I gazed at him with narrowed eyes. Tarquin never did anything without a reason – and that reason always served his own interests. The building where Eve and I live is lovely, but old-money people like Tarquin don't live there. It is neither pretentious, nor stupidly expensive nor up-and-coming. 'Have you fallen on hard times?' I could only hope.

He laughed. 'Don't be ridiculous. Father just thought it was time that I stopped relying on the family. I'm striking out on my own.'

I watched him carefully. I doubted that was all there was to it. The more I thought about it, the more it seemed likely that his new address was about giving the appearance that he was an everyman in the hope that the Order seniors would look favourably upon him.

After the kerfuffle and corruption surrounding Order promotions, they probably wanted to make it very clear to the world that their system was based purely on merit. They didn't want to be seen promoting someone from a wealthy, well-connected family. Affirmative action, Order style. Tarquin was slumming it because he was worried that his privileged position wouldn't permit him to get to Second Level until the dust settled. It probably didn't hurt that he'd moved to the same building where Eve lived, given that she'd already been promoted beyond him.

'Where's your car?' I asked. He prided himself on showy numbers that wouldn't look out of place on a racetrack. There was no way he'd have given up whatever swanky vehicle he was currently driving. His postcode, maybe. His car? Never.

'It's in the garage.' He wrinkled his nose. 'I may have wrapped it round a tree last weekend.'

I wasn't even slightly surprised. 'Plonker,' I dismissed.

He didn't argue with me, he simply leaned forward, a familiar smile tugging at his mouth. When I was a teenager, he'd managed to get me to do just about anything he wanted with that expression. But I wasn't a teenager any more.

'Come on, Ivy. I want to talk to you so let's make bygones be bygones. We could be friends again.' He placed a certain emphasis on the word 'friends' which made me grimace in disgust.

'Been there, done that, got expelled,' I said.

He leaned back and shrugged as if it were entirely my loss. 'Fine, then. But you will drive me home. I really do want to talk to you.'

Tarquin was probably enjoying the chance to order me around. As tempting as it was to turf him out, it was more tempting to take his money. It wasn't as if I had to go out of my way to get it either.

I pursed my lips. Fine. There was no way I was going to put up with his inane chatter for the whole journey back, however. I sketched out another rune, putting up an invisible barrier between him and myself. It would effectively block out any noise and I could drive home in peace. I'd already tortured myself enough for one day.

***

When we finally pulled up outside my block of flats, Tarquin's lips were still moving. I didn't think he'd stopped talking for more than a few seconds during the entire journey. I congratulated myself on my forward planning and released the spell.

'...and that's when I told him he was wrong,' he said with a dramatic flourish.

'Excellent,' I murmured. 'That's fifty quid.'

He looked startled. 'How much?'

'Fifty quid,' I repeated, silently adding on a tax for the benefit of customers like him who annoyed me.

Tarquin shrugged and handed over the money. I wasn't surprised that there wasn't a tip; in my experience the wealthier the customer, the less generous they were likely to be. It made me feel less guilty about charging him far more than I should have.

I got out of the car. Tarquin didn't move. Tapping my foot, I glared at him through the window. 'Get a move on then.'

He looked startled. I wondered whether he'd been waiting for me to open the door for him like some kind of private chauffeur. As if. Belatedly getting the message that I wasn't going to bow and scrape, he pushed the door open himself and got out. I locked up the taxi and spun away. My duty was done.

'So did I do the right thing?' he asked, calling out from behind me.

I ignored him and picked up my pace. He had to get the message sooner or later.

'Ivy...'

I marched ahead. Unfortunately, Tarquin's legs were far longer than mine and I'm rather unused to moving quickly. He caught up within seconds, grabbing my elbow and swinging me around. 'Get your hands off me,' I hissed.

He dropped them as if he'd been burned. 'Sorry,' he muttered. 'But I do value your opinion. Just let me know what you think and I'll leave you in peace.'

Obviously I still hadn't the faintest idea what he'd been wittering on about. I sighed. 'Yeah, sure. You did the right thing.'

He looked relieved, which surprised me. 'Really? That's great.' He took a step forward and gazed down at me. 'Thank you.' For a moment he seemed sincere then he reverted abruptly to type. 'You could come up to my place and I'll show you my gratitude in person,' he purred, drawing even closer. He reached up and brushed the back of his hand against my cheek, his touch feather-light.

Ick. Ick. Ick. My fingers itched to draw a rune that would teach him never to come near me again. Instead I told myself to stay calm and coyly looked up at him through my eyelashes. I pushed onto my tiptoes until we were nose to nose. 'Tarquin,' I breathed.

He tilted his head, his hair falling across one eye, and deepened his own voice to a husk. 'Yes, Ivy?'

'I think I've made it clear,' I said softly, 'that I despise you. Don't ever come near me again. Don't get in my taxi, don't even say hello to me in passing if we meet in the corridor. I'm a far better witch than you and if you bother me again, you'll regret it.'

I never got chance to hear his response. There was a loud cough from behind us. Somehow I knew who it belonged to without check- ing.

I turned round slowly. It was even worse than I thought.

Before I could say anything Tarquin, with wide eyes and a de- lighted expression, all but bowed. 'Ipsissimus Collings! How won- derful of you to call on me at my new abode! And you brought along Adeptus Exemptus Winter. It's a pleasure to see you both.'

I had the feeling that the Ipsissimus was looking at Tarquin as if he were trying to remember who he was, but I wasn't paying the Or- der Head much attention. All my focus was on Winter. Unfortunate- ly, his expression was completely unreadable. He was also wearing a red robe, suggesting he was here on official business rather than for a social call, which didn't exactly fill me with the joy that his presence should have.

'Villeneuve, is it?' the Ipsissimus asked. He looked at Tarquin in confusion. 'Aren't you the one who was assaulted by Ms Wilde?'

'That was years ago!' Tarquin burbled happily. He put his arm round my shoulders as if to prove that we were the best of friends now, before abruptly remembering my threat of just seconds earlier and hastily removing it. 'Why don't we go upstairs? I have the most wonderful twenty-year-old malt that I'm sure you'll love.'

'Actually, we are here to speak to Ms Wilde.'

Tarquin blinked rapidly. 'What?' He coughed. 'I mean, of course! What have you done now, Ivy? Been getting into mischief again?' I glared at him. With the looming presence of the Ipsissimus, however, Tarquin barely noticed. 'I'll walk up with you. Maybe you can come and partake of some whisky when you're finished with her.'

Winter's jaw was set. 'We are very busy. Run along now.' There was no mistaking the patronising edge to his tone. I could have hugged him. I *should* have hugged him.

Tarquin looked at the Ipsissimus as if expecting him to disagree but when the Order Head simply knitted his hands together and stayed quiet, he inclined his head and started walking away. Even I could tell that he was dragging his feet. His curiosity about their visit was greater than his respect for their positions and he obviously wanted to eavesdrop.

I eyed the pair of them. 'Do you want to go inside?'

For the first time, the Ipsissimus smiled. 'Thank you, Ms Wilde. That would be prudent. We don't anyone eavesdropping on our conversation. Why don't you lead the way?'

I nodded once, feeling surprisingly awkward. I didn't have the faintest idea what the pair of them were doing here but I doubted it was going to be because Winter wanted to take me to bed and smother me in kisses while the Ipsissimus had tagged along merely to give his blessing to our coupling. The idea did amuse me, though.

I turned and headed for the main doors, veering round to call the lift more out of habit than conscious action. Winter immediately sighed as if irritated. I glanced at him. 'Would you rather take the stairs?'

It was the Ipsissimus who answered. 'Oh my goodness, no. My bones have become remarkably creaky of late. That's what happens when you get to my age. You young folks have all that joy to look forward to. Frankly, it's a blessing to have some technology to help me get around. In my Order dwelling, of course, there's nothing like this. One day we'll find a way to combine twenty-first century advances with ancient magic but I don't expect it will be in my lifetime.'

He was being remarkably verbose, not to mention friendly. It didn't appear that I was going to be clapped in chains for abusing magic outside of the Order or anything like that. Intrigued now, I gestured to them both as the lift doors opened and then followed them in.

The lift is rather small and cramped so I was forced to stand very close to Winter. I brushed against him, by accident rather than by design. He flinched and drew away and my heart dropped down to my toes. Well, I guessed that answered one question.

I kept my eyes trained dead ahead, relieved when we reached my floor and I could step out and give him some space. In stiff silence, the three of us walked down the hallway to my flat.

Brutus was lying flat on his back on the sofa, all four paws in the air and his immense belly on show. He opened a lazy, slitted eye as we entered. 'Man,' he said. 'Good.'

I cleared my throat. 'Ipsissimus Collings, this is my familiar.'

The Order Head stared at Brutus. 'Yes, Adeptus Winter did tell me about him. I must confess I didn't quite believe him. A talking cat! How extraordinary.' He walked over and addressed Brutus. 'May I sit here?'

Brutus ignored him.

I licked my lips. 'Please do sit. Can I get you anything to drink? I have, um, water.' I hadn't been shopping for a while and I wasn't sure whether the milk was still drinkable.

'No, thank you.' The Ipsissimus carefully lowered himself, making sure not to disturb Brutus in any way.

I glanced at Winter. He'd shoved his hands in his pockets and was looking rather bored. 'Would you like a drink?' I asked him.

He shook his head and sat down on the chair opposite. I took up position on the other end of the sofa. Brutus rolled over onto his front and began batting at the edge of the Ipsissimus's cuff. Then he lashed out, scratching his hand and drawing blood.

Arse. 'Sorry!' I leapt up and grabbed Brutus, whose tail was swinging violently from side to side. 'He's not always good with strangers.' He struggled in my arms, wriggling free so he could immediately jump up onto Winter's lap. We all watched as he turned round twice and then curled up and went straight back to sleep. I scratched my neck. Okay.

The Ipsissimus exchanged a look with Winter then focused back on me. 'The reason we are here, Ms Wilde, is to ask for your help.'

I started. Of all the things I'd been expecting, this certainly wasn't one of them. I slowly closed my hanging jaw and told myself to reserve judgment for now. I sat down again cautiously but I didn't lean back; I'd make a run for it if I had to. Brutus would just have to look after himself. 'Go on.'

'Adeptus Winter was most effusive in his praise of you. Despite the circumstance under which you were thrown together last month, he holds you in high regard.'

I couldn't help my smile from blossoming but, when I looked at Winter, his gaze was fixed on a spot on the far wall. Why the hell wouldn't he look at me?

'We worked well together and solved some serious crimes.' I paused. 'But I still don't want to be in the Order.'

The Ipsissimus chuckled. 'Oh, that's not why we're here. Don't worry.' He leaned forward slightly, shifting his hands as he did so. He was still bleeding from Brutus's unwarranted attack. That wasn't a particularly good sign, despite the warmth currently emanating from him. 'Tell me, have you heard of *Enchantment*?'

I stared at him, wondering whether I had heard him correctly. 'The television programme?'

He nodded in satisfaction. 'That's right. I'm told it's rather popular.'

Popular? It had been the highest-rated show across the country for years. I hadn't missed a single episode. A sudden thought occurred to me and I sat up straighter.

'If you're looking for someone to watch it carefully for signs of potentially powerful witches, I'm your man. Or woman. Or whatever. I should tell you that the majority of their contestants have very little magic. It's more about their interaction and the situations they're put in than what spells they manage to cast. But I'm prepared to let you pay me to watch it. It'll be hard,' I said, 'but if it'll help you out, I'm prepared to make that sacrifice.'

Winter snorted. 'We're not going to pay you to sit on your arse and watch television, Ivy.'

Shame. I met his bluer-than-blue eyes. 'It was worth a try.'

'Yes, because you wouldn't put in an effort for anything else, would you?'

The castigating nature of his words hurt. I crossed my arms and looked at him in confusion. Winter was a lot of things but he was never callous or mean. Even the Ipsissimus seemed rather shocked.

Somewhat belatedly, Winter appeared to realise he'd gone too far. 'Sorry,' he muttered.

'Yes, well,' the Ipsissimus coughed. 'The thing is that the producers of *Enchantment* are planning a new series. Instead of twelve would-be witches in London, they're going for some kind of wilderness expedition. They've already selected their participants but during pre-production on location one of them met a rather, well, unsavoury end.'

I ripped my gaze away from Winter and tried to focus. 'One of them is dead?'

'Alas, yes. And under highly suspicious circumstances. This was not a natural end.'

I sucked in a breath. 'That's terrible. I imagine you're concerned about it because you believe magic was involved?'

The Ipsissimus grimaced. 'There are no primary traces. Benjamin Alberts, the poor man who died, was essentially ripped apart and found strewn halfway across a moor.'

I winced. That sounded nasty. 'No primary traces,' I said slowly, thinking about what he'd said. 'But there are secondary suggestions of magic?'

The Ipsissimus nodded. 'Whoever killed him didn't use magic but they'd recently come into contact with it. The residue was faint but definitely there.'

I tried hard not to think about who would tear a living, breathing, human person apart. 'What do the police say?'

'They don't believe there's enough evidence that magic was involved to call us in. Neither do they have any evidence to suggest the death is connected to the television show.'

I absorbed this. Without direct evidence of any spells, the Order wouldn't automatically be involved in the investigation and couldn't demand to be part of it. Somehow I didn't think this sat well with the Ipsissimus.

He continued. 'The production company behind *Enchantment* wields considerable power. They have connections in high places and they've pulled some strings to be allowed to continue with the show. They already have a replacement for Benjamin Alberts and are all set to begin filming next week.'

'We put in a request,' Winter said, 'for an Order representative to be present at all times to ensure the safety of the other contestants. Even though they don't appear to possess enough magic ability to enter the Order, the rest of the country doesn't see it like that.'

'If more of them die, then the Order will be blamed,' I said slowly. 'Because they're supposedly witches.'

'Indeed.' A muscle in Winter's jaw throbbed. 'It will reflect very poorly on us. Not to mention that we don't want more of them to die.'

Well, yes, I supposed there was that too. 'Let me guess,' I said drily. 'The company has refused your request. They don't want anyone from the Order messing with their most popular programme.'

'You have grasped the situation accurately, Ms Wilde,' said the Ipsissimus. 'We cannot afford any more bad press right now. We'll be blamed for not acting sooner if there are further deaths but we are not being permitted to investigate the first one, or to be present to guard against any more. The large audience that this programme apparently commands means that this is a situation that merits close attention. We need someone who is not associated with the Order to go undercover and find out exactly what's going on.'

A slow thrill descended down my spine. 'Me.'

Winter shifted slightly, causing Brutus to growl in his lap. 'You will do nothing other than report back. You will be there to observe and nothing else.'

'Just watch what's going on?' I grinned. 'I can do that.' In fact it seemed right up my alley. Besides, just because one contestant had met an untimely death didn't mean there would be more. It might just be bad luck. Very bad luck, admittedly.

Before Winter could comment yet again on what he believed to be my lazy nature, the Ipsissimus spoke up. 'We do appreciate it. You are the perfect candidate, Ms Wilde. You fully understand the nature of magic but you have no current affiliation with the Order. Even if your past history with us is discovered, no one will have reason to think you are working for us.'

'Because first I was expelled and then I was forced to work for you against my will,' I said.

The Ipsissimus inclined his head. 'Just so.' He met my eyes. 'Will you help us?'

'Sure. It doesn't sound too hard.' I glanced at Winter. 'I can put in the effort.'

He looked away. The Ipsissmus clapped his hands. 'Excellent. I knew we could count on you.' He checked his watch. 'I shall leave Adeptus Winter to go through all the details with you. Unfortunately, I must take my leave.'

We all stood up. Even Brutus seemed keen to act politely, although he still watched the Ipsissimus depart with narrowed eyes. Apparently deciding that he needed to make sure that the Order

Head was definitely leaving, he stretched before following him out to the corridor.

Then the door closed and Winter and I were alone.

Chapter Two

For several seconds after the Ipsissimus left, neither of us said anything. The silence lengthened, filling the atmosphere with a heavy, uncomfortable feeling.

'How have you been?' Winter asked eventually.

'Good.' I hesitated. 'You?'

'Good.'

There was more awkward silence. I scratched my neck and sighed. This could be going better. 'How's Princess Parma Periwinkle?' I asked, referring to Winter's daftly named familiar.

'Fine. Although she will be staying behind in Oxford for the duration of this investigation. She doesn't travel well.'

'Mmm.' I racked my brains for something else to say. 'Have you changed jobs?' I enquired finally. Winter's brow furrowed. 'You used to deal with stolen property. Murder seems an entirely different proposition.'

He raised his shoulders in a vague shrug. 'I was reassigned. Obviously I'm still in Arcane Branch but, given that our assignment together involved the death of an Adeptus Exemptus and we managed to solve the case...'

'...then,' I finished for him, 'your superiors have seen your abilities and granted you an even more prestigious position.' He nodded while I arched an eyebrow. 'Are you being groomed for Department Head?' To be in charge of Arcane Branch was to enjoy heady heights indeed.

Winter tapped his foot. 'There are many talented witches in Arcane Branch. And it doesn't look like Magus Phelps is retiring any time soon. I'm still only Second Level, Ivy.'

'Plenty of Department Heads are Second Level.'

'Not Arcane Branch.'

I pursed my lips. 'So you're looking to move up to Third Level?' It was the highest any witch could go. I had no doubt that Winter would achieve it sooner or later, regardless of his relatively young age.

'Are you suggesting that I shouldn't?' His tone was cool. 'Ambition isn't a disease, you know.'

I held up my hands. 'Heavens forbid I would think such a thing. I think you'd be a good Department Head, Rafe.' I used his first name deliberately just to see how he'd react. There was nothing more than a faint flicker in his eyes. 'And I'm sure your skills are more than up to the task.' He watched me as if he thought I were somehow taking the piss.

Unsure how we'd reached this point, I half grimaced. 'Are you sure you don't want anything to drink?'

'Do you have tequila?' There was an odd note in his voice. I hardly needed reminding that tequila was what we'd both been drinking before we ended up in bed together.

I sucked in a breath. 'I don't have any. But I can go out and get some if you...'

He forestalled me. 'It was a joke, Ivy. I'm fine.'

I laughed unconvincingly.

Winter sat back down on the same chair, took out a manila folder and opened it up. 'Despite the production company's recalcitrance,' he said formally, 'we have managed to procure you a position via one of the recruitment agencies they use. You will be working for them for the duration of filming.'

The thought of being on set for *Enchantment* was almost enough to make me forget the strange awkwardness between us. I had sudden visions of operating a camera or snapping a clapboard and yelling 'Action!' It might be work but it also sounded fun.

I grinned in delight and shook out my hair. 'I'm ready for my close-up, Mr de Winter.'

He gave me a blank look. 'You will be a runner with duties involving—'

Whoa. Hold on a minute. I interrupted him. 'What did you say?'

'You'll be a runner.'

My shoulders slumped. 'That was what I thought I heard.' I shook my head. 'I don't think myself and running go together.' I raised my eyebrows pointedly. 'You should know that.'

Winter sighed. 'You won't actually be running. It's an entry-level position, which is all we could get you with your lack of experience. You'll mostly be completing errands for the crew. It works out very well because it means you'll have plenty of reasons to be in all sorts of places. You can get to know everyone on set and you'll be well placed to discover any anomalies.'

'I'm afraid I'm still focused on the word runner.'

'Ivy...'

'What?'

He pressed his lips into a line. 'You'll be fine.'

I wasn't so sure of that. 'There must be something else I could do.'

'There's not.' He checked the sheet in front of him. 'You will report each morning at 5am.' I began to splutter but Winter completely ignored me and carried on. 'Your contracted hours will run until 6pm.'

'That's thirteen hours!'

'You get a break for lunch,' he informed me, as if that made all the difference.

'Thirteen, Winter! I know you don't believe in superstitions but come on! You need to get that changed.'

'You can finish at 7pm if you prefer. Sometimes there will be night shoots so you may well be expected to stay for longer.'

'No way. I'm not doing it.'

He looked up. 'Are you complaining that you have to work for thirteen hours or that you have to work?'

'It's slave labour!' I protested. 'No one should have to work for that length of time. Even Order geeks probably don't...' My voice faltered when I saw the expression on his face. I gritted my teeth. 'Fine.' I'd just have to seek out a quiet corner where I could snooze for a few hours each afternoon. If all I was doing was 'running', that shouldn't be too hard.

Winter took out two pieces of paper. 'Here are Benjamin Albert's details. It's your job to find out more about him and whether his death is connected to the show itself or to anything magical. If you can find evidence of the latter, the Order can get involved. You'll also need to keep any eye out for any suspicious behaviour, particularly involving the remaining contestants. We can't have anyone else getting hurt. Check out the crew. I have details here about all of them and basic information on their backgrounds. We've not uncovered anything worrying yet – but that doesn't mean it doesn't exist.'

I stared at him. 'I assume you want me to have time to eat and breathe as well.'

'Don't be facetious.' He pointed to yet another piece of paper. There was a photograph in the right-hand corner. I craned my neck, catching a glimpse of a man in his thirties and who was wearing a witch's hat of all things. I grinned. I knew instantly who he was.

'This is Trevor Bellows,' Winter explained. 'He's the magical consultant for the show. Any spells are run through him and he'll sniff you out in a second if you're not careful.'

'I know. I'm a fan of the show, remember?'

'Indeed. Do you know his background?'

I thought about it. Nope. He was obviously not much of a witch or he'd be in the Order rather than working for *Enchantment*. He'd always struck me as more of an actor than a magician.

Taking my silence as an answer, Winter continued. 'This is his official background story, which was released by the production company several years ago. He's not an Order witch and never has been, so we have no way of knowing what his actual abilities are.'

I put aside the long list of orders from Winter for now and focused on Bellows, glancing down at his meagre biography. 'He grew up in Tibet? Seriously?'

'His story is that his parents were seconded there by the British government.'

I looked up. 'You don't believe it?'

Winter's lip curled. 'We have traced him so far to Slough. It appears that the nearest he's been to Tibet is getting his photo taken with a yak at a local petting zoo.'

Hmmm. 'I'm not convinced he possesses much magical ability. I've seen him perform a few spells in previous series but they never really amounted to much.'

'As I said, we have no idea what he's capable of. I don't think he can do much either but, until we know otherwise, you should assume that he's dangerous and has a battery of abilities and knowledge at his fingertips. He has, after all, been the main consultant for *Enchantment* for years. There must be something to his claims.'

I frowned. 'The target audience isn't witches. All the magic is fairly low-level stuff which is designed to provoke loud whistles and create big bangs but isn't really anything of substance. The challenges don't require much in the way of magic knowledge either.' I tapped my mouth thoughtfully. 'For example, the big show-stopper last season when it came down to the final two contestants was to create a spell to make as many people as possible stop in their tracks and watch. One contestant designed a light show that failed epically because it was high noon and there was too much sunshine for it to make an impact. Most of what she created was simply enhanced fireworks. The other one turned the Thames pink.' I shrugged. 'It was more of a murky purple really.'

Winter blinked at me. 'And you actually watch this? Regularly?'

'It's not about the magic,' I said earnestly. 'People want to see showy shebangs but they prefer it when the contestants fail spectacularly and when they fall out with each other. It's about making good television, not about who can create the best spells, regardless of what the producers might want you to think. It's highly entertaining. You should watch it. In any case, there's not enough evidence from the programmes themselves to suggest what Trevor Bellows can do.'

'Well,' Winter said with a dismissive grunt, 'there will be plenty of opportunity for spectacular failures and fallings-out in the Highlands of Scotland.'

'That's where the expedition is happening?'

He nodded. 'I'm still working on a way to regularly debrief you.' He reached into his pocket and took out a neatly folded map. Jabbing at what looked like a massive mountain, he started to explain. 'Most of the filming is taking place here but there's a small village where the crew will be based.' Winter squinted. 'Tomintoul. It looks like it's pretty.'

'It looks like it's in the middle of nowhere.'

'It is supposed to be the wilderness, Ivy.'

I wrinkled my nose. I'd been hoping for the sort of wilderness that involved a tropical island with swaying palm trees and butlers carrying multi-coloured drinks with mini-parasols in them. Up a freezing mountain in the Scottish Highlands didn't sound like my kind of thing.

'Anyway,' Winter continued, 'in Tomintoul, there's a small square. Each night, at the stroke of midnight, we will meet there and you can tell me what you've discovered.'

'Wait a minute,' I said slowly. 'You want me to start work at 5am. As a runner. I'll be on duty for thirteen hours. And then you expect me to come and find you at midnight?' My voice was getting higher and higher.

'It's the safest way.' He checked the map again. 'Everyone else will be tired out and sleeping by that time, so there's no chance you'll be seen.'

'*I'll* be tired out! *I'll* need to sleep!' I shook my head. 'Nope. I've changed my mind. Get the Ipsissimus back here. I'm going to stay at home instead.' I patted the sofa. 'I'll stick to the original plan and watch it from here then report in afterwards by telephone.'

The tiniest smile played around his lips. It was the first time since he'd shown up tonight that he'd looked at me with anything other than irritation, annoyance or downright disdain. 'You did say you were willing to put in the effort.'

I growled at him. 'I can change my mind. It's a lady's prerogative.'

'Too late. We're counting on you now, Ivy.' There was a faintly mocking edge to his words.

I narrowed my eyes. 'Have I done something to annoy you?' I asked. 'We were getting on well last time I saw you.' I softened my voice. 'Very well.'

'What could you possibly do that would annoy me?' Winter's fleeting amusement vanished and he glanced down, pretending to inspect the map again.

'You keep looking at me like ... like...' I fumbled for the right words. 'Like I've disappointed you or something.'

'I have no idea what you're talking about.' Winter stood up. 'I should go. There are still lots of preparations to put into place before filming starts.' He pointed at the folder. 'And you've got homework to do.'

No. I wasn't going to let this go. 'Winter, just tell me. If you're angry that we slept together then I'm sorry. I didn't do it to try and compromise you or your position.'

His jaw clenched. 'I am not angry that we slept together.'

Hope flickered. 'You're not?'

'I'm not angry at all, Ivy.'

I remained still. 'Yes, you are.'

Winter's expression shuttered. For a long drawn-out moment he didn't say anything. Finally he took a deep breath and gazed down at me. 'I just don't understand why you're carrying with that Villeneuve fellow after everything he's done to you.'

I stared at him. 'Pardon?'

'It was obvious what was going on tonight when we showed up. The very fact that he's even living here...'

I felt a flash of sudden understanding – and glorious happiness. 'I didn't know he'd moved here until tonight. He got into my taxi and demanded I drive him or he'd make a formal complaint. There's nothing between us. There never will be.' I tilted my head. 'Were you really jealous?'

Thinking about it now, it was clear how compromising the scene had probably appeared, considering I'd been a hair's width away from Tarquin when the Ipsissimus and Winter showed up. Not to mention that it had probably looked like I'd been whispering sweet nothings into his ear.

Winter turned away from me. 'Why would I be jealous?'

A massive smile split my face. 'I can't imagine.' I touched his arm. 'There's nothing going on between Tarquin and me. I promise, Rafe. You'd know that if you'd been in touch since last month.'

He grunted in response. I hoped he was going to say something else, or at the very least turn back around and face me. Unfortunately, Brutus took that opportunity to stroll back in.

'Fooooooood.'

'In a minute.'

'Food. Food. Food. Food.'

'I should go,' Winter said quickly. He glanced over his shoulder. 'I'll see you next week, Ivy. Read through the files before then.' He hesitated then turned round, leaned down his head and kissed me gently on the cheek. 'Take care.'

I was left standing in my own living room with my skin burning and my thoughts awhirl. Now what was I going to do?

Chapter Three

I took Brutus with me. It wasn't that I didn't trust Eve to look after him while I was away so much as I didn't trust Brutus with Eve. He was none too impressed at being shoved into his cat carrier like an ordinary cat, although he did cheer up somewhat when I informed him that we weren't going to the vet. What I neglected to tell him was just how long it was going to take us to get to Tomintoul. All these witches around and not one of them had ever managed to make a broomstick fly. One day, perhaps.

In any case, so that I could maintain the fiction that I was a poor non-witch willing to work nonsensical hours for the minimum wage I took the train, ostensibly travelling on my own. It was a long trip up to the north of Scotland, with several changes. It was nice to just sit back and relax. With the cart coming by every hour or so selling all manner of junk food, not to mention tea so strong you could stand up a spoon in it, I decided there were far worse ways to pass my time. Until, that was, someone came along and sat beside me after we'd passed Crewe.

I'm not averse to people. While I'm aware that my apathetic tendencies can sometimes be mistaken for misanthropy, I'm really not that bad. I'd not be much of a taxi driver if I were. However, when I end up sitting next to a man who spreads out his legs almost as wide as they'll possibly go, squeezing me against the window, before falling asleep with his head dropping uncomfortably onto my shoulder, I happen to get rather tetchy.

I twice attempted to shove him away from me but, despite my best efforts, he stubbornly remained put. Even worse, when I sharply nudged him the second time, he just started to snore. It wasn't a delicate little wheeze either. No: this man sounded like a warthog on a mission to wake up the devil.

Brutus appeared equally disgruntled by his presence, edging out a sharp claw from inside his cage to swipe at the space-hogging fiend. He had as little effect on the man as I did which, given just how sharp my familiar's claws were, was quite something. I shook my head. This simply wouldn't do. I'd have knocked my lukewarm tea off the little tray table onto his lap if it didn't seem like a terrible waste of a good drink.

What I really needed was something organic. I'd dabbled in herblore for a week or two after my magical binding was removed, not because I enjoyed that particular strain of magic but because Winter was rather fond of it. In the end, however, it became too irritating when I never had the herbs I required to hand and I soon abandoned my efforts.

I dug around in my jacket pockets on the off-chance that there were a few sprinkles of something still lingering around. Unfortunately they were empty apart from a twisted sweet wrapper. Then I caught sight of the crisps trodden into the floor under the seat in front of me. Not perfect but, if I got lucky, they'd be one of the more pungent flavours. I was hoping for cheese and onion. The discarded corner of an egg mayo sandwich or a few lost scampi fries would be better, but the train was just a bit too clean for that. I'd have to work with what I had.

I stretched out one toe, arching it past Brutus's carrier and snagging a few of the crumbs. Bringing them closer to me, which was no mean feat given just how little space I had to work with, I began drawing out the rune I required.

It didn't take long for the magic to do its job. I'd barely finished the rune when the most godawful reek began to rise. Rotten vegetables with an extraordinary odour of foul fish. It appeared whoever had been sitting here before me had gone one better than cheese-and-onion crisps – they'd been munching on prawn cocktail flavour. Not my snack of choice but it was perfect for this scenario.

The smell grew into a cloud of foul air. My annoying companion choked in mid-snore and opened his eyes. Yep. It was pretty disgusting. I turned my head in his direction and looked as embarrassed as I possibly could. 'I'm so sorry,' I said. 'I have a dodgy tummy and simply the worst case of wind.'

The corners of his mouth turned down and he looked faintly nauseous.

'Don't worry,' I assured him. 'It's contagious but it rarely lasts for more than a few hours. By mid afternoon I promise you won't be able to smell a thing and the odds of you catching it from me aren't too bad. Five to one at worst.' I paused. 'Well, maybe three to one.'

The man's mouth tightened and he let out a guttural grunt. Then, without a word to me, he grabbed his bag, stood up and walked away to find another seat, preferably in an entirely different carriage.

Way to go, Ivy, I grinned to myself, although the smell I'd created was becoming quite overpowering and I could see a family down the other end of the carriage looking very disturbed. I hastily cancelled out the rune, sure that the nasty odour would disappear quickly. That's when a familiar head popped up from one of the seats and fixed me with an icy blue glare.

'Manspreading,' I called out by way of explanation. 'It's a recognised phenomenon but there's very little you can do to combat it. The easiest way is to get rid of the offender as quickly as possible. The less confrontation the better.'

Winter's glare only grew. I guessed he was pissed off that I was talking to him directly instead of wholeheartedly throwing myself into our concocted story that we didn't know each other.

I shrugged. If he really thought that this production company was so thorough that they'd bother tailing a nonentity like me, then he thought too highly of them. No one would go that kind of trouble. All the same, he really didn't look very happy.

Deciding that this would be the perfect time to put my head down and take a nap, I leaned back into my seat and avoided looking at Winter again. But it was nice to know that he wasn't far away.

***

Winter might have said that Tomintoul looked pretty but when we finally arrived, it was difficult to make out much of anything at all. It was dark, it was cold, and there weren't any helpful chauffeurs with limousines to pick me up and take me to where I needed to go. I wasn't even sure *where* I was supposed to go, if I were being honest.

The crowd of other passengers who'd disembarked appeared to disappear almost immediately whilst Winter strode off without so much as a glance in my direction. It occurred to me that he'd probably used his almost perfect memory to map out every street of the small town in his head. He'd have a nice little B&B set up and waiting for him. I had a heavy suitcase, Brutus and his cat carrier, and absolutely no clue.

With no one around to ask for help, I set off at a shuffle down what looked like a main street. At that time of night, there appeared to be nothing open. I passed a few tearooms, an art gallery and a pub that seemed to be dark and dead. Brutus growled in irritation.

'I know, I know, but I can't remember the name of the damn hotel,' I muttered to him. My excitement at being part of the *Enchantment* team had long since dissipated.

I was just about to turn on my heel and head back to the station to demand to be returned to civilisation when a young guy in his twenties ambled out from a side street, pausing to light a cigarette as he went. Feeling hopeful, despite his somewhat unkempt appearance, I trotted up to him. 'Hello!'

He lifted his head and looked at me, glancing up and down with an assessing eye. 'Tourist or TV?' he asked in a heavy Scottish brogue.

Excellent. 'TV!' I beamed. 'I'm here for the *Enchantment* filming but I'm not sure where the rest of the crew are staying.' I stuck out my hand. 'Ivy.'

He shook it briefly but there was very little enthusiasm behind the effort. In fact I had the distinct impression that he wished I'd go away and leave him in peace. 'Gareth.' He raised a bushy eyebrow. 'You important? Some TV bigwig or something?'

'Of course! I'm vital to the entire production. Without me, they'd all be lost.'

He considered this. 'But aren't you the one who's lost right now?' he finally enquired.

Ha! Gareth was smarter than he looked. 'You've got me. Between you and me, my driver didn't show up to pick me up from the station.' I leaned in closer and added with a dark edge, 'Heads are going to roll.'

He watched me for a moment. 'Interesting choice of words,' he murmured.

I frowned. 'Why?'

'Because heads have already rolled. Literally.'

Hang on a minute. 'Are you referring to...?'

'The contestants. Or, more specifically, that bloke who managed to get himself killed here just last week. There's not been a suspicious death here in decades then, within days of your company showing up, there are body parts strewn across the Highlands.' He reached into his jacket pocket and withdrew a small flask before taking a swig and shuddering.

'How do you know about it?' I asked, treading carefully. Contrary to expectations, I had actually read the files and I knew that the circumstances of Benjamin Albert's death were being kept quiet by both *Enchantment* and the police. This might be a small town where gossip spread like wildfire but Gareth still knew that the victim had been decapitated and dismembered – and I was certain that little titbit had been withheld from all but those closest to the investigation. I'd avoided thinking about it too much; it was simply far too gruesome.

Gareth let out a tiny snarl. I inadvertently took a step back. 'They didn't tell you about me? I found him, didn't I? Out looking for a lost sheep and...' His voice drifted off and his pupils dilated as he remembered what were no doubt the horrors of unexpectedly come across a brutalised body.

Suddenly his night-time wandering and hip-flask gulping were starting to make sense. I winced. 'I'm sorry.'

He dropped the cigarette and ground it under his heel. 'I gave up three years ago. I don't even like nicotine.' He bared his teeth and looked at me, his shoulders sagging slightly when he seemed to realise my sympathy for him was both heartfelt and honest. 'Seeing something like that can make you question everything you think you know,' he muttered.

I could well imagine. I pulled my shoulders back. Winter would probably be ecstatic that I'd already managed to make contact with a vital witness like Gareth. I had to tread very delicately, however. Judging by his state of mind, if I went in too hard or was too pushy I'd simply scare him off.

'I know a little about what you've experienced,' I said quietly, thinking of Adeptus Diall's corpse which Winter and I had both seen. It still gave me the odd nightmare. 'But nothing nearly as bad. If you ever want to talk about it, come and find me. Sometimes it can help to talk to a stranger and I don't imagine there are many trauma counsellors up here.'

He blinked, as if surprised that I could care that much. I quashed my wave of sudden guilt. I was here to do a job, after all. I didn't have to like it but if Winter and I were going to get to the bottom of the murders – and prevent any more from happening – I'd simply have to toughen up.

'Thank you,' Gareth said in a low voice. He pointed up the street. 'All your colleagues are staying at the Hook and Eye. It's about a mile down that way, just on the edge of town.'

A mile? Good grief. I choked back my response and murmured my thanks. 'Come on, Brutus,' I said with a sigh. 'Let's get a move on.'

Brutus didn't answer, probably because he was fast asleep. It was alright for some, I huffed to myself. I waved to Gareth and shambled off. I really needed a bath and a bed. I might have only been sitting around on a train all day long but I still felt bone weary. At least I wasn't like poor Gareth though, I mused, strengthening my resolve to do everything I could to find out just what in hell was going on here. Someone bloody did.

***

I was woken up by someone vigorously shaking my arm. For a strange, sleep-sodden moment, I thought it was Winter and I squeaked in dismay, attempting to shield myself from what could only be the icy onslaught of water about to be flung at my face. It took a moment or two for me to realise that my human alarm clock was speaking with a female voice. Somewhat belatedly I realised it had to be my room-mate, who'd already been crashed out by the time I'd arrived.

I peeked upwards cautiously, gazing up at the anxious face of a brunette. I swept my bleary gaze over her. Although she was wearing fairly casual clothes – jeans and a blouse – she looked remarkably smart. Her hair was carefully pulled back into a neat bun and the glasses that were perched on her nose were so shiny I could see my reflection in them.

'Urrrgh,' I said. It was supposed to be good morning but I knew that wasn't what it sounded like, even to my own ears.

'You need to get up,' the woman urged, with wide, owl-like eyes. 'The bus is leaving in ten minutes.'

I groaned. I had at least another seven minutes of snooze time then, I reckoned. My new roomie wasn't giving in, however.

'You've missed breakfast. I thought it would be better to let you sleep in. But Armstrong will fire you in a heartbeat if you keep everyone else waiting. The last runner got the boot just for forgetting to put milk in his coffee.'

I already knew that Armstrong was the new director of *Enchantment* and the man whose brainchild it was to shake up the usual format and include a survival element.

While I should have been concentrating on doing what I could to get up, given that he was the last person I wanted to annoy, it was the mention of coffee that really helped me out. I struggled up to a sitting position and looked around. There was indeed a small kettle in the corner. Maybe if I was quick...

'I'm Amy,' she said. She reached down and hefted my suitcase upwards, landing it on my knees with a painful thump. 'Come on!'

'Ivy,' I murmured, giving her a half-hearted wave in greeting. 'Can you put the kettle on, please?'

Amy threw me an anxious look. 'There's no time! I'll see you down there. Remember, don't be late!' She all but sprinted out of the room, the door banging behind her as she left.

Well, she was energetic. I yawned and tried to pull myself together. 'Brutus,' I murmured. 'Could you put the kettle on? I could really do with a coffee. The stronger the better.'

As far as I could tell, it was still pitch black outside. But then it wasn't even 5am. I shuddered at the thought and unzipped the case, looking for something to wear.

'Brutus?'

There was still no answer. I clipped on my bra, hooked a sweater over my head and glanced round. There didn't seem to be any sign of him. I frowned. Contrary cat. Then the phone on the bedside rang, startling me so much I let out a strangled yelp.

'Ivy,' said Winter's voice on the other end, 'you need to get up now or this assignment is over before it's even begun.'

I wrinkled my nose. Winter might make my toes curl up in delight every time I thought of him but did he have to sound quite so chipper this early?

'How did you know I was still in bed?' I asked suspiciously. 'Are you watching me?'

'I'm not anywhere near you. I'm staying somewhere else. I just *know* you, that's all.'

I shook out a pair of jeans and wiggled into them at high speed. 'Well,' I tutted, 'for your information, I'm wide-awake and raring to go. And I even made contact with an extra-special witness last night. I bet you didn't manage that. His name is Gareth and...'

'You can tell me later. Ivy, if you're not on that bus in the next sixty seconds, then you'll need to run.' He hung up. Always with the running. I had the sinking sensation that I was going to very tired of that word very, very quickly.

I stood up, pulling the jeans up over my hips just as there was a loud toot from outside. The bus. Grimacing, I ran my hands through my hair, decided there was nothing else I could do about it and dashed out of the door.

The bus's engine was already running and the seats were jam-packed with people. I received more than a few strange looks. When one of the more helpful passengers pointed down at my crotch, I realised it was because I'd not done up the zip. Grinning like an idiot, I pulled it up then squeezed into an empty seat.

Breathless, I smiled a quick hello at the woman next to me and checked the rest of my attire. My sweater was on inside out. Oops. Shrugging, I pulled it off, doing what I could not to elbow the woman in the process, turned it right the way around and pulled it back over my head. Nobody blinked an eye – but then this was the world of reality television. They were probably used to displays of nudity.

'I slept in,' I told my companion unnecessarily, once I'd righted myself.

'So I see,' she murmured. She glanced down at my ID, which I'd just managed to grab in time. Apparently clocking that I was no one of consequence, she turned away and looked out of the window instead. I'd have thought she was being rude if it weren't for the fact that that no one on the bus was talking. It was almost as if we were monks on a vow of silence. Either that, or nobody here was a morning person. Suited me.

The bus trundled its way out of the town and down a single-track road. I shook out my hair and craned my neck round to look at the other passengers, wondering whether there was anyone I could recognise on board. It appeared that Belinda Battenapple, the host of *Enchantment*, and the other on-screen regulars, including the enigmatic Trevor Bellows, enjoyed other transportation. I hadn't missed a single episode of *Enchantment* in my life and I would have blithely walked past any of these people on the bus without recognising them. That was probably a good thing.

Warning myself that acting star-struck probably wouldn't be a good idea even if I did meet Belinda, I settled back into my seat and closed my eyes. I was just drifting back to sleep again when the bus came to a juddering halt.

'Briefing in two!' yelled an overly enthusiastic bloke towards the front. 'Let's get moving, people!'

I heaved myself up and followed everyone else off the bus, trying to appear as if I knew exactly what I was doing. It didn't last long. The second I stepped outside and got a good look around the set, all my attempts at looking nonchalant fell by the wayside.

People were scurrying about everywhere, some carrying equipment, others clipboards. There had to be at least forty of them, and every single one was busy. From almost every angle, I could see the trademarked *Enchantment* signs emblazoned across lorries and cars and strung up between trees. I stood in the centre of it all, gawking like an idiot with my mouth hanging open.

'The main quad!' the man from the bus shouted. 'Now!'

All at once, everyone seemed to stop what they were doing and head off. There were some grumbles; it appeared I wasn't the only one who didn't appreciate early rising. I kept hoping someone would tell me where I could find the industrial-strength coffee; instead we were ushered forward where an elaborate stage was already set up.

A harried-looking woman clambered up with the aid of a few of the others before grabbing hold of a bullhorn and facing all of us. 'Good morning!' she bellowed. 'And welcome to the very first day of filming for *Enchantment*: Highlander edition!'

If she'd been expecting a raucous response, she was sorely mistaken. There was some ragged applause but no one appeared particularly thrilled by her words. Unlike me: I whooped loudly, ignoring the frowns I received from the people around me. There were a few eye-rolls as well but I smiled happily. This was brilliant. It took a lot to get me to smile before 11am but being on set for *Enchantment* was definitely enough.

Someone from the side of the stage called up to the woman. She nodded and yelled into the bullhorn again. 'Now for our esteemed director and man of the hour, Morris Armstrong!'

This time, the applause was slightly more enthusiastic. For some reason, however, I still got the impression that it was because of what was expected rather than out of any real desire to cheer on the supposed captain of the most popular show on television.

I watched with interest as a large man leapt onto the stage. With his back to the crowd, he murmured something to the woman. From behind me, I heard someone else mutter, 'Apparently he's in a bad mood. He was down south completing some last-minute budget negotiations and couldn't get first-class tickets for the train yesterday, so he had to join the rest of the cattle instead.'

There was a choked snigger. A bout of snaking dread assailed me. Uh-oh. Then, when Morris Armstrong turned round to face us, I bit my lip and raised my eyes to the heavens. Of course, the new director was the man who'd sat beside me on the train and who I'd managed to chase away with my supposed bad smell. Not only had I missed the perfect opportunity to find out more about what was going on, I'd made him think I was walking petri dish that should be avoided at all costs.

I slumped my shoulders in a bid to hide from his roving eyes. The chances were that I wouldn't have to go near him; I was just a lowly runner and completely beneath his attention. The likelihood that he was involved in the murder was slim to none.

I dreaded to think would Winter would say if I was given the boot before I even managed to open my mouth – although his icy irritation on the train was now making more sense.

Armstrong didn't bother with the bullhorn. 'I know most of you have been here for a few weeks already completing pre-interviews with the talent and setting everything up. I also know that things have been more difficult than they should have been and that there have been ... complications.' Complications? Well, that was one way of describing a horrific murder, I thought. 'The police are still investigating the matter and I urge you to give them your full cooperation.'

He nodded over to a small contingent at the side who, now I looked at them more closely, did appear more grimly official than any of the film crew. 'However,' Armstrong continued to shout, 'nothing will stop *Enchantment*. We are the best television series on this planet! We have millions of viewers! We are going to go from success to success and nothing is going to stop us.'

There should have been someone in the back with a drum kit. At the very least he deserved a cymbal crash to add to his dramatic flair.

'You all know what to do and what needs to be done. At precisely midday the talent will arrive and the cameras will start rolling. We are making history, people! Don't you forget it!' With that, Armstrong punched the air and left the stage.

Mrs Bullhorn returned to her spot, clapping the director ostentatiously as he walked away. 'Wonderful, just wonderful! We're so lucky to have such a hands-on director. All runners need to report directly to Armstrong's trailer now as he wants to brief you all in person. The rest of you get back to work!'

Arse.

Chapter Four

There were three other runners besides myself. One was Amy, my helpful room-mate, while the two others looked young enough to have just stepped out of high school. I eyed the first one's acne and shook his hand when he introduced himself with a mumble as Mazza. I sincerely doubted that was the name his parents had christened him with.

The other one was almost as posh as Tarquin, with the kind of floppy hair and expensive clothes that marked him out as defiantly upper class. I was betting that he was called George or William or Henry but, when he gave his name as Moonbeam, it took everything I had to maintain a straight face. That couldn't be his real name – could it? He was clearly used to painful reactions at his name, judging by the way he rolled his eyes at my stifled smirk, but at least he seemed to be enjoying himself.

We hustled towards a large silver contraption that I took to be Morris Armstrong's trailer. I did my best to stay behind the others but, with only four of us, it was obvious that I couldn't stay hidden for long.

Moonbeam took the lead, marching up the steps and knocking on the door. There was a muffled yell from inside and he shrugged then entered with the rest of us on his heels.

The trailer's interior was considerably more spacious and luxurious than I imagined. I gazed round in awe at the plush decorating and shiny surfaces. I could easily live like this, I decided.

I wasn't the only one who was impressed. Mazza's expression was something akin to a small child being introduced to ice cream for the first time. He let out a low whistle and then blushed immediately. He flicked a quick look at Amy and blushed even more. I decided that I liked him the most.

Armstrong appeared from the far end, wiping his hands on a towel. He tossed it to the floor and stared at our little group as if he'd completely forgotten the reason why he'd asked us here. Then his expression cleared. 'You're the runners.'

Moonbeam again stepped forward. 'We are.' He put out his hand. 'I'm Moonbeam.'

Armstrong gazed at him with a blank face. 'No, you're not.'

'I am. It's a strange name but...'

The director held up a palm and Moonbeam fell silent. 'I will not call anyone Moonbeam. You are Number One. That is what you will answer to from now on.' He pointed at Amy then at Mazza. 'Number Two. Number Three.' His head turned to me. As soon as he registered my face, his mouth snapped shut.

'Number Four,' I offered helpfully, in case his arithmetic had suddenly deserted him.

Armstrong's eyes narrowed. I held my breath and waited for him to throw me unceremoniously off his set. Instead he muttered something under his breath and gave a barely perceptible nod. He recognised me from the train – of that there was no doubt – but for some reason he was declining to mention it just yet.

'Your job is going to be the most vital of all,' he barked. 'You might only be runners but everyone has to start somewhere. I was once like you, you know.' His eyes took on a faraway cast as if he were fondly remembering his golden days of being a dogsbody when he didn't have to worry about large gleaming trailers and lots of money.

Armstrong shook himself. 'As runners, you have access to all areas. Naturally we have security on hand to deter any trophy hunters or rabid fans or,' he shuddered, 'the press. But that doesn't mean that the more cunning of them will not find ways of gaining access. This is supposed to be a closed set. In my experience there is no such thing. This area was chosen because of its longstanding historical links to witchcraft. It's certainly not the sort of place I would have chosen if

I'd had the choice. There are simply too many opportunities for outsiders to sneak in. We can't completely barricade ourselves off. More's the pity.'

Amy nervously raised her hand. 'Sir? Mr Armstrong?'

'What is it?' he barked.

'Doesn't everyone have identification tags?'

He drew himself up, looming over her in an almost sinister fashion. 'That's what makes their kind so insidious! And where you come in. One of your tasks will be keep track of those tags. You will frequently be approached by crew members who have misplaced their badges. I have already sent out an email to everyone. If your ID tag is lost, then so are you.' He glared at her as if she'd already dared to forget her own. 'Got that? There will be no duplications or replacements. I will not have my set sullied by anyone not of the industry who might have stolen a tag for their own ends.'

He wagged a finger at her in further admonishment. 'Keep a particularly close eye out for anyone who might be a journalist. The last thing we want is their kind here revealing all our secrets to the world before we are ready to broadcast them.'

This time it was Moonbeam who dared to speak up. 'What about the murder?'

'What murder?' Armstrong snapped with such ferocity that Mazza took a step backwards, colliding with me.

'Er... the contestant who was...'

'I know who you mean!' Armstrong bellowed contrarily. 'But what happened to him is nothing to do with us. Nothing, do you hear me? His death was unfortunate but completely unrelated to *Enchantment*. There will be no further discussion on this matter. Get out of my sight!' For a moment we all just stood there. 'Get out!' Armstrong roared.

I twisted round and made for the door while I still had my eardrums intact.

'Not you, Number Four! *You* will stay here.'

Uh-oh. I guessed I'd not managed to slide by after all. Maybe I should be grateful that I'd be fired out of earshot of the others.

I sighed and moved to the side to let them leave. Amy looked especially worried on my behalf. I gave her a small reassuring smile as she left, with Mazza biting his lip and Moonbeam blithely unconcerned. The door banged shut behind them and I tilted up my chin. Morris Armstrong might be shouty but I wasn't intimidated. Not much, anyway.

He sank down into a chair, his heavy frame making it a tight squeeze. 'Moonbeam,' he muttered. 'Where on earth do they dig these idiots up?'

I licked my lips, wondering whether I was supposed to answer him or not. Fortunately, he didn't give me much chance. He raised his head and looked at me with suddenly tired eyes. In a flash of insight it occurred to me that, with the contestant's death and his new role as director, he was under a great deal of pressure. If this new and supposedly improved version of *Enchantment* went tits up, there was no doubt that the blame would be laid firmly at his door. The revelation didn't make me feel much sympathy for him but I did understand his violent swings between enthusiastic encouragement and terrifying rage a little bit more.

'Ivy Wilde.' Armstrong rolled my name round his mouth. I rather thought I'd preferred Number Four; at least then I'd been anonymous. 'You're a witch.'

The plain, unvarnished truth. So much for my undercover work. Still, there was no point in lying about it now. 'I am,' I said cautiously.

'Why are you here?'

'I'm a big fan of the show.' I paused. 'I've been watching it from the beginning.'

Armstrong's lip curled. He clearly didn't believe me for a second. 'Who's been your favourite contestant?'

That was easy. 'Ally,' I answered.

He snorted. 'She's everyone's favourite.'

I couldn't win. 'Ask me something else.'

'What do you think has been the greatest magic trick ever seen on the show?'

The fact that he called them tricks told me far more about him than he probably wanted me to know. 'Most people would say the second series,' I said in earnest, 'when three contestants banded together and used their powers to make it snow in Knightsbridge in May.'

'You disagree?'

'The weather was already cool for that time of year and the snow shower was localised. Any Order Neophyte could do that. The actual best spell was series four when Jonathon was the first contestant to get voted off. He used magic to heal a cut on Becky's finger.'

'He slept for three days afterwards.'

'True,' I agreed. 'But there are very few witches of even Second or Third Level who have mastered healing. The human body is too complex and there's too much potential for disaster. We're talking about knitting together skin and ensuring that blood flow isn't hampered. In fact,' I said, warming to my subject, 'closing a tiny cut is harder than fixing a broken bone because of the delicate touch it requires.'

Armstrong scratched his chin. 'Do you know what happened to Jonathon?'

Yeah, I did. 'He entered the Order on a fast track to Second Level and he's currently working in the depths of South America helping out the tribes there.'

Armstrong's eyes half closed but I was aware that he was still watching me with all the attention of a hawk eyeing up a mouse. 'Are you with the Order?'

I didn't hesitate. 'No.'

'They want to come here but they don't understand what it is that we do.'

I didn't imagine that they did. 'Would their desire to come here be as a result of the Benjamin Alberts' murder?'

Armstrong opened his eyes fully again. 'What happened to him is a terrible shame. But nothing to do with *Enchantment*.'

'How do you know that?' I pressed, half expecting to get my head bitten off and spat out for asking. 'He was only here because of *Enchantment*.'

For the briefest moment Armstrong seemed to shrink into himself. 'Because if Alberts died as a result of our show, I'm sunk before I get started.' He ran a hand through his hair. 'And the police have found no evidence to suggest his passing had anything to do with us.'

I reiterated my point. 'Apart from the fact that he was a contestant, you mean.'

He gazed at me. 'You seem to know a lot about what happened.'

I gestured uneasily to where the others had been standing. 'There's been a lot of gossip.'

Armstrong's mouth tightened. 'Yes,' he said. 'I suppose there has.' Then he apparently remembered who he was and why I was here. 'There was an Order witch on the train yesterday.' His voice grew hard. '*You* were on the train yesterday.'

I swallowed. At least he'd not made any reference to my allegedly smelly contagion. 'I was.' I made a quick decision. It was highly possible that he'd clocked me talking to Winter. 'Adeptus Exemptus Raphael Winter. I'm sorry. He's following me. We were temporarily forced to be partners last month and now he seems to think I'm up to no good.' I dropped my eyes. 'I understand if that makes my position here untenable.'

'You think he's here for you?' Armstrong spoke sharply.

I looked up, mentally crossing my fingers. 'I do think that, actually. Unless you believe he's here because of the death.'

He folded his arms. 'The Hallowed Order of Magical Enlightenment doesn't like programmes like ours. They'd prefer to keep the magic to themselves.'

I refrained from pointing out that what *Enchantment* did involved such weak magic spells that the Order wouldn't give a toss what they did, as long as their name was kept out of it. But it was time to keep my mouth shut and see what Armstrong was going to do.

'Can I trust you, Ivy Wilde?' he asked.

It was make or break time. I pulled back my shoulders and met his gaze. 'Yes,' I said. 'You can. Check my background. I'm no Order flunky.' I had no doubt that he already knew my history but it was worth mentioning to labour my point.

Armstrong rolled his tongue across his teeth and stood up. 'You will make contact with this Winter. You will watch him and find out what he's doing and report back to me. I won't stand for Order interference, regardless of the circumstances.' He glared. 'Got that?'

I blinked rapidly. 'Er, okay. But...'

'Just do it. If you want to get anywhere in television, you will move every mountain to find out what he's up to and keep me appraised.'

Winter wanted to me spy on *Enchantment* and report back to him and *Enchantment* wanted me to spy on Winter and report back to them. How very messy. I hoped that didn't mean I'd have to work harder. There were already far too many threads to keep track of.

'Okay. I'll do that.' I hesitated. 'I might need some extra time away from my runner duties to...'

'You'll do it in your time off,' Armstrong barked. 'We don't need the rest of the crew alerted to the fact that there's a damned Order witch watching our every move. They're on edge enough as it is.'

It had been worth a try, I supposed. 'Sure. Whatever you say.' I added a smile to show him that I was on his side but he was no longer watching. Instead, his attention was caught by something out of the window.

'Brilliant,' he said under his breath. 'Just bloody brilliant.'

Before I could crane my neck to see what he was talking about, the door to Armstrong's trailer opened and a man strolled in wearing the most extraordinary set of clothes.

Trevor Bellows. Even if I hadn't recognised his face, his outfit would have given him away. He had on a long purple robe that didn't look a million miles away from the outfits the Order geeks wore, except their robes didn't generally include embroidered stars. Perched on top of his head was a conical witch's hat with an artfully crooked tip. Frankly, I was surprised that he wasn't carrying a broomstick. When I saw what he was holding in his arms, however, my mouth dropped open.

'Greetings and salutations,' Bellows said with an oddly squeaky voice that didn't match either his attire or his demeanour.

Brutus purred.

Armstrong's eyebrows flew up. 'Is that a cat?'

Bellows pushed his spectacles up his nose and flashed the director a smile. 'There's no pulling the wool over your eyes! Why, yes.' He held Brutus up in the air. If I tried to do that to him, I'd lose an eyeball. 'This is indeed a cat. I need a familiar to help me with my spells and this is the perfect creature.'

I stared in astonishment as *my* cat delicately licked Bellows' hand as if to show his admiration for all the world to see.

'Where did you get it from?' Armstrong enquired.

Good question. Bloody good question.

'It was fate,' Bellows said smugly. 'When I woke up this morning, he was right there on my doorstep. Cats can sense powerful magic, you know. He was obviously drawn to me.'

I reached out one hand towards Brutus. I was going to throttle him. His head whipped towards me and he hissed.

Bellows turned to me, a glint in his eyes as he looked me up and down. Something about his expression made me feel rather grubby. 'He doesn't like you,' he proclaimed. 'Don't feel bad. It's not your fault you don't have magic like I do.'

My fingers curled into tight fists while Brutus looked away from me and head-butted the so-called witch's chest in apparent adoration.

'Who are you anyway?' Bellows enquired. 'I thought all the contestants were being kept away from here until filming starts.'

'This is Ivy Wilde,' Armstrong said. I didn't think I was imagining his sudden hint of glee.

All suggestion of friendliness vanished from Bellows' features. His eyes narrowed as his gaze continued to sweep me up and down. 'You're blonde,' he said.

My mouth twitched. 'Why, yes, I am.' How ... astute of him to notice.

He sniffed. 'And messy.'

I crossed my arms. If I looked like I stuck my pinkie in an electrical socket then that was my business. 'I had a late night,' I said stiffly, biting back the urge to turn his elbows inside out. It would do the magical investigation no good if I offended the show's only magical consultant.

'Now, now children,' Armstrong said. He was clearly enjoying every minute of this. 'I have phone calls to make. The two of you should run along.'

Bellows pouted. Actually pouted. 'But I want to talk to you about the plans for next week when we...'

'Later. We'll discuss it later.' Armstrong grabbed both our elbows and propelled us towards the door. He glanced at me meaningfully. 'Report to me with your first findings before filming tomorrow morning,' he said. And that, apparently, was that.

Back outside, Bellows wasted no time. He drew in close to me, with Brutus still in his arms. 'Listen up, girly,' he hissed quietly to avoid being overheard. 'No one is taking my job away from me. I'm the magical expert around here and if you so much as think about commenting or showing off or doing anything that even ventures towards a spell, you'll be out on your ear before you can so much as say abadarabacadra.'

I blinked at him. 'Don't you mean abracadabra?'

'I meant what I said. Watch your step.' And with that, he picked up his robe and flounced off. Brutus popped his head up from over Bellows' shoulder. I could have sworn the damn cat was smirking.

Chapter Five

Despite half the world seeming to want to me to become some kind of bizarre double-agent, I spent the next few hours doing nothing more than menial work. Winter had been wrong. There was considerable running expected of a runner and I was growing mightily tired of it.

First of all, the sound technicians wanted coffee. They reeled off their orders at machine-gun speed and then got irritated when I asked them to slow down and repeat what they'd said. I was trying to do what they'd asked and to move quickly, but I still managed to arrive back with a latte instead of a cappuccino and the wrong sort of herbal tea for the hipster with the silly man-bun.

I was on my way back across muddy ground with the correct drinks when a prop guy hailed me and demanded that I send a message directly to wardrobe and tell them that the magical wands they wanted were useless and he didn't care if they clashed with the contestants' bandanas. When I relayed this information to two women surrounded by clothing racks, they looked at each other and burst out laughing, saying with a mocking sneer that he would use whichever colour of wand they decided. They shooed me off to tell him that but, when I tried to find the prop guy again, I was assailed by a member of security who growled darkly about the sheep that was breaching the far perimeter. He wanted to know whether he had permission to shoot it or not. I was sent dashing from one end of the set to the other and there didn't appear to be any rhyme or reason to my movements.

'This is madness,' I muttered to Amy when I passed her with an armful of last-minute herb displays to decorate the staging area.

She grinned. 'Is this your first gig?'

'Yes.' And it was most definitely going to be my last.

'Don't worry,' she said. 'It's just the last minute pre-filming panic. Once the cameras start rolling, things will settle down and you'll be assigned somewhere permanently.' She paused. 'See if you can avoid being assigned to Bellows though. He does better with the male of the species.' She shook herself. 'This is my third time as a runner. I've been told that if I stick around and do a good job, I'll be promoted to junior researcher.' She beamed. 'I need to go. Belinda's shoes have some mud on them and she wants me to scrub them until they gleam.' She checked her watch. 'Less than thirty minutes to go till showtime!'

Yay. I can barely wait, I thought sarkily as she darted away. I'd not seen any of the contestants yet but I already had the feeling that if I ever saw anything about *Enchantment* again I'd be tempted to hurl my television set out of the window.

It didn't help matters that I frequently caught sight of Moonbeam schmoozing instead of moving. I tried on several occasions to get close enough to hear how he managed to avoid doing so little work but, every time I did, someone called for me and I was sent off on yet another errand.

Even Mazza seemed to be in his element, a happy, eager-to-please expression written all over his face whenever I passed him. I noted that he reserved a sweet smile for Amy. If he were the murderer, I'd agree to clean the Order Headquarters from top to bottom with my toothbrush. As for everyone else, I was keeping my options open. I didn't have any choice; there was no spare time to catch my breath, let alone have a quiet 'chat'.

By the time everything was in place and ready for the show to start, I was footsore and very irritated. At least with the contestants arriving, things should slow down somewhat. I avoided the eye of one of the boom operators who was summoning me and slunk round the corner of a van to watch as each witchy wannabe was offloaded. Twelve lambs to the slaughter, I thought sardonically, as they trooped off their minibus and gazed round with the same awe that had been plastered all over my face a few hours earlier. They were dressed in all manner of outfits designed to proclaim their inner personalities. The geek. The temptress. The macho guy. So predictable. I loved it.

One of the producers led the merry band round. From where I was, I could hear every word that was said to them. I leaned back and listened.

'Remember, this is your chance to make a good first impression. The only person who can screw this up is you. We might not be airing for another couple of weeks but you still need to keep the audience in mind at all times. Get them on your side and the rest will be plain sailing.'

'I'm freezing,' a female voice complained. 'Can't I get a cardigan or something?'

'Don't be ridiculous. You're the totty. That's your role. We need more cleavage not less!'

'Suits me,' a man said. 'I'm rather enjoying the view.' Ick.

'Is there security here?' another one asked. 'Because I'm still worried about...'

'Nothing is going to happen to you. You'll be absolutely fine.' There was a pause. 'It's time. We need to head to the stage.'

There was the sound of several pairs of feet shuffling. I pushed myself off the side of the van and edged round. I could do this, I decided. Besides, if I were focusing on one of my secret missions, I'd have good reason to avoid making anyone else a cup of coffee.

I fell in near the back of the small group. The last contestant turned round with a start, smiling nervously when she saw me. 'Hello!' I beamed at her. 'I'm Ivy. I work here.'

'Hi.' Her hands plucked at her tight tweed skirt as she struggled to keep up with the rest of them. I guessed she was supposed to be the shy, retiring, librarian type. I pegged her for the win. People love an underdog. 'Harriet.' Then, 'I'm one of the contestants.' She didn't seem very happy about it.

'How are you doing? Are you feeling nervous?'

'No. Not so much.' The slight tremble to her fingers belied her words. 'Are we going to get lunch soon, do you think?'

A woman after my own heart. 'I'm not sure,' I admitted. 'You should tell Morris Armstrong that you're hungry. He's a lovely guy and he won't mind making sure we stop to eat if it's going to help you out.' I wasn't trying to drop her in it, not really, but my stomach was rumbling too.

'They didn't give us breakfast,' she said. 'And they made me put these stupid clothes on. We're going to be spending the next four weeks out here in the wild and I have to do it in a skirt I can barely walk in.'

I eyed her sympathetically. The contestants had been here for ten days already and, apart from the replacement, they'd have met Benjamin Alberts albeit briefly. The more I could ingratiate myself with them, the more chance I had of finding out information that Winter might find useful.

'Stop a second,' I told her.

She shot a nervous look at the other contestants who kept moving but she did as I asked. 'I don't want to be left behind,' she said.

'This will only take a moment.' I concentrated on her legs. It helped that she'd been shoved into a pair of woolly tights. Between those and the skirt, I could do something. Using both hands, I drew out a transmogrification rune. The woman gasped and stared down as the fabric around her lower half altered itself. I stepped back and cast a critical eye. The seams were a bit wonky but I reckoned it was an improvement, at least for tramping around the Scottish Highlands.

She smoothed down her new tweed patterned leggings. 'These are brilliant! Thank you so much!' She looked at me in awe. 'You're a witch. A real witch.'

I smiled at her. 'You're a contestant on *Enchantment*. You're a real witch too,' I lied.

She shook her head. 'I'm not. I'm only here because I want to break into TV presenting. My agent told me that the sort of exposure I can get on a show like this is priceless.' Her face fell. 'But I can't do any spells at all.'

I revised my opinion; maybe she wouldn't win after all. The contestants had to have at least a smidgen of magical ability to get to the later stages. All the same, I patted her arm. 'You should get a move on,' I advised. 'It's about to start.'

Impulsively she reached across and hugged. 'Thank you,' she said again. 'Thank you so much.' She jogged to catch up to the rest of them, able to move more quickly now. I high-fived myself. Awesome work, if I said so myself.

Peeling away from the group of contestants, I weaved through various boxes of equipment and busy looking crew members until I reached the clearing in front of the main stage. Belinda Battenapple was already there and I goggled up at her. Although her make-up was caked on, no doubt for the benefit of the cameras, she looked as glamorous in person as she did on screen – although slightly shorter than I'd expected. To emphasise our location, she was wearing a short tartan kilt. Somehow I didn't think the original Highlanders had ever paired their kilts with knee-high stiletto boots.

I managed – just – to resist letting out an almighty squeal and rushing up to demand her autograph. But it was a close run thing.

'Bitch.'

I stiffened and turned to see Moonbeam standing beside me. 'I hope you're not referring to me.'

'Hardly.' He jerked his chin over at Belinda. 'Her.'

I raised an eyebrow. It was the first time his voice had sounded anything other than chirpy and enthusiastic and I was taken aback by the vitriol he injected into his words.

'Why? What has she done?'

He looked at me as if I were stupid. 'Made me take this stupid job for one thing. I shouldn't have to start out at the bottom,' he complained. 'What's the point of being television royalty when you're forced to work as a runner?'

A whole lot of things suddenly slid into place. I switched my gaze between both him and her, belatedly registering the resemblance. 'She's your mother.'

No wonder he had such a daft name – he was a celebrity's kid. The fact that he'd been managing to get away with doing so little work also made sense; he probably knew half the crew. Not to mention that everyone would be walking on eggshells around Belinda Battenapple's only son. Except for Morris Armstrong. I wondered whether he'd been deliberately left out of the loop about Moonbeam's heritage because someone was hoping Armstrong would mess up and piss off La Battenapple herself. He might be the director but she was legendary.

Moonbeam's mouth turned down. 'Yeah, she's my mother. She said she'd cut me off if I didn't get a *real job.*' He sketched out air quotes and snorted. 'As if what she does is real.'

Poor put-upon baby. I should have told him to grow a pair; instead, I put a soothing hand on his arm. 'How awful for you.'

He sniffed. 'Thanks. But I won't be doing this crappy job for long. Don't worry about me too much.'

Yeah, okay, I wouldn't. Moonbeam didn't seem to realise that I was doing the same crappy job. 'You're going to quit?' I enquired. Maybe I'd join him.

'A contestant has been murdered,' he said. 'And the word from the minders is that more than a few of this lot are running scared.

They've already used up their standbys. I just need to have a word in the shell-like ear of one or two of them and then there will be a new position that needs to be filled at the last minute.' His eyes gleamed.

I wrinkled my nose. This time I couldn't even attempt to hide my disgust. 'You're going to scare someone into quitting?'

'If they choose to leave the show, that'll be their decision. I'm not forcing anyone to do anything.' He spoke with the petulant air of a spoiled brat.

My distaste for him was growing. 'There's no guarantee that if someone drops out you'll be given their spot.'

'Of course there is.' He leaned down to my ear. 'That's how nepotism works.'

Well at least he wasn't pretending he'd become a contestant through merit. I wondered idly whether I was just jealous. If my family were rich and powerful and I could get away with doing very little for a lot of reward, then I probably would. I reminded myself once again that I was here to get on with people and find out anything I could which was related to Alberts' murder. I didn't want to antagonise anyone who I might need in the future.

'Good luck,' I murmured.

A loud inarticulate shriek rented the air, causing me to leap half a foot upwards. I whipped my head round, certain that something terrible must have just happened.

'What is *she* wearing?' It was one of the women from wardrobe. She was pointing at Harriet with one hand while flailing the other around in the air. Oops.

Everyone stared as she stalked up to Harriet and began pulling at her new tweed trousers. 'I did not give you these! Why are you wearing them? Where did you get them from?'

I shuffled behind Moonbeam, trying to hide. Harriet, looking flustered, searched round before pointing in my direction. 'She did it.'

Arse. So much for trying to conceal myself. Or for trying to help the poor woman out. This was why laziness was not a bad thing. If I'd left her appalling skirt alone, I wouldn't now have the wardrobe lady's mean stare fixed on me.

With her hands on her hips, she marched over in my direction. 'You! What did you do? And who are you anyway?'

Moonbeam unhelpfully stepped to the side, doing everything he could to make it clear that he barely knew me.

'I was just trying to be of assistance,' I began.

'Assistance?' Wardrobe Lady shrieked. 'Do you have any idea how long it took to get that ensemble together? Do you?'

I reckoned she'd plucked it out from a nearby charity shop without even looking at it, but she probably didn't want to hear that. 'Um,' I said, shuffling backwards, 'I can change it back if you like.'

She didn't hear me. She was already on a tremendous tirade that didn't involve listening to anything I had to say. 'You idiot! There's no time to change it now!' She glared at my badge that proclaimed to the entire world that I was a mere runner, the lowest of the low. 'Where is Armstrong? You're going to get your marching orders! Nobody interferes with my work. Nobody! First they want the wands changing and now this. It won't wash, I tell you. You'll regret the day you crossed me, little girl.'

Wardrobe Lady really was very, very angry. It didn't help that virtually every crew member was watching us – and that most of them were enjoying the show. I caught more than one snicker of amusement.

From out of nowhere, Armstrong appeared. 'What's the problem here?'

Wardrobe Lady raised one long, henna-covered finger and jabbed it at me. 'Her! She changed Number Ten's clothing!'

Armstrong raised his eyebrows. 'Did she?'

'Yes! She needs to be fired immediately.'

Uh-oh. I hoped the secret mission Armstrong had given me would supersede Wardrobe Lady's desire for revenge. 'I didn't mean anything by it,' I said. 'I can change her clothes back if you really want.'

Armstrong looked round. Harriet was still standing apart from the others, her cheeks flushed. He swept his gaze up and down her figure and shrugged. 'She looks fine to me. She's still mousy enough.'

Harriet went even redder. If she'd had any doubts before as to her place on this show, she hadn't now. Maybe it would be the making of her but more likely she'd curse me until the day I died for supposedly ruining everything. I know people; if they can find someone to blame for their woes then they will – and a runner like me was an easy target.

'She does not look fine!' Wardrobe Lady yelled.

Armstrong patted her on the arm. 'Yes, she does.' His voice was firmer this time. 'Off you go and sew some hems or,' he paused, 'whatever it is you do around here.' He twisted round on his heel and walked back towards the stage.

The woman's mouth tightened. If I'd thought she was angry before, it was nothing compared to now. Her expression contorted with unsatiated rage. 'I'm not done with you,' she promised me in an undertone before whirling off.

Well that hadn't exactly gone to plan. How to win friends and influence people by Ivy Wilde. Or not.

I ignored the stares I was garnering from everyone else and resolutely turned back to the front. Moonbeam was already off, chatting away to one of the producers and occasionally throwing looks in my direction. I lifted my chin and gave him an enthusiastic wave. It didn't make him very happy.

I really was going to have to try harder if I was going to find out any useful information from this lot before I antagonised them all into avoiding me for good. The only positive thing was that no one seemed to want me to run off on yet another errand. At least I'd get to watch the show's opening without interruption.

Belinda Battenapple, who'd barely lifted a perfectly manicured eyebrow at all during the commotion, was shaking herself in what could only be some kind of pre-show ritual. She started with her feet, raising one then the other before allowing her jiggles to travel up her body. Her actions made her look more like a dog who'd been for a swim than a world-famous television presenter – though I was hardly in a position to judge.

When she began flicking her head from side to side, the morning sun caught a glimmer of something round her neck. Frowning, I edged closer for another look. She was wearing a silver necklace with a small vial attached to it. It was certainly pretty, but that wasn't what had grabbed my interest. The contents of the vial were what were really fascinating. From this angle, it appeared to be some kind of liquid, not dissimilar to mercury. There was also a strange etching on the glass. Before I could read what it said, she realised it was dangling out of her shirt and hastily tucked it away. Interesting.

From the far corner of the stage, Armstrong checked his watch. The show wasn't going out live so I could only imagine that he was trying to stick to a strict schedule to make sure nothing was missed. He strode forward and made an incomprehensible gesture in the direction of the cameras. The operators seemed to understand what he meant because they immediately straightened their backs.

'Quiet on set!' someone yelled.

The bustle of activity stilled. Armstrong murmured something to Belinda and she nodded. It was time.

'Remember folks,' he said, to everyone and no one in particular, 'we are making history here.' And with that, he stepped off the stage and headed for a chair with his name emblazoned on the back. A delicious shiver ran down my arms. It was showtime.

A crew member gave Belinda's invisible microphone a final check before she shooed him away and stepped up to her mark. Her features visibly transformed as she glowed into the cameras. 'It's Friday,' she breathed. Actually it wasn't. It was Monday but I wasn't going to argue with her. 'And we are here in the stunning Highlands of Scotland for the most epic, most unique and most special series of *Enchantment* every created. Twelve new contestants are waiting in the wings and all of them have special skills and abilities. All of them want to win the coveted Trophy of Spells. And all of them know that,' she paused for dramatic flourish before she launched into her catchphrase, 'Magic. Is. In. The. Air. Welcome back to *Enchantment*!'

This was awesome. At least until the screaming started.

Chapter Six

At first, I thought it was Wardrobe Lady again. Maybe Belinda had committed some terrible infraction by wearing the wrong tartan on her miniskirt. It wasn't her though – it was one of the assistant directors who had emerged from a trailer at the far end of the set.

He ran a few metres towards the crew, all of whom stared at him frozen in shock. I didn't think it was because of the strangled sounds still coming from somewhere deep inside him, although they were awful enough. The crew's combined lack of movement probably had more to do with the blood that was dripping from his hands and staining the patchy grass in front of him.

I ran to his side. Despite the blood, which seemed to be drenching him, I couldn't see any visible wounds. It didn't even appear to be his blood. If he wasn't in immediate physical danger, there were other pressing concerns. It was vital not to touch him and contaminate any possible evidence, but I also needed him to calm down or he'd give himself an aneurysm. He was still wearing his ID badge and, although it was splattered with blood, his name was visible.

'Marcus,' I said softly. He kept on screaming. 'Marcus,' I repeated. 'Look at me.'

As if my words had broken the statue-like shock of the others, several people rushed towards us.

'Back off!' I yelled. 'And don't touch him!'

Security appeared from all directions. Most were running towards us but some were scanning the perimeter, as if expecting to see a horde of attackers appear. *Enchantment*'s medical team also arrived from the other side of the stage and I was shoved out of the way.

'Marcus! Are you alright?' People swarmed around him. The contestants were being ushered away to safety but I spotted a pale-faced Armstrong point to one of the mobile camera units. Without a second's hesitation, they came running over, already in the process of filming. Somehow I didn't think this was an appropriate candid-camera moment.

'He's fine,' I said over the hubbub. Physically anyway.

Nobody heard me. I gritted my teeth. Whatever evidence that had been clinging to poor Marcus had already been compromised by the people checking him over. I raised my head and glanced at the trailer he'd emerged from. The door was hanging open; from this distance, there was nothing to be seen inside other than darkness. I flattened my mouth into a grim line. Whatever had spooked him had come from there.

I veered round the crowd and strode over, taking care not to step near Marcus's bloody footsteps. I didn't have to get near before the smell of the blood overtook me. It had been strong enough around Marcus, but the reek coming from the trailer was choking. There was also an odd sour tinge to it, which I couldn't make sense of. One thing was clear: there was no way that the still-screaming Marcus had walked into the trailer while it was like this. Whatever had happened took place when he was already inside.

A gust of wind caught the hanging door, momentarily swinging it shut. The name taped onto it, along with a purple trail of stars for added effect, was Trevor Bellows. For a moment I forgot to breathe. Was that whose blood this was? Sudden fear for Brutus drenched me – although if my contrary cat had got himself killed he could only blame himself.

Rather than risk walking up the steps and entering the trailer, I slipped round to the side so I could crane my head round and peer in. All the curtains were closed and no lights were on so it was difficult to see much but the amount of blood was clear. It covered almost every corner. I couldn't see a body – Bellows, Brutus or otherwise. On the opposite wall, however, there was something that gave me pause. I stepped back to get a better look. A pentagram. It was lopsided and rather messy but since it had been painted with daubs of blood that was hardly surprising. Winter had wanted evidence of magic and here it was.

'What the bejesus...?'

I half turned, clocking Bellows. He was staring into his trailer with a horrified expression. Thankfully, Brutus was by his side. The cat sniffed the air then recoiled. Without a sound, he ran away, tail between his legs. Despite the relief I felt that he was alright, the question remained: if it wasn't Bellows' blood and it wasn't Brutus's, then who the hell did it belong to? There was far too much of it to signal anything other than a brutal and untimely demise. The only saving grace was that I couldn't see any dismembered limbs.

Bellows took off his hat, dropping it to the ground and running a hand through his hair. Either he was the world's best actor or he was as shocked as I was. He stumbled forward as if to enter but I grabbed his robe by one trailing cuff and yanked him back. 'You can't go inside,' I said. 'The police will need to examine the scene first.'

Given the pentagram on the wall, so would the Order but I figured it would be better not to mention that just yet. 'And we don't know whether there are any traps. If you enter you could trigger something else.'

Bellows blanched, going even paler than before if that were possible. 'Uhhhhnnn,' he said.

I nodded. 'Yeah, I know.'

Two of the security detail marched up. 'What is in there?' the first one asked, even though he had exactly the same view as I did.

His partner had considerably more *savoir faire*. 'We need to seal this area off immediately,' he barked. 'Someone call the police too. No one is to enter.' He twisted back towards the still-moaning Marcus. 'Find out what the hell happened!'

Morris Armstrong, looking surprisingly gentle, took control. He ushered everyone else back and crouched next to Marcus. 'What happened?' he asked softly. 'We need to know, Marcus. You need to pull yourself together.'

Marcus hugged his arms to himself and continued to moan.

'There are no injuries that we can see,' said one of the medical team. 'But he should be checked out anyway.'

Armstrong nodded and tried again. 'Marcus, tell us what happened. Why were you in Trevor's trailer?'

It was the implication that he'd been up to no good that finally broke through Marcus's brain and encouraged him to pull himself together. Somewhat. He was still shaking like a leaf and his voice was little more than a hoarse whisper. 'I went to fetch Mr Bellows' stick,' he said.

We all looked at the wannabe witch. He swallowed and nodded, his purple robes flapping gently in the breeze. 'My staff. I'd left it here and asked Marcus to get it for me.'

His staff? Who did he think he was? Gandalf?

'Good,' Armstrong said. 'That's good. What happened next?'

Poor Marcus looked like he was about to keel over. 'I went inside. I was sure no one was there and it looked empty. I went to the corner and picked up the sti— I mean the staff, and then something hit me on the back of the head. When I came round, I was surrounded by blood. It was everywhere.'

He began to moan. Any second now he'd be screaming again. Someone probably ought to fetch him a cup of sugary tea but I wasn't going to suggest it. If I said anything, I'd be the one sent off and I needed to find out everything I could about what had happened. Winter would not be happy if I missed the salient details of another murder because I was waiting for the kettle to boil.

Armstrong glanced up at Bellows. 'What time did you send him to get your staff?'

Bellows scratched his head. 'It was just after the final sound check so that would have been...'

'Just after ten.'

Bellows jerked his head in assent. 'Yeah, I guess.' He cleared his throat and tried to sound more confident. 'After ten.'

I tapped my mouth thoughtfully. This was supposed to be a closed set. Either someone who was already a crew member had sneaked inside when no one was looking or someone from outside had found a way in.

It seemed impossible that someone could have created that kind of bloody mess and stayed clean themselves and there was certainly no one here – other than Marcus, of course – who looked like they were splattered in O neg. I stepped back and edged away from the rest of the crowd, most of whom were still wringing their hands. It was inconceivable that our murderer had just blithely strolled out of the front door with no one noticing.

The intelligent security guard was giving instructions to the others. I tapped his arm. He paused in mid-sentence and looked down at me. 'You need to find out who's not here,' I told him. In other words, who had been drained of their blood.

He gave me a grim nod. 'That's what we're doing.' I watched as Mazza appeared, handing him a clipboard with a long list of names on it. The police would get here before he got even a quarter of the way down it.

I let him get on with it and headed towards the back of the trailer, sucking in a breath when I spotted the open window. It was definitely large enough for a person to squeeze through. There was also a trickle of blood dripping down from its edge. Here was the point of entry. Beyond the blood, I couldn't see any other clues.

I sketched out a quick rune designed to reveal that which was hidden but all it revealed was a rabbit hole by the trailer's left side. Without forensic analysis, there was nothing else to be seen here.

I abandoned my scrutiny of the trailer for now and turned round in the other direction. There was a makeshift fence and, beyond that, a copse of pine trees. I studied the fence. Given that it had probably only been erected recently by the film crew, it was surprisingly sturdy – but it wasn't all that high. Even I could probably scale it.

I scanned its length, eventually spotting something that had snagged along the top several metres along. I frowned and picked my way through the long grass to get a closer look.

Tufts of straggly white hair had caught in several places. I raised myself on my tiptoes just to be sure. What had happened inside the trailer – and why – was still a mystery but it wasn't quite as disastrous as it had first appeared. I nodded to myself and backed away, just as the first sirens began to sound.

***

The police who arrived might have been from a small local force unused to dealing with elaborate television productions and murder cases, but they seemed to know what they were doing. They immediately cordoned off the site and took down the details of everyone who'd been present. Naturally, the big show-stopping opening of *Enchantment* was postponed, if not cancelled for good.

Eventually we were all allowed to leave. I might have been persona non grata on the journey in, but the fact that I'd been the first to approach Marcus meant that I had suddenly gained a raft of new buddies. Several people wanted to sit next to me to go over in detail what I thought had happened and who had died. No one yet seemed to have clocked that every crew member was accounted for.

'It's just as well we don't film live,' someone behind me said. 'Can you imagine?'

'It doesn't matter,' another person dismissed. 'It'll be front-page news tomorrow morning. This show is scuppered for good. I just hope we still get paid.'

I suspected that all of this would boost *Enchantment*'s ratings rather than diminish them. This was reality television, after all; it invited voyeurism. I kept mum, however, sitting next to Amy who I felt I could count on to be at least a little circumspect.

'This is just terrible,' she said, over and over again. 'Simply terrible.'

I took off my shoes and started to massage my feet. 'Yeah,' I agreed. 'I've got at least three blisters. And the next person who complains because I've got their coffee order wrong is likely to end up with it upended over their head.'

She blinked. 'I meant the murders.'

Oh. I bit my tongue and nodded. It would probably be easier to keep my mouth shut.

It would have been nice to get back to Tomintoul and put my feet up for a bit but news travelled fast. There was already a crowd of townsfolk waiting for us when the bus pulled up outside our hotel. Moonbeam was more than ready to regale them with the whole story. That boy sure loved an audience.

I was prepared to sidle past the lot of them and go to my room for a well-deserved nap but Winter was hovering on the other side of the street, trying to look inconspicuous and failing massively. The sight of him was more than enough to perk me up. I trotted over. 'Hello!'

He glared at me with icy intensity. 'What the hell are you doing? We can't be seen talking to each other like this!'

'It's okay,' I assured him. I leaned in and lowered my voice. 'I'm on a secret mission. Not your secret mission, Morris Armstrong's secret mission.'

'Huh?' He gave me a blank look. I didn't blame him.

'I'm to get close to you and find out what you're up to,' I said cheerfully. 'Then I have to report back to him.' I paused. 'He wants me to seduce you to gain access to all your secrets. I'm the new Mata Hari. You can call me Ivy Hari.' I frowned. 'No, wait. Mata Wilde.' That sounded better.

Winter's astonishment was palpable. His blue eyes flared and he took a step backwards. 'You're kidding me.'

'Yeah. Well,' I amended, 'about the seduction part.' Unfortunately. 'But he does want me to pretend to be your friend so I can pass on information about you. He knew you were here from the start, so I told him you were spying on me rather than the show.' I grinned. 'Pretty awesome, huh?'

Winter's jaw clenched. 'He must know we're working together. He's testing you.'

'You're saying that he has a secret mission to put me on a secret mission in order to stop our secret mission?' That made my brain hurt. I shrugged. 'Either way, I have permission to talk openly to you.' I looked at him meaningfully. 'And we have a lot to talk about.'

He drew in a deep breath. 'So I hear. It's all over the town.' He glanced from side to side. Amy was looking curiously at us but no one else seemed to care.

Winter shook his head and then yielded. 'Meet me at the Dog and Whistle in twenty minutes. I'll order a drink and sit at the bar so it'll appear that you just bumped into me.'

'Can we have a secret handshake?'

'Don't be ridiculous.' He raised his voice. 'I told you, Ivy Wilde. If I find out you've been using magic, there will be hell to pay. The Order will see to it that you're kept off the streets for good.' He jabbed his finger sharply into my chest for good measure and stalked off.

I watched him go while Amy sidled up. She let out a low whistle. 'Who was *that*?'

I made a show of looking unhappy. 'My old partner. He just can't let it go that I don't want to be in the Order.'

'The Hallowed Order of Magical Enlightenment?'

Was there any other? I nodded. 'Yep. I'm a witch. But I don't want to be with them.'

Amy's eyes widened. 'You're really a witch? That's why you're here on *Enchantment*! You want a job with Trevor Bellows as a magical consultant.'

Er, no. 'Yeah,' I said. 'Sure.' I warmed to my topic. 'He's amazing.'

'Is he?' Amy's nose wrinkled. 'He knows a lot about magic, I suppose.'

I thought about the strange pentagram drawn on the wall of his trailer. Maybe Bellows did have a smattering of talent after all. I smiled at Amy. 'I'm going after him,' I said, pointing to Winter. 'He needs to butt out of my life.'

'He's gorgeous,' she said. 'He can butt into mine any time he wants.' Then she suddenly looked sorry. 'I didn't mean that to sound the way it did. It's not fair to talk about someone like that.'

'You wouldn't want him anyway,' I snapped. 'He has terrible halitosis. And he's lazy. Really lazy. Plus, he's deformed. He has a wooden leg.'

My tone must have been harsher than I thought because Amy looked slightly hurt. 'Uh, okay then.'

I felt a flash of guilt – but not enough to make her think that Winter was worthy of her attention. 'I'll catch you later,' I muttered. Then I walked off in the same direction as Winter.

Chapter Seven

Winter smelled good. Really good. I hopped up onto the barstool next to him and inhaled deeply. Then I raised my arm and sniffed an armpit. I grimaced. I guessed he'd have to smell good enough for the both of us.

'Fancy meeting you here,' I drawled. 'Do you come here often?'

He threw me an irritated glance but didn't comment. Other than the barman, this place was empty no doubt because everyone else was still out and about trying to find out what on earth was happening with *Enchantment*.

I gave up trying to get Winter to smile and got to the point. 'Things are afoot. I don't know how much you've heard, or how accurate it is, but Trevor Bellows' trailer is covered in blood. Drenched in it, in fact.'

'Do we know whose it is?'

'It's not human.'

A frown marred Winter's forehead. 'That's not what everyone is saying.'

'I reckon the lab results will be out by early morning tomorrow. The blood belongs to a sheep.'

'How do you know that?'

'Not magic, if that's what you're thinking,' I said airily. 'I know it because I'm a super-awesome sleuth with immense powers of deduction.'

Winter exhaled. 'Ivy...'

'The set is closed,' I explained. 'It's pretty hard for someone to gain access to it. Not impossible, but difficult. I wouldn't bother. But then, that's me. However there are a few blind spots around the back of the trailers where it's possible to clamber over the fence.' I began to tick off on my fingers. 'First of all, none of the crew members are missing so the blood doesn't belong to anyone involved in *En-*

chantment. Secondly, security was complaining earlier about a sheep trying to get inside. Thirdly,' I finished with a flourish, 'on top of the fence and almost directly behind Bellows' trailer, there's evidence that wool has snagged.' I paused. 'And we all know how much you love evidence.'

Winter stared at me. 'So what you're saying is that a sheep tried to get access and was foiled by security so climbed over the fence instead, which is ... how high?'

I considered. 'About two metres.'

'So this sheep climbed over a two-metre high fence, walked through Bellows' door—'

'Went through the rear window, actually,' I interrupted.

Winter gave me a long-suffering look. 'Fine. Went through the window, hit a crew member over the head, slit its own throat, disposed of its own body and created enough havoc to stop *Enchantment* from filming.'

I smiled. I hadn't told him about my *pièce de résistance*. 'This sheep also drew a pentagram on the wall of Bellows' trailer.'

His spine stiffened. 'A pentagram?'

'Yep.' I reached over and grabbed his pint glass, taking a long swig and smacking my lips. I deserved it. 'A crude one but definitely a pentagram. Obviously, someone bewitched the sheep to do all this.'

'So, in your infinite wisdom, Ivy,' he said, 'what's the motive for all this?'

I shrugged. 'I don't know. I figured I'd leave that part to you.'

Winter snatched his drink back from me. Boo. 'Have you ever tried to bewitch a sheep?'

'No. I don't meet many sheep in Oxford. I tried it on Brutus once. I attempted to bewitch him so that he'd go and buy his own cat food.'

'You attempted?'

'Yeah. It didn't work.'

Winter rolled his eyes. 'You're probably the most naturally talented witch I've ever met, Ivy, even if you do let those talents go to waste. If you can't bewitch your own familiar, how would someone else manage to bewitch a sheep? Even if they could, how could they bewitch a sheep to scale two-metre high fences?'

I opened my mouth to speak but he held up a hand to forestall me. 'If it really is sheep's blood, then someone brought the sheep over and killed it in Bellows' trailer.' He rubbed his chin. 'Although what they did with the body is anyone's guess. Perhaps Bellows is the next target and this is a warning.'

As much as I liked my theory, Winter's did make more sense. 'It would have to be someone strong to get a damn sheep over the fence and through the window.'

He grunted in agreement. 'Probably male, then.'

'And,' I added, 'probably a witch, given the pentagram.'

'Or someone who *thinks* of themselves as a witch. When was the last time you used a pentagram?'

I tried to think. Then I remembered: it was when I wanted to go out with Mickey Jones, the best-looking guy at school. The theory was that he would fall in love with me instantly and invite me to be his date at the end-of-school dance. It hadn't worked. Too embarrassed to tell the truth, I just shrugged. 'It's been a while.'

'Yes. They're more trouble than they're worth. It's good intelligence though, Ivy. The pentagram means the Order has to be involved. I can get on set and you can go home.' He gave a self-satisfied smile.

I sat up bolt upright. 'Go home? Why would I do that?'

'Oh, come on. We both know you don't want to be here.'

'It's been barely a day,' I argued. 'And I've discovered a damn sight more than I've just told you. I'm the lynchpin of this entire operation.'

'Really?' he said drily.

'Really! For example, the presenter, Belinda Battenapple, who is all things fabulous and wonderful and who I would one day like to grow up to be, is wearing some kind of magical vial round her neck.' I described it in great detail, including how she'd hastily hidden it when it accidentally revealed itself. Winter didn't appear particularly impressed. 'That's not all. Her son, Moonbeam—'

'Moonbeam?'

I waved a hand at him. 'Don't interrupt. Moonbeam told me that he wanted to scare the contestants so that one dropped out and he could take their place. He really wants to be on the show. The sheep thing might be completely unconnected to the murder. It might just be him trying to create enough of a stir to get what he wants.'

Winter looked at me. 'Was he gone for any part of the day before the blood was discovered?'

I wrinkled my nose. I'd been watching him every chance I'd had to find out how I could copy his avoidance of work. Moonbeam hadn't left the set. 'Um, no. But he might have had something to do with it.'

'All the same, Ivy,' Winter said, 'I think it's best if you leave this to the professionals now.'

For just a moment, he lost some of his allure. 'What? You plonker! You can't say that! I can be professional. I've not even told you about Gareth yet. He's the one who found the body – or what was left of it. He's bound to have some good information to spill and I bet he'll only want to tell it to me. I've already developed a relationship with him.'

Winter growled. 'What kind of relationship?'

'The kind where he thinks he can trust me,' I shot back. 'You need me, Winter. You can't cut me loose.'

A tiny smile played around Winter's lips. It was so fleeting that, once it was gone, I wondered whether I'd imagined it. 'You're asking to stay on and work?'

'Yes! Not as a runner though. You should get me a different position. Maybe ...' I thought about it '...as a food tester. We've had dismemberment. Poison is the next natural step.'

'Is it?'

'It could be!' I'd have kept on arguing with him but I had the feeling that I'd already won. Then a thought occurred to me. 'Hang on,' I said suspiciously. 'Have you just been trying to manipulate me into staying?'

'Of course not! I wouldn't dream of doing such a thing.'

I watched him. The spark suddenly gleaming in the depths of Winter's eyes told me I was right: he wanted me around.

A miniature starburst of joy exploded in my chest. 'Of course you wouldn't,' I said. I leaned in towards him with a serious expression. 'I'm glad you have a reason to be on set now,' I told him. 'It'll be good to be working close together again.'

Winter's gaze met mine. 'Yes,' he replied with a ring of sincerity that made my toes curl. 'It really will be.'

He finished his drink and gave me a little nudge. 'You should toddle off. See if you can find this Gareth and learn more about what he discovered. The more details we can get first-hand about the murder, the better.'

I'd rather hoped that he was going to suggest we have a couple of drinks to celebrate the re-forming of our relationship but I should have known he'd want to stick to work. All the same, I was feeling more optimistic where Winter was concerned.

Wanting to show that I was prepared to listen to him and do as he asked – to an extent – I gave him a quick bob of my head and slid off the stool. I was halfway to the door when I turned round and caught a glimpse of him smiling to himself in the bar mirror. Boom.

***

I trudged back through the streets of Tomintoul towards my hotel, ignoring the curious looks I was getting from the locals – and the odd hissed comment. They'd probably all been delighted when they'd found out *Enchantment* was coming here but I'd bet Brutus's tail that they thought differently now.

I couldn't see any sign of Gareth and I didn't know where to start looking. It would be a waste of breath to ask around for him, even if this were the kind of place where everyone knew everyone else. I knew that this lot would be taciturn and unwilling to point him out to me. I had to find someone who was still dazzled by *Enchantment* and not put off by the grisly goings-on. Teenagers.

'If I were fifteen years old,' I muttered to myself, 'where would I hang out?' Bike sheds seem somewhat passé these days. No doubt there would be some kids hanging around the hotel, hoping for a glimpse of someone famous but I didn't want any of the crew catching sight of what I was up to.

I had to think laterally. It was coming up for six o'clock, so school was out of the question. I doubted there would be a handy skate park around here – but there was a sign for a leisure centre nearby. I shrugged: it seemed as good a place as any. And it was only round the corner. I wanted to please Winter but I did have limits – and I hadn't been lying to Amy about those damned blisters.

Fortunately, I was in luck. As soon as the leisure centre came into view, a pair of boys on bikes rode by. Concentrating, I threw out a quick rune, causing the chain on the lead bike to come undone. It wasn't one of my best ideas – the kid on the bike behind collided with his mate with a loud clunk of metal and an even louder curse. Oops.

I darted over to help them. 'Are you alright?'

'Fine,' the first one muttered from where he was entangled with his bike.

Good. I didn't want to have to mess around with putting the chain back on for him.

He extricated his feet from the bike's frame and pulled himself up. 'You idiot,' he hissed to his friend.

'It's not my fault, Al. You're the one who stopped.'

'Because my bleeding chain came off, didn't it?'

Both boys realised I was watching them and glared. 'Why are you still here?'

I held up my hands. 'I thought you might need some help.' I paused. 'I don't know much about bicycles but I helped fix the axle on one of the camera equipment trucks last week and they can't be that different.'

My oh-so-subtle hint did the trick. The second boy's eyes widened. 'You're with *Enchantment*.'

I clapped my hand over my mouth and looked guilty. 'I wasn't supposed to say anything. Pretend you didn't hear me.' I started walking away.

'Wait!'

I grinned to myself and turned slowly. 'Yes?'

'What do you do for *Enchantment*? Do you know Belinda? Did you see the dead body? Was there a lot of blood?'

The questions came so thick and fast I didn't know which one to answer first. 'Er ... I shouldn't say anything. It's a closed set and we're not supposed to talk to the public about what's going on.'

'We won't tell anyone,' Al said slyly.

'Yeah,' added his mate. 'Tell us about Belinda. She's hot.'

She was also old enough to be their grandmother. 'Between you and me,' I said, 'she's a bit worked up about the murder and what happened this afternoon. She likes to get a handle on things, you know? The police won't talk to her about the death and she feels she can't settle until she knows all the details.'

The boys exchanged looks. 'We know who found the body,' the one called Al said.

His friend nudged him knowingly. 'Yeah. Al knows him *real* well.'

Al snorted. 'Not through choice. He's loony tunes. She'd do better to stay away from him.'

'Who is he?'

'Gareth.' The other boy smirked slyly at his friend. 'McAllan. He lives at Glen Bart Farm.'

'She won't find him there though,' Al added. 'He's not been back home since it happened.' He gave a derisive snort. 'Baby.'

It was easy to judge when you were a kid and you hadn't seen what Gareth had seen. 'So where is he then?'

A calculating expression crossed Al's eyes. 'Buy us a pack of fags and we'll tell you.'

'Smoking's bad for you.'

'Not as bad as working for a television company where everyone keeps dying.' The spotty one had a point.

I shrugged. 'Okay.'

'Fags first. Then we'll tell you.'

Arse. These two were smarter than they made out. I nodded in agreement and they directed me towards the nearest corner shop, although they kept out of sight. I had the feeling that the shopkeeper was probably wise to their tricks.

Buying the first packet I saw, I handed over a crumpled ten-pound note and marvelled at the cost. Then I palmed the packet and went back outside again, finding the boys scuffing a nearby wall. I held up the packet. 'Here you go. You have to tell me where I can find Gareth before I hand it over though. Belinda will be really keen to meet him.'

'Back there.' Al jerked his head at the leisure centre. 'He's in the gym. Thinks if he bulks up he'll be in with the ladies. As if.'

Gareth hadn't struck me as the kind of person who enjoyed a good workout. I shuddered slightly. Even the mention of the word brought me out in hives. It was also somewhat galling that he was so close; I could probably have found him without the dubious help of these two.

'Thanks,' I beamed. Then, before either of them could reach for the cigarettes, I drew a rune and set the whole packet ablaze. 'Up in smoke,' I said sadly.

'You...' Al stared at me like I'd just killed his puppy.

I shrugged. 'It really is bad for you. You should get a new hobby.'

He lunged for me but his friend grabbed him and held him back. 'Leave it be. She's obviously some kind of witch.'

Something flashed in his eyes. 'No wonder she's so ugly. Do you ride a broomstick? Will you turn us into frogs?'

I smiled. 'No. But I will tell your parents if you don't piss off.'

I received identical glares of vicious hatred. I raised my hand as if to draw out another rune, however, and they got the message quickly enough, taking their bikes and sloping off with only a few scowls over their shoulders in my direction. They'd get over it. One day they might even thank me. I watched them go then turned round. Gareth was waiting.

Chapter Eight

My unhappy confidants hadn't been lying. Gareth was indeed in the gym, heaving a barbell even though the pallor of his skin suggested he might do better to lie down for a week or two. He certainly didn't look like he was having fun.

'Hey!'

He jerked in shock and almost lost his grip on the weight.

'Sorry,' I said. 'I didn't mean to startle you.'

'You're looking for me? How did you know I was here?'

'Some kids outside.' Gareth flinched. I pretended not to notice. Teenage boys like Al and his buddy could be intimidating but neither of us needed to admit it out loud. 'How are you doing?'

He put the barbell down and looked at me woefully. 'Great. Just great. I can't sleep no matter how much alcohol I throw down my throat. All I can think about every time I close my eyes is,' he glanced around in case anyone was listening, 'well, you know. I can't eat because every time I smell food I want to throw up. And all I get are people wanting to hear the grisly details. Vultures.'

Ah. It was unfortunate that I would be classed in that category. For the right reasons though, I comforted myself. I sat down on a bench next to him. 'I'm really sorry to hear that. Maybe it would help to talk about it. If you got it off your chest, it might make you feel better.'

He flicked a dribble of sweat from his forehead. 'Why are you here? Don't tell me it's to work out.'

I sighed. Sometimes the truth is the only way out. 'There's been another incident on set,' I told him. 'I don't think anyone has died but there's a lot of blood. The police are doing their best but I can't help thinking that magic has to be involved somehow.' I met his eyes. 'I'm here because I'm a witch. I'm not with the Order or anything like that but I think I can help with the investigation. Whoever did

81

that to Benjamin Albert will probably try again with someone else. You don't just dismember someone then walk away and forget about it. The police won't let any witches into the investigation but the fact it involved a contestant on a magic show...'

My voice trailed away. There wasn't any real evidence that magic was involved, regardless of what the Ipsissimus had told me about secondary sources. But it still seemed very plausible. This was no ordinary killing.

'I want to stop it from happening again, Gareth, and if you tell me what you saw then I might be able to do just that. I can look at it from a fresh perspective. And,' I added, 'I really do think that talking about it will help.'

Gareth watched me for a long moment. 'I believe you,' he said finally.

'That's because I'm telling the truth. Look, I wasn't lying before when I said I know a little about what you're going through. My experience was wholly different to yours and far less brutal, but it still took me a long while before I could get it out of my head. Even if you won't talk to me, you should talk to someone. You need professional help.'

His head dropped. 'The police gave me a number for Victim Support but they also interrogated me as if they thought I'd done it. Ripped someone apart.' He squeezed his eyes shut. 'No one with a soul could do that to another human being.'

I waited. The music piped into the gym changed to an upbeat number, no doubt to fool people into believing that working out was fun. It didn't seem to be doing much for Gareth. For a long moment he didn't say anything. He didn't even move. Then he grabbed a small towel, wiped his face and looked up at me.

'What do you want to know?' he asked quietly.

I didn't smile because this wasn't a cause for celebration. Regardless of the reason I was here, my heart still went out to him. I touched his arm gently to show that I appreciated what he was doing and kept my voice quiet. 'How did you find the body?'

'I work at Glen Bart farm. One of the sheep had escaped from a field so I went to try and find it.'

A sheep. I couldn't help wondering if it was the same one that had bled out in Bellows' trailer. I kept my mouth shut though, and gave him a small encouraging nod.

'There was a trail. I'm no tracker, but there were marks made by some shoes that didn't look like they matched those of anyone else from Glen Bart.' At my questioning glance, Gareth elaborated further. 'We all wear wellies or steel-capped boots. These looked...' He shrugged. 'I dunno. Smart.'

'You could tell that from the footprints?'

'It had been raining so there was quite a lot of mud. One of the prints had a logo on it. Some kind of weird squiggle.' He stood up and walked to a nearby mirror, then breathed on it before drawing the logo in the steam. I squinted. It looked oddly familiar but I couldn't place it. 'We've had quite a few problems in the past with sheep rustling. Only one animal seemed to be missing but that didn't mean whoever took it wouldn't be back for more.'

'Sheep rustling? That's still a thing?'

'You'd be surprised,' he answered grimly. 'Anyway, I tracked the footprints for a mile or so up an embankment and onto Dead Man's Hill. It's called that because it's not far from the cemetery.' His expression took on a morose cast. 'Or that used to be the reason.' He sighed heavily. 'The first thing I saw didn't make any sense. I thought it was a stick at first. But when I got closer there were some ... bits attached to it.' He looked green. 'Flesh,' he whispered. 'Blood. I think it was a rib. I still didn't have any reason to believe it was human. In fact, I wondered if a dog might have got hold of the sheep somehow. Old man Jones at the other end of town has a bloody husky which ... never mind.'

I wasn't sure I wanted to hear any more but I'd promised Winter. 'So you kept on going?' I asked.

'Yeah,' he said. 'I wish to God I hadn't. I really do. It wasn't much further before there was more blood. A lot more blood. When I saw the hand, I knew for sure that this wasn't about the sheep.'

I swallowed. 'It was … dismembered?'

'And chewed. At least three of the fingers had definite bite marks.' He looked at me. 'They didn't look like they'd been caused by an animal.'

'You think they were human?'

He was so quiet I had to strain to hear him. 'I do.' His voice cracked. 'Just beyond the hand there was a head. The eyes...' He shook his head, the horror too great to put into words. 'And the smell was horrific. I've dealt with dead animals before, it comes as part of my job. But this was something different. It feels like the reek of it is still caught in my nostrils. Decaying and sickly sweet.' He stared at me. 'I don't know if it will ever go away.'

That was interesting. I knew from the files that Benjamin Alberts had been missing for less than five hours before his body was discovered. Even with the little I knew about forensic pathology, it didn't seem possible that he could have already smelled that badly. Unless Gareth had magnified it in his mind because of the trauma of what he'd seen.

'For a second, I couldn't move,' he told me. 'It felt like an hour but it was probably only a minute or two. Then I turned and ran back down to the farm and called the police. They did the rest.'

'I'm so sorry it was you who found him,' I said softly.

He avoided my gaze. 'I keep thinking I shouldn't be feeling like this. After all, I'm fine. I didn't get hurt. I didn't know the guy who was killed.' He pressed the base of his palms against his temples as if he could drive out the images of what he'd seen by sheer physical force. 'But I can't get it out of my head. It's always there. I don't know what to do. Can't you help me? If you're a witch, maybe you can make me forget. There must be some potion or herbs you can give me which will make all this go away.'

There were certainly herbs that could dull the sensation of memory. They were a weak salve at best, however; once they wore off, the returning trauma was often worse than before. And runes wouldn't help. Not here.

'There's no magic spell,' I told him honestly. 'But I do know someone who might be able to help. Just give me a few moments.'

I slid my phone out of my pocket and stepped away from him. There was a heaving grunt from a man straining to lift a set of weights so I moved further towards the door.

'Hey Iqbal,' I said, once he answered.

'Ivy, baby! How's it hanging?'

'Not too bad. How's that thesis?'

He sounded smug. 'I've managed to get an extension. I told my supervisor that my grandmother had died.'

'Didn't she pass away a few years ago?'

'You're thinking of the time I skipped lectures for a fortnight and told everyone she'd been attacked by a shark while surfing in Australia. She's still very much alive. More's the pity. She keeps trying to throw girls my way. She can't wait for me to settle down and have a gazillion kids. And she makes me wear these horrid knitted jumpers all year round. I swear she must think I'm ten-stone heavier than I am. They're always massive. And I reckon she makes a special effort to buy wool that is specially itchy.'

'How terrible for you.'

'I know, right?' I could almost hear him grinning. 'Anyway, I'm going to assume because of the late hour that this is not a social call. You want my help again, right?'

'I do. Not for myself this time, though, so no karaoke requests.'

'But the last one went so well! If it hadn't been for that night, you and sexy Raphael Winter would never have got it together. How is he doing? Have you set a date yet?'

I snorted. 'Hardly. Listen, do you still have the number for that counsellor woman?'

'Julia? The pneumatic kisser?'

'That's the one.' Iqbal might have found her a bit overly energetic but she was damned good at her job. And I was sure I'd heard she had moved up to Scotland. 'I could do with getting in touch with her.'

Iqbal dropped all his joking. 'Why? Is everything alright?'

'Like I said, it's not for me.'

'Hang on a minute.' I waited a few beats before he came back on the line and reeled off a phone number.

'Thanks.'

'No problemo. Are you sure you're okay?'

'Yeah, yeah. Although...' I paused. I'd trust Iqbal with my life but what I was about to say made me feel like an idiot.

'What?'

'Well, I'm with Winter on a job. Things are pretty awkward between us. I think he likes me and I *know* I like him. But how do I broach the subject without scaring him off? I'm not with the Order and I'm not technically his partner any more, so there's no real reason why we can't be together. You're a guy. Should I wait for him to make a move? What if he doesn't?'

'Ivy?'

'Yes?'

'This is Ivy, right? Ivy Wilde? The woman who does whatever she wants when she wants?'

'Uh...'

'You really do like him.' Iqbal's voice was full of wonder. 'When have you bothered this much about a guy before?'

I coughed. Raphael Winter had sneaked into my head and, with his typical tenacity, he wasn't letting go. 'Never mind.'

'Ivy Wilde, are you in love?'

'Let's talk about something else.'

'*Is* there anything else?'

'No.' I hesitated. 'Actually, wait, there is something.' I told him about the vial Belinda Battenapple wore around her neck. 'Do you know what it is?'

'No. I can look it up, if you want.'

'I'd appreciate it.'

'I'll do what I can and get back to you.' There was a beat. 'Ivy, are you sure you're alright? You sound ... different.'

I shrugged. 'I'm fine. I'd better go.'

'Look after yourself.'

'Always. Cheerio, Iqqy.'

I jabbed in the number for Julia, whose last name completely escaped me. When she answered with a purr, it was clear she'd been expecting someone very different. I hastily re-introduced myself and outlined Gareth's problems without telling her any real specifics.

'He needs to see someone, Ivy,' she said. 'Someone professional. I know someone who works up in that region. She's brilliant. Give me your friend's number and I'll get her to give him a call.'

'You're the best.'

'I know.'

I strode back to Gareth and passed the phone over to him so he could give her his details. He was somewhat taken aback that so many strangers seemed willing to help him out, but I knew that if I didn't force him to get help he'd keep going on his own until he cracked completely. I could manage a few phone calls. He was the one who'd have to really work hard. Maybe sometimes we all need a bit of a nudge.

Chapter Nine

I snuggled up into my duvet feeling pretty damn pleased with myself. All in all, I reckoned it had been a good day's work. I might have run around like a mad thing for the first part but I'd played the role of runner to perfection. I'd potentially saved two teenage boys from cancer, not to mention that I'd found Gareth the help he needed to return to a sane and normal life.

Of course, I didn't want to have to work this hard every day. I probably ought to give myself the day off tomorrow after doing so well. It was only fair.

I stretched out, enjoying the sensation of drifting into to blissful sleep. This was what I needed. This was what it was about. Glorious, uninterrupted slumber. I sighed contentedly.

'Ivy!'

I frowned. As much as I liked Amy, there were limits. I ignored her whisper. I was sleeping; this was not the time for girly chats. If she wanted a bedtime story, she could go and find Mazza. I was sure he'd be very happy to oblige.

Unfortunately, my room-mate wasn't about to give up. 'Ivy! Can you see that?'

No. I was sleeping. My eyes were closed. I couldn't see anything. I didn't want to see anything.

'It's right outside our window!'

Whatever was there, she was starting to sound alarmed. As long as it was outside, I didn't care.

Then the room phone rang. Amy yelped. I heard her pick up the receiver and answer cautiously. 'Hello?'

Didn't she know anything? You should never pick up the phone at night time. It only invited problems that could almost always wait until daylight. Preferably after noon.

'She's sleeping.'

Uh-oh. I felt an unpleasant squirm deep in the pit of my stomach.

'What? I can't throw water over her!'

Arse. I sighed and sat up. 'Give it here,' I said reluctantly. Wide-eyed, she passed over the phone. 'Winter,' I said. 'I love you to bits but it's the middle of the night. I need to sleep.'

'How did you know it was me?' he asked.

Because I'm not a complete idiot; no one else would be rash enough to try and phone me at this hour. I tutted into the phone.

'Never mind,' he said. 'I need to know what your new friend told you. The one who found the body. I waited ages for you to show up.'

'Really?' I grinned.

His response was terse. 'Of course. We're here on serious business, Ivy.'

As if I'd forget. 'I know that. That's why it's very important that I get enough sleep to function like a human being instead of a zombie tomorrow. He didn't say anything you wouldn't expect.'

I shot a glance at Amy. She was watching me with her arms around round her knees, apparently concerned that this was some type of family emergency. I had to be careful how much I said on the phone; I didn't want to give the poor girl nightmares that might interrupt my sleep even more. 'What he saw was very nasty.'

'Did he give you a location?'

Hang on a minute. There was a businesslike tone to Winter's voice that had me worried. He'd better not be planning what I thought he was. 'Yes.'

'Good. That's what I was hoping for. Meet me downstairs in five minutes and we can go and check it out.'

Before I even began to tell him what a plonker he was, he hung up. I stared at the silent phone, half-expecting Winter to start speaking again and tell me he was joking. Of course, that didn't happen.

I replaced the handset and lay down. There was no way I was going out at this hour to meet him. Midnight trysts were not my thing, even with Winter.

'Is everything okay?' Amy asked tentatively.

'Fine.' Hopefully my terse response would encourage her to lie down and go back to sleep. I closed my eyes. Back to dreamland.

A moment later, I sat back up again. Huffing, I swung my legs out of bed and scrabbled around for my clothes. All I was going to do was to tell him what an idiot he was and that tramping around the Scottish Highlands at this hour was a stupid idea. *Then* I was going back to sleep.

It might have been close to summertime but this was Scotland. My breath clouded in the air and the shock of the cold was almost enough to wake me up. Almost.

Winter was waiting for me underneath a street lamp, looking for all the world like some kind of old-school detective. Or crazed stalker. Frankly, it could have gone either way. I yawned in his direction.

'I really don't think this is a good time to go wandering about a great big hill,' I told him in no uncertain terms.

He didn't acknowledge my complaint; instead, he cast a critical eye up and down. 'You can't wear your pyjamas. Even with that coat on, you'll still get cold.'

'I'm wearing my pyjamas because I'm going back to bed. Winter, even you can't think this is a good idea.'

His expression was blank. 'There's no other time. You'll be busy working during the day. In fact, now there's been a bloody pentagram, I will be too. If we want to check out the murder site, this is the only time we can do it.'

Except I didn't want to check out the murder site, I wanted to go back to bed. 'The police will have been all over it with a fine toothcomb. There won't be anything to see. Not any more.'

Winter arched an eyebrow. 'No witches have been permitted access, Ivy. Do you really think that the police, regardless of how competent they are, will be able to recognise spell traces? Do you think they'd notice if there were some stray herb sprinkles amongst the grass? Would they...'

Bloody hell. 'Enough,' I said. 'Give me five minutes and I'll change my clothes.' This was an argument I wasn't going to win.

***

Just about the only positive to this venture was that Winter had somehow managed to procure a motorbike. He muttered something about borrowing it from the proprietor of his B&B. When he initially refused to let me drive it, I pointed out that driving was what I did for a living and that I hadn't told him where we were going yet. What I didn't mention was that I'd never driven a motorbike before. There was a first time for everything.

'I'd have thought,' Winter shouted in my ear as I revved the engine, 'that you'd take the opportunity to sit back and not do anything. If I drove, you'd be able to relax.'

True. But if he drove, we'd go at snail's pace and he'd probably want to stop to examine random trees or pick rare herbs just in case they would come in useful in the future. With me in charge, we'd get there and back much more quickly. After all, I had to get some sleep at some point.

It was also rather nice having Winter hold my waist. When he almost fell off the back and took me with him, however, I decided I was less enamoured of the situation.

'Slow down!' he yelled in my ear as we careened away from the hotel.

'I can't hear you!' I shouted back and sped up. This was fun. It helped that the roads were empty. Maybe I should get out and about in the Highlands of Scotland in the dead of night more often.

Nah.

From what Gareth had told me, I had an idea about how to get to Dead Man's Hill. There were enough signposts for the cemetery and, when we reached it, I spotted a small dirt track leading up the slope behind it. That had to be what we were looking for. It looked less like a hill and more like a damn mountain that would give Everest a run for its money.

Yet again I pretended not to hear Winter when he shouted that we could walk from here and nudged the bike upwards. I was going to use horsepower to get as close as we possibly could. I kept going upwards, stopping only when I was forced to.

'What the hell?' Winter ground out when I turned off the engine and he slipped off the back.

'There's too much mud. The wheels are spinning.'

He peered at me through the darkness. 'That was not what I meant and you know it. You drive like a demon, Ivy.'

'Thank you.'

Winter growled, 'You should have left the bike at the bottom of the hill.'

I blinked. 'But then we'd have had to walk all the way.'

'Now the bike is all dirty.'

'So wash it when we get back.' Preferably while wearing a white T-shirt, which would quickly get soaked, and when I was watching from a comfortable vantage point. I patted him on the arm. 'Come on. I think it's this way.'

'Then let's get going.' With his usual gait, Winter took off at a tremendous speed, scaling the hill as if it were nothing more than a gentle incline. I followed after him, my determination to get this over and done dissipating in the face of the immediate ache in my calves.

'Slow down,' I called to Winter.

His response was immediate. 'I can't hear you!'

Ha. Ha. Ha. I gritted my teeth and ploughed upwards. Who the hell murdered someone up a mountain? It would have been far more convenient to use the cemetery – at least then it would have been a one-stop shop.

Huffing and puffing, I glanced back down. With the gravestones just visible in the moonlight, it looked more picturesque than creepy. 'It can't,' I heaved, 'be a coincidence,' I paused again for breath, 'that the murder took,' I gasped, 'here.'

Winter finally stopped and turned. 'What on earth is wrong with you?'

I doubled over and tried to bring more air into my lungs.

He snorted. 'If you went to the gym...'

My bottom lip curled. 'Yeah, yeah.' I straightened up. 'The locals call this place Dead Man's Hill. It's probably got nothing to do with the graveyard and everything to do with the fact that you feel like a dead man when you climb it. In any case, it can't be a coincidence. This spot is poetically apt.'

'So you think our murderer is a local?'

'Not necessarily. But I bet it's someone with local knowledge.'

'I think that's a given.'

I clutched my chest. Winter peered at me. 'Are you having a heart attack now?'

'I might be. I'm just so shocked that you agree with me.'

His eyes fixed on mine, their brilliant blue piercing, despite the darkness. 'Stranger things have happened.' He held out his hand. 'I'll help you up the rest of the way.'

Never one to look a gift horse in the mouth, I gladly accepted his help. His hand was warm and firm and, as we walked further up the hill avoiding the odd rabbit hole and clods of random turf, I couldn't shake the delicious shiver that was running down my spine. 'What kind of moisturiser do you use?'

'Huh?'

'Your skin is very soft.'

Winter paused before speaking. 'Sometimes, Ivy Wilde, you are very strange.'

'But you like me really.'

This time there was an even longer silence. 'Yes,' he said finally. 'I do like you.'

I took in a deep breath. It was now or never. Act your age, Ivy, not your shoe size. 'Rafe,' I said quietly. 'Can you stop a minute?'

He did as I asked, turning to face me. 'What is it?'

A cloud passed in front of the moon, blocking out the last of the little light. For once, I was glad that I couldn't see Winter's face. This would be easier, I decided, when I couldn't judge his immediate reaction. Not to mention that he wouldn't be able to see how red my cheeks were, although they felt hot enough that I was probably casting my own glow.

'I've been meaning to say this for some time but,' I gulped in more air, 'I was a bit scared. The thing is that I like you too.' I swallowed. 'What I mean is I...'

From out of nowhere, a huge shape emerged from the darkness to our left. It collided with Winter, throwing him to the ground. I caught the barest glimpse of dark skin, a mane of hair and long claw-like nails flashing towards him with murderous intent before I acted. Screeching like a banshee, I threw out three runes in quick succession.

The first sent out a single gust of wind strong enough to send our attacker off-balance. He swayed violently to one side as the second rune took hold and the roots of a nearby clump of heather rose up and wrapped themselves around one bony thigh and completed the job of pulling him off Winter. The third was a protective barrier, shielding both of us from the bastard's next move.

I yanked Winter to his feet. He was breathing heavily and there were four raked cuts down his cheek, blood dripping from each one. 'Get back, Ivy.'

I moved in front of him. He was injured; this wasn't the time for gentlemanly heroics. There was a rustle as whoever had attacked us broke free from the heather and sprang up again to face us. I stared at him, horror reverberating through my veins. Yes, he was male. And, yes, he looked vaguely human – but the emphasis was on vaguely.

He had long straggly hair that covered his face, which was probably just as well given the state of the skin on his hands. There were pus-filled sores and his nails were an extraordinary length. He was on all fours, like some kind of animal. A continuous guttural snarl emitted from his throat and the reek that wafted from him was almost enough to make me pass out.

None of those were the worst things about him, though. What really sent a chill through me was that he was wearing a smart double-breasted suit, complete with red-spotted tie and a matching handkerchief peeking out from his top pocket. It was like being faced with a monster from Savile Row. A real monster.

I barely had time to take in all these details before he lunged again. His body smacked against my magical barrier and I felt the magic in it waver. It wouldn't last long.

Winter stepped up next to me. 'Goddamnit, Ivy, get back!' He raised his hands, drawing his own runes.

'They won't...' I began. I didn't get the chance to finish. Fire plumed upwards, singeing the ward and falling short uselessly. There was no such thing as a one-way barrier. It protected us from the monster man but it also protected the monster man from us.

Winter hissed out an expletive. 'Release the ward spell,' he yelled as we were subjected to another frustrated attempt at an attack.

'If I release the spell,' I argued, 'then we're dead.' I wasn't even sure why I was bothering to refuse. It'd probably take the bastard facing us fewer than three attempts to bring it down completely.

Winter's jaw clenched. 'Fine. On the count of three, you start running back down the hill. Go and get help from the town. I'll hold him off until then.'

That was about the most nonsensical thing I'd ever heard – for many reasons. 'You know I can't run,' I told him.

'Ivy, this is not the time.'

I drew back my shoulders. 'No, it's not. Because if you think I'm leaving you here alone with that thing, then you're doolally.'

'Doo what?'

The monster man threw his head back and screamed. For a fleeting moment, his face was visible – what remained of it. I saw a swarm of maggots in the soft flesh of his cheek and little more than dark holes where his eyes should have been. I swallowed hard and tried not to vomit.

'Doolally,' I whispered. 'Whatever this thing is, it's going to take both of us to bring it down.'

Winter didn't answer immediately. I wondered whether he was still going to argue the point. Instead he gave me a small, tight nod. 'Fire,' he said. 'Fire will stop it in its tracks. If you release the ward, I'll cast out enough fire to cremate it to kingdom come.'

I shook my head. 'It'll die with fire but it'll take too long. It'll be on us before it collapses and we'll end up getting burnt too.'

The monster man snorted, as if he thought both of us were being ridiculous. Still on all fours and moving with the litheness of a cat, he began to circle round us apparently searching for weaknesses in the ward.

'We're running out of time. We need something.'

'Tell me something I don't know.'

Winter reached into his pocket. 'Calendula flowers. They'll offer us some protection.'

Not much. I nodded, however. The energy I'd expelled in order to cast the three runes was costing me and my whole body felt drained and weak. Even if I wanted to run away and leave Winter to it, I wasn't sure I could. 'We have to work together,' I said in a strained voice.

Winter shot me a quick look of concern. 'Yes.'

'We need to stop the thing. We don't necessarily have to kill it.'

His left eyebrow twitched slightly. I had the feeling there was something he wasn't telling me but there wasn't time to pursue it now. 'Not fire then.' He paused. 'Ice.'

That could work. I stretched out my hands. There was enough moisture in the air, I reckoned. Just.

The monster man began to growl. He was preparing for something. He threw himself down to the ground and began to scrabble in the earth at the base of the barrier, as if he'd decided that he couldn't go through it so he might as well go under it. Every time he touched the ward, the magic flickered. We had seconds.

'Use the calendula. I'll release the spell.'

Winter agreed. 'I'll draw on the water in the air.'

'And I'll draw a rune to drop the temperature.' I nodded. This could work.

Winter reached out, grabbed my hand and squeezed it. 'We'll be fine.'

'Sure.' I smiled unconvincingly. 'No problem.'

'Aim for its feet and legs,' he advised.

The monster gave up on its scrabble and reared back before launching itself at the ward once more. The second after it crashed into it I sketched out the rune to dissipate the barrier; at the same time Winter threw the calendula in an arc in front of us. The monster grunted and heaved itself back onto its hands and feet. Winter drew his own runes and the molecules in the air almost immediately coalesced. The monster threw back its head, displaying a slashed, maniacal grin, then it lunged just as a wash of water rose up to meet it.

'Now, Ivy!'

I wasted no more time. Hastily flicking out a double-handed rune, I forced Winter's water to freeze. The magic was fast. Winter pulled me backwards as the monster's claws scraped towards us. Then it fell heavily to the ground with its feet and legs encased in a large chunk of ice.

It groaned – but it wasn't giving up. It stretched out its arms, flailing towards both Winter and me as if it thought it could still catch us. There was enough ice to hold it in place for an hour or two. That would give us time to work out what to do next.

I walked over and crouched down beside its head. It wasn't easy; the smell of putrefying flesh surrounding it was extraordinary. A troubled thought pricked at the back of my mind but I pushed it away. This monster man was unlike anything I'd ever dreamt of but that didn't mean I should start thinking the impossible.

'Careful, Ivy!'

I gave Winter a faint smile. For all the creature's flapping, it was an easy thing to stay away from those claws now its body was trapped. I tilted my head towards it. 'What are you?' I asked. 'Why are you doing this?'

'There's no point in trying to communicate with it,' Winter said. 'It's not going to respond. It can't.'

It appeared Winter was right – the only answer I received was a snarl. Just to be sure, I tried again. 'Can you speak English? Did you kill Benjamin Alberts?'

I looked down, noting that the soles of its shoes had the same squiggle of a logo that Gareth had drawn for me. This was definitely our culprit. This ... thing had ripped Benjamin Alberts apart.

I sensed rather than saw Winter come up beside me. Before I could say or do anything, he raised his hands. Too late, I registered the rock he was holding. A second later, he brought it down onto the monster's head, smashing in its skull and spraying me with dark co-agulated lumps of weird monster blood. There was one short spasm and then the thing stopped moving. Forever.

I stared aghast at Winter. He shrugged at me, although there wasn't any ambivalence in his expression. 'It was already a corpse, Ivy. It's an animated anomaly. Whatever we're dealing with here involves necromancy. Someone is raising the dead to attack the living.'

Chapter Ten

I felt like death warmed up. Given the circumstances, that probably should have been funny but I definitely wasn't laughing. I managed a muttered good morning to Amy and that was about it. When we were ushered onto the bus pre-dawn, I simply kept my head down and ignored the speculation around me about whether *Enchantment* would be able to continue.

I'd spent almost an hour under the scalding shower and I was sure I could still smell the damn monster on me. Every time I thought about it, a shudder rippled through my very bones.

When we arrived on set, we gathered out by the main stage as we had done the previous day. There was no sign of any of the contestants but all the *Enchantment* bigwigs were there. No crew members were rushing around or making preparations; everyone simply waited to hear what we would be told. It might have been my favourite television show but, frankly, I was praying that they'd shut the whole thing down for good. I felt like I could sleep for a week.

Surprisingly, it wasn't Morris Armstrong who took the microphone. He was there on stage but he gave the floor to Belinda. She was dressed more simply than yesterday but, as she was wearing a silk scarf wrapped in an elaborate knot around her neck, it was impossible to see whether she was wearing her vial necklace. Whatever.

I cast a tired eye around for Moonbeam and spotted him lounging against a tall box on the far side. He was doing his best to appear disdainful but his body language was too relaxed. He didn't know any better than the rest of us what was about to be said – and he was just as curious. Mommy dearest wasn't keeping him in the loop then. I wondered why. I closed my eyes and decided I really didn't care.

'Dearest people.' Belinda's voice filled the air. Despite her saccharine-sweet words, she somehow managed to sound wholeheartedly sincere. I opened one eye slightly; she was charismatic enough that

I'd give her that much attention. 'You all know, of course, of the traumatic time we have faced over the past few weeks. Losing one of our contestants was a genuine shock and I have no doubt that you felt the tragedy just as deeply as I did.'

She paused, as if in memory of the dear friend she had probably not even met, and continued. 'Of course, things got even worse yesterday when our own set was attacked.'

Trevor Bellows reached forward and grasped her hand. As if to give credence to the sombre mood, he was no longer wearing fancy dress. Oddly, however, the high-waisted jeans and T-shirt made him look far weirder than the Halloween witch's get-up that he had on yesterday.

'I'm fine,' Bellows said, bobbing his head up and down several times. 'It was a terrible experience but, if I can find even some of the strength which you wonderful people have, I will get through this.'

Unfortunately for him, Bellows didn't have the same aura of honesty that Belinda managed to convey. Perhaps it was because his words were so patently ridiculous. There was more than one scoff from the watching crew. If Bellows noticed, he didn't react.

Any dregs of sympathy I might have felt for him at apparently being targeted by a murderer vanished the instant Brutus leapt on stage and curled up on one of his shoes. There was a soft murmur of delight from the crowd. I crossed my arms and glared. Not that it did any good; Brutus didn't even glance at me.

Bellows passed the microphone back to Belinda and she continued. 'What most of you don't know,' she said in honeyed tones, 'is that there were significant developments overnight.'

There was a collective intake of breath. Even Moonbeam seemed to stand up straighter. I yawned. Significant developments? I'd say.

Belinda cleared her throat, more for dramatic effect than because she needed to. It was hardly necessary. You could have heard a cat's whisker drop to the ground. 'The murderer has been brought to justice.'

I snorted. The tool had been destroyed but its maker was still out there.

Belinda carried on blithely. 'Not just that, but the blood which was discovered on set belonged to a sheep, not a human. We no longer have anything to fear. No doubt it was simply a prank. And,' she smiled, 'it is apparent that *Enchantment* was not the target of the original attack. Benjamin Alberts, may his soul rest in peace, was simply in the wrong place at the wrong time. Filming will start afresh this afternoon at three o'clock. We are behind schedule but, if we pull together as a team, we can bring everything back to where it should be. We are, after all, the greatest show on television.'

There was a loud cheer from the watching crew members. As far as I could tell, everyone was delighted. I wrinkled my nose. Yeah, yeah.

Morris Armstrong stepped up. For a moment it looked as if Belinda wasn't going to relinquish her hold on the microphone. Rather than cause a scene, however, she eventually let it go. There was no denying who was really running things around here – and Belinda was perfectly content to make sure everyone knew it. Given that yesterday Armstrong had spoken to everyone without a microphone, it was clear that his bid to take the microphone from her was a power play on his part. A failed power play at that.

'I would like to thank Belinda for her gracious words. Be assured that I share every sentiment,' Armstrong said. '*Enchantment* is most definitely the greatest!' He fist-pumped the air. More than a few of the crew aped his actions but there was definitely less enthusiasm than there had been for La Battenapple. 'To prove it, for this time ever, this series will have a member of the esteemed Hallowed Order of Magical Enlightenment on board!'

A ripple of shock ran through the crowd. As Winter stepped onto the stage, looking for all the world as if he wished the ground would open up and swallow him, Trevor Bellows appeared rather nauseous. If he'd been worried about me as competition, he couldn't begin to fathom what it would be like having Winter judging his every move.

'This is Adeptus Exemptus Raphael Winter!' Armstrong began to applaud and gradually everyone else joined in. Even Bellows.

Winter forced a smile. His eyes scanned the crowd until eventually they landed on me. I raised my arms and clapped enthusiastically until the corners of his mouth crooked up slightly. I wasn't oblivious to the many lascivious looks he was receiving from most of the female – and some of the male – crew members. I resisted the urge to yell out that he was hands off and contented myself with the fact that at least he was here. And at least it was me he was focused on.

But there were limits to how much Winter was going to be allowed to do. The microphone in Armstrong's hands went nowhere near him and the director quickly regained everyone's attention. 'We have seven hours until showtime, everyone! Let's get this set shipshape and ready once more.'

And with that, they all trooped off the stage.

***

'*Enchantment* is most definitely being targeted,' Winter told me in an aside when I caught up with him near the main producers' tent.

I raised an eyebrow. 'What makes you say that?'

'There were some herbs found on the body last night. They were matched to a clump discovered in Bellows' trailer. And,' he reached into his pocket, 'I found more of the same scattered around the perimeter.'

I sucked in a breath. 'All the way around?'

Winter nodded, his expression grim. There were only two reasons why you'd encircle an entire area with herbs. To protect it – or to attack it.

'So we're looking for a witch again.' Except why would an Order witch care about a reality television show that used only the weakest forms of magic?

Surprisingly, Winter disagreed. 'I don't think a witch is behind this.'

'But you just said...'

'The amounts are all wrong.' He trailed his index finger through the herbs in his hand. 'In every location I've checked, there are two parts cinquefoil to one part mandrake, with a tiny amount of prickly ash bark thrown in. I can't see how that would have an effect on anything. Even in small quantities, the prickly ash bark would completely negate the mandrake. And there's no known spell that uses mandrake and cinquefoil together. I've spent the best part of the night on the phone to the Herblore Department back in Oxford. They agree.'

I pursed my lips. 'Is the Order being set up?'

'Either that or we have a dangerous amateur on our hands.' Winter swept a hand around. 'Given where we are and who we're surrounded by, that's not a great shock.'

'But the thing that attacked us last night was a damn zombie. A zombie!'

He sighed. 'I explained that to you already. It wasn't a zombie. It was an animated anomaly.'

'Of course it was a zombie! It was a dead body which clawed its way out of its grave and attacked us!' I still found it difficult to believe but the evidence had been there.

'Keep your voice down.'

I put my hands on my hips. 'Seriously? You don't think that the people here have a right to know about this? There could be an army of the dead on their way!'

'There's no army.'

'You don't know that!'

'Ivy, it's impossible to raise more than one un-dead being at a time. Unless there's an army of necromancers, which is not going to be the case, there's no army of the dead.'

I met his gaze head on. 'I bet,' I said, 'that if I had asked you last week if it were possible to raise one dead body, you would have said that was impossible too. Except that's already happened. How could an amateur manage it?'

'I don't know yet. Necromancy is so rare that we don't know much about it. There's very little written in the Cypher Manuscripts because any spells designed to get the dead even to twitch are highly unreliable.'

'I wouldn't call what happened last night as a corpse merely twitching!'

Winter placed a hand on my arm. 'I know you're concerned. I am too. But one of the conditions of being permitted on set is that no one finds out what's really been going on.' I opened my mouth to continue arguing but he didn't let me start. 'The Ipsissimus agrees. We can't have the world and its dog knowing that necromancy is real. We have to deal with enough conspiracy theories as it is. Not to mention that people up and down the country will be trying to raise their loved ones. Or worse.'

'But the people *here* could be in danger, Rafe.'

Winter's voice softened. 'I know. It's up to you and me to make sure they're safe until we find out who's really behind this.'

'Can't you do one of your herby spells to find out what happened in Bellows' trailer? That'll give us something to work with at least.'

He sighed. 'I tried that first thing. There have been too many people coming in and out of the trailer for it to work. All it conjured up was a mess.'

Fat lot of good that was, then. I tried a different tack. 'Morris Armstrong said that they chose this area for filming because there are historical links to magic.'

He nodded. 'I heard. But it was one family a long time ago. While their descendants are still in the area, they don't have any discernible magic. They've already been interviewed. They don't have any links to the animated anomaly that attacked us last night either. I've already checked. The truth is that none of this started until *Enchantment* came to town.'

'And with the traces of crap magic we've found around the set...' I sighed. It did seem likely that the television show and at least one of its crew were connected.

'The situation is different now. Even if the production company agreed to shut down *Enchantment*, we'd have to start from scratch again. At least this way we're in the right place to catch the bastard who's doing this.' He squeezed my arm. 'There are back-up teams already on their way from Oxford. They'll stay out of the way unless we really need them but we know that they'll be there.'

My bottom lip jutted out. I really didn't like this. 'Can I at least stop being a runner now?'

'Your cover remains in place. We need to provide for every eventuality and you can sneak around less noticeably than me if you're just another crew member.'

As if to add credence to that irritating sentence, someone shouted to me from the other side of the path. 'You! You're wanted in the tent!'

'I have a name!' I yelled back.

'Ivy,' Winter warned.

'Yeah, yeah. I don't see why you get to be the expert swanning around while I have to be the dogsbody.'

He lowered his head to my ear as the ghost of a smile crossed his face. 'Join the Order and become my partner for real then maybe things will change.'

Not in the way I wanted them to. I lifted my head and breathed in Winter's musky scent, filling my lungs with it. Good grief, he smelled divine.

'Get a move on!' bellowed the same plonker from before.

I cursed. 'I'd better go.' A few drops of rain began to fall from the sky. I supposed at least I'd be inside for a while. Small mercies.

Winter's hand still lingered on my arm. 'Be careful, Ivy. If you see or suspect anything, you come and find me first. Don't put yourself in *any* unnecessary danger.'

There was something about the look in his eyes that made me think he was very earnest. I nodded and tried to smile.

'I mean it,' he growled. 'No matter what it is, if there's any hint of danger then we investigate it together. Promise me.'

'I promise,' I whispered. Very, very reluctantly, I plodded off to the entrance of the producer's tent. I was pretty certain that Winter watched me the entire way and I couldn't help injecting a tiny bit of extra sashay into my stride. Unfortunately, it seemed to be about the only part of all this I had control over for now.

***

First of all, I had to sweep the floor. Then re-arrange the schedule board to show the updated version. Then make copies of the new schedule and deliver them to *all* the crew. When I got back to the tent just about ready to collapse, I was ushered into the main space and told to make coffee for all the producers who were sitting around a large table and too deep in discussion to manage a please or thank you.

I plonked myself down in the far corner and sat cross-legged on the floor. It was all becoming too much. I tried to will my legs to work but it wasn't happening; instead I pushed my head back so I could see the top of the refreshments table. Then I used a quick series of runes to set out the cups and saucers.

There must have been quite a rattle of china because several of the producers' heads turned in my direction. One blonde woman nudged the man next to her and the pair of them watched as I lazily lifted my hand. At least there was a decent-sized urn with enough hot water in it to do the trick. I ignored their stares and continued. Some of us had real work to do. The group eventually gave up on the Ivy Wilde Show and continued their discussion. I was too tired even to listen, despite their tones of worry and displeasure.

I'd just finished magically dispensing teaspoons to each saucer from my vantage point on the ground when Belinda entered with a young man who I took to be her assistant. He was holding an umbrella over her head and, rather than fold it up, he left it open. I squeaked in dismay. This might only be a tent but we were still indoors. I'd already had all the bad luck I needed for this year.

Abandoning the coffee cups, I lunged for the still-dripping brolly. The man gave me an astonished look.

'What the hell do you think you're doing?' I yelled at him. 'Don't you know anything?' I snapped the umbrella shut and flung it back at him. His reactions weren't fast enough to catch it and it fell uselessly to the floor.

Belinda raised a perfectly manicured eyebrow in my direction. 'Is there a problem?'

'I should think,' I said through gritted teeth, no longer caring that I was talking to one of my idols, 'that a magical show would know better than to tempt fate.'

A flicker of amusement crossed her face and she exchanged glances with the seated producers, as if to tell them that they'd employed a crazy person. Honestly. I was surrounded by idiots. Famous well-paid idiots, but idiots nonetheless.

She sat down. 'I'm afraid it's bad news,' she began.

I snorted to myself. If she went around indoors with open umbrellas that was hardly surprising. I stopped paying her attention and collapsed in the corner again. My small spurt of energy meant I'd need to sit down for at least another half an hour.

Using some carefully designed runes, I transported each cup to the urn and filled it up before sending it through the air to each seated person. One by one, they all fell silent as my bippity-boppity-boo ensured they were appropriately watered.

'What?' I snapped. 'You said you wanted coffee.'

Morris Armstrong, whom I'd barely noticed near the end of the table, inclined his head. 'And we thank you for it.' He reached down and took a sip. 'It tastes even better for the magic.'

'Is she with the Order too?' asked a dapper bloke with slicked-back hair.

'No.'

'But...'

'Let's just get on with this. You say there's bad news, Belinda?'

I continued depositing my floating cups. Belinda stared then shook herself. 'Billy is right. The Bitch is dropping out.'

There was a loud chorus of disapproval. 'We need her!'

'I've tried. She's adamant. Apparently she got on well with Benjamin Alberts and his untimely death has hit her hard. With what happened to Trevor's trailer, she's decided enough is enough and can't be swayed. She's already on her way home.'

Another producer hissed through his teeth. 'She had the most magic out of this lot. Not that that's saying much.'

'At least she's dropped out before filming began,' Armstrong interjected. 'We can use another standby.'

'Except several of the standbys have already left too. And none of them have the temperament we're looking for. If we don't get the fireworks we need, this series will fall flat. We needed the Bitch to cause arguments. We needed some magic. She was a sure bet for the final and now she's out the door and on the train.'

The woman nearest me caught my eye and pointed to the sugar. I bobbed my head and started a new dance, sending a line of sachets tipping through the air. Casting unnecessary runes like this could be exhausting but I was willing to forego some of my remaining energy for the sake of staying off my feet a little while longer.

'Your son is champing at the bit to get in,' Armstrong said.

'Pah!' Belinda flicked back her hair with such force that she almost got hit by several sugar sachets. I only just diverted them in time. 'I won't have him as a reality show contestant. He's far better than that.'

'He's very keen…'

'No.' Her voice was flat and brooked no argument. 'Besides, we need a female or there will be a gender imbalance. And we need someone who the others are going to hate.'

A tentative hand went up at the far end. It wasn't seeking Belinda's attention, though. 'Could I get some milk?'

I gave a dramatic sigh of irritation and sent a little jug flying over, inadvertently spraying half of its contents across several of the others. A few of the producers leapt out of the chairs in alarm. Belinda, however, turned towards me with a brilliant smile and pointed one long, bejewelled finger. 'She's perfect.'

'Ha ha.'

She tutted. 'I'm serious. This … runner has got magic.' She glanced at Armstrong. 'She's definitely not with the Order?'

'No. I had her checked out. She has been with them in the past but she's not now.'

Belinda nodded happily. 'Excellent. So there's no chance that our new resident Adeptus Exemptus can get pissed off. She's obviously not afraid to say what she thinks. Not to mention that the other contestants will despise her for coming in at the last minute. Wasn't there some wardrobe kerfuffle because of her as well?'

A few smiles spread across the others' faces. 'Yes. The Mouse hates her.'

I took 'The Mouse' to mean Harriet, who I'd attempted to help. Yeah. She probably did hate me – but not as much as I hated this stupid job. And there was no way I was going to be one of their contestants. I might love watching the show but I had zero desire to be part of it.

'Thanks,' I said, 'but no thanks. Find someone else.'

Belinda rose gracefully to her feet and directed her gaze at Armstrong. 'Make it happen,' she declared. Then she swept out, her assistant throwing me a nervous look and scooping up the offending umbrella before dashing out after her.

With an effort, I stood up and glared. 'I am not going to be a contestant.'

Morris Armstrong smiled at me. 'I think the lovely Ms Battenapple is right,' he murmured. 'You're perfect.'

'No. Nuh-huh. Absolutely no way.' I hardened my eyes, hoping he'd remember that I had a secret mission to complete for him. Just because Winter was now on the team didn't mean I couldn't still be a useful spy. 'You need me for other things.'

'Not any longer.'

I pointed at the cups. 'Someone has to make you coffee.'

'I'm sure one of the other runners can do that.'

'But...'

Armstrong held up his hand. 'Would you rather be fêted as one of the contestants on the greatest show on earth or run around in the rain on errands?'

I'd rather lie on my sofa and eat chocolate. 'I thought you had fond memories of your time as a runner.'

'I lied. It's horrific. We all know that. We've all been there.' There were several murmurs of agreement from around the table. 'This is a fast track to the top, Ivy. You'll be amazing. You're just what we need. You could clean and get blisters and bow and scrape. Or,' he deepened his voice to show just what a fabulous opportunity I was supposedly getting, 'you could be a contestant on *Enchantment*. Do you know how many applicants we get?'

'So choose one of them.'

'We don't have time. You'll have a far easier time on the show than behind the scenes.'

He had a point. But it would be hard to do any proper investigating if I were being filmed at every moment. Winter probably wouldn't like it either.

'Nope. Still not doing it.'

Armstrong stood up. 'Do you want to be here?'

Not really. Not with zombies running around the place. 'Yes.'

'Then become a contestant.' He shrugged. 'Or get out.'

Arse. His eyes didn't waver. He wasn't bluffing. 'But Adeptus Exemptus Winter...' I began.

'I'll worry about him from now on. It's not as if you've told me anything about him yet anyway. He probably found out about the pentagram in Trevor Bellows' trailer from you.'

I was prevented from giving an answer by Mazza, who burst in with a newspaper in his hands. 'I was told to show you this!' he gasped breathless.

I glanced at the headline. *Battenapple's Horror*. I peered closer. It appeared to be a story about how disturbed she was by the death of Benjamin Alberts. My heart sank when I spotted the photo underneath the headline of two familiar teenage boys who were quoting a 'special on-set source'. Bloody hell.

Armstrong transformed in an instant. His cheeks puffed out and a vein started bulging in his forehead. 'Where did this come from?'

We did not want that at all. With considerable reluctance, I allowed him to drag me into the tent. Apparently the women there had been forewarned because Barry's delight was nothing compared to their glee. The woman who'd shrieked hellfire at me for daring to alter Harriet's clothes had a particularly nasty gleam in her eye.

'Well, well, well,' she purred. 'Look who's now a contestant!' She drew me in close and whispered in my ear, 'I hope you get voted out first, you little harlot.'

Harlot? I wasn't sure what that had to do with anything. That was until she reached out for my costume.

'We've thought long and hard about what would suit you best in the ten minutes since we were informed of your new status. And we know exactly what will work for you.' She held up what could only be described as a scrap of fabric. 'Mr Bellows was kind enough to bespell it for us so that you can't alter it with your magic.' She sneered the last word, somehow forgetting that this was supposed to be a magic show.

I doubted whether Bellows' magic would withstand what I could produce if I really wanted to, but I had the feeling that if I tried to change my designated outfit I'd be given something far worse. Not that there could be much that was worse than this, I thought miserably.

Wardrobe Lady all but threw it at me. 'Go on, then. Go and get changed. Time is ticking away!' She let out a peal of laughter. At least the others looked slightly guilty at what they were forcing me into.

Was it too late to back out now? I frowned down at the poor excuse for clothing and shrugged. 'It's stunning,' I lied. 'I'm so lucky!'

Her smile faltered. 'Glad you like it.' Her voice hardened. 'Put it on.'

I plodded round to the changing area. The dress looked as if it were about two sizes too small for me. I stripped off and squeezed into it. Make that three sizes too small. It was a strange combination of something Snow White would wear coupled with a dominatrix's favourite costume.

I stared down at my cleavage. *Enchantment* was supposed to be a family show. Not only did I look as if my breasts were about to fall out at any moment but I also had a built-in leather corset contraption to contend with. The bottom section only reached mid-thigh, but if I hiked it down to cover some of my wobbly flesh all I succeeded in doing was displaying more skin up top. The billowy sleeves were sort of pretty, I supposed, but they were made from sheer material. We were in the Highlands! How was I going to get any protection from the notoriously wet Scottish weather while wearing this?

'Are you ready?' Wardrobe Lady called out.

I grimaced and drew back my shoulders. I wasn't going to let her break me. I'd flaunt this ridiculous garb to the very best of my ability. With my head held high, I strutted out.

Even Barry appeared shocked. He didn't know where to look: his eyes drifted from my face to my chest and back again. He eventually fixed his gaze on a midpoint around my collarbone. 'That's, uh, that's pretty.'

Wardrobe Lady tapped her mouth. 'Something's missing.'

Several yards of fabric?

She squinted and then her expression cleared. 'I know!' She bent down, reached into a chest and drew out a pair of knee-high boots. With stiletto heels.

'No.' I folded my arms across my chest. Even I had limits. I wouldn't be able to walk three feet in those things without toppling over.

Wardrobe Lady smiled. 'Yes. I'm in charge here, darling.'

I shook my head. 'This show needs me more than I need it. No heels. If you're that desperate to get your revenge on me by making me wear this, fine. I'll let you have your moment. But I won't put on those shoes.'

Her mouth tightened fractionally. Whether it was because I'd called her out on her petty plan or because I was refusing to tramp around muddy Scottish moors in those boots, I wasn't sure. She'd be sorry if she ended up getting her face eaten off because I couldn't get to her in my heels in time for a rescue.

Seeming to realise that she'd gone too far, she relented. 'Fine,' she snapped. She reached into the chest again and took out some ballet pumps. 'Will these do her highness?'

Nah. Too flimsy. I glanced over her shoulder and spotted a heavy, scuffed pair of Doc Martens. 'I'll take those.'

Wardrobe Lady opened her mouth to refuse so I forestalled her. 'You've seen a tiny amount of what I'm capable of,' I said softly. 'But changing a few seams isn't what I'm really good at. My magic skills are far beyond anything you can imagine. You might think you know magic from working on *Enchantment*. The truth is that you don't have a clue.' To emphasise my point and make sure she didn't mistake my meaning, I added a close-mouthed smile. It didn't reach my eyes.

Wardrobe Lady swallowed. 'I think those will look good,' she said eventually.

I clapped her on the shoulder. 'Great minds think alike!' I bent down and put them on. A perfect fit.

Gazing in the mirror I decided that, despite her best efforts, I looked rather cool. The Doc Martens made me seem more like a grunge princess than a showy hooker. At least that's what I was going to tell myself.

When I finally left the trailer, with Barry still firmly by my side, a gust of cold air immediately gave me a serious bout of goose pimples. And it was clear from my producer's embarrassed cough that the flimsy material was doing little to hide my reaction to the cold in other areas as well.

I spotted Winter on the far side of the set. He glanced over and beckoned me. It took him a moment but, when he finally realised what I was wearing, his mouth slowly dropped open.

'We need to get to make-up,' Barry told me.

'Just give me a minute. Stay here.'

'But...'

I ignored his protests and set off. When I reached Winter, he was trying hard not to stare. I twirled for full effect, almost losing my balance in the process. Winter reached out and grabbed me before I fell over. Slightly breathless, I grinned at him. 'Whaddya think?'

Winter's jaw worked. 'What...?' For once he was lost for words.

'I've been press-ganged into becoming a contestant,' I informed him. 'I think I'm to play the role of evil slut.' I grinned at him. 'Of course, I'm sure you know where the word slut comes from.'

'Huh?' He blinked rapidly.

'Slut,' I said, rather enjoying myself. 'What's the etymology of the word?'

Winter shook his head in disbelief. 'I have no idea. It's not something I've ever thought about.'

'Well,' I informed him airily, 'technically it's of dubious origin and possibly generates from the German word *schlutt* meaning slovenly woman. But there's also an argument to be made for the Swedish term *slata* which translates as idle woman.' I beamed triumphantly. 'It's like these people see right through me.'

Winter's mouth flattened into a grim line. 'I can see right through you! Right through that dress anyway. You can't wear that!'

'Wardrobe Lady made me put it on. She doesn't like me very much.'

Winter looked even more annoyed. 'Every man on set will be leering at you!'

I shrugged. 'That's their problem. Not mine.'

'It's...' He suddenly halted. 'Hang on,' he said slowly. 'What did you say? You're a contestant?'

'It was either that or be thrown off set.' I tried to look apologetic. 'Sorry.'

'No, this is brilliant. Well done, Ivy.'

I smiled again. 'Thank you.' Then I hesitated. 'Why is it brilliant?'

'We've not been able to get close to any of the contestants. After Alberts was killed, I'm sure the police interviewed them all but the Order hasn't been given access. Considering it was a contestant who was murdered, and that the contestants are all here ostensibly because they can use at least some magic, it's quite possible that one or more of them is involved.' He rubbed his chin. 'Even if they're not, they might still be targeted by our would-be necromancer. If you're one of them, you'll be able to investigate them and protect them at the same time.'

I hate multi-tasking. 'Or I could make them all my bitches and have them running at my beck and call.'

Winter frowned in exasperation. 'Did you see the papers this morning? Someone has been talking to the press. Not to mention allegedly buying cigarettes for some children. You should take some time before this afternoon to find out who. Anyone who would stoop that low is bound to have sneakier plans. Perhaps not necromancy, but it's a slippery slope to evil, Ivy.'

'Mmm.' I started to fidget. I needed to change the subject. 'Do we have any information on who our zombie was?'

Winter muttered something under his breath at the z word. 'He was a local man who died just over two years ago in a farming accident. I have spoken to his family and there's no magical connection with them and no reason to believe he was specifically targeted. The Order will keep looking into it but I don't think we're going to draw any leads that way.' He shrugged. 'All indications suggest his rising was due to chance and perhaps opportunity. There is nothing to suggest he was chosen for a reason.'

For some reason that disturbed me more than if his body had been specifically selected. Lack of clear motive meant that the person behind this could have much grander designs for bringing the dead back to life. Grander designs that I doubted would be warm or fluffy for the rest of us. I tugged at the bodice of my dress, irritated by the scratchy material, and sighed.

'Do you really have to wear that?' Winter enquired.

'It's not that bad.'

He harrumphed. 'You look like you're serving yourself up on a platter.'

Wincing slightly, I smoothed down the skirt. 'Let's not talk about humans as food while there are zombies around, shall we?'

'I told you,' he began, 'it's not zomb—'

'What gives?' Moonbeam marched over, interrupting Winter and glaring at me. 'I'm supposed to be the replacement! All that work I put in and they chose you instead?' His voice dripped with disdain. 'You!'

I shrugged. 'Unless there's something you're not telling us, you're not quite what they're looking for.'

He rose up, even more piqued than before. 'I'm exactly what they're looking for! I can fill any role!'

'They want a woman, Moonbeam.'

'I...' He deflated. 'Damn it.'

'Sorry.' I wasn't but he looked so dejected that I figured I could say it.

Moonbeam ran a hand through his hair. 'All that work.' He sighed and glanced at Winter. 'You're the Order witch.'

Winter was staring at Moonbeam in fascination. 'Yes, I am.'

From behind, I saw Barry desperately try to catch my eye and point to his watch. I played dumb and looked confused.

'I'm a big fan!' With an impressive mood change, Belinda's son switched from looking pathetic to complete enthusiasm. 'I love the Order! How difficult is it to get in? I can do magic, you know.'

Both Winter and I gazed at him with sudden interest. 'Can you?' Winter asked. 'Have you ever performed any spells?'

'Like raising the dead and creating an army of zombies?' I butted in.

Winter jabbed me sharply in the ribs. 'Ignore Ivy,' he said with an irritated glance in my direction. 'We used to work together and she seems to have delusions of grandeur where her magic ability is concerned.'

It was my turn to frown. 'But you said...' Winter's glare intensified and I paused. 'Yeah, okay. I'm crap at spells,' I lied.

Moonbeam wasn't interested. His attention was wholly on Winter. 'You know I have friends in the Order? They're very highly placed.'

I could tell from Winter's expression that he was about to snap. It might have been because of Moonbeam's overly earnest nature or the fact that he'd interrupted us. Either way, it seemed appropriate to get Moonbeam to a safe distance. The last thing any of us needed was the Order making an enemy of Belinda Battenapple's son.

'Time to go!' I chirped. 'Come on, Moonbeam! I need your help.'

He dragged his eyes away from Winter. 'What with?'

'Tactics,' I said, trying to think of something that would entice the poor boy away. 'I want to talk strategy with someone who has your intellect and capacity for dissembling.'

Moonbeam looked pleased. Thank goodness. 'Is that Barry?'

I nodded.

'First of all, you don't want him as your producer,' he said, as I linked arms with him and drew him away from a still-gloweringing Winter. 'You need someone with some real bite if you want to go far.'

Again with the damned eating analogies. The only difference this time was that I couldn't tell Moonbeam off. Winter obviously didn't want word of last night's zombie getting out. And it definitely had been a bloody zombie, regardless of how much he protested. 'Tell me more,' I murmured.

Unfortunately, Moonbeam was only too happy to oblige.

***

With his diabolical plan to usurp one of the contestants almost certainly sunk, Moonbeam seemed to have moved on to trying to take Barry's place. Every time the producer opened his mouth, Moonbeam jumped in. He stuck to our sides like a limpet. I'd have done something to get rid of him but he actually had some useful information to impart. Besides, I was curious to know if he was aware of what his mother had hanging around her neck.

'See,' he said, clutching at my arm in order to emphasise his point, 'you need to ensure you have as much camera time as possible. That means you need to be out there. Do you get me, Ivy?'

'I have to be out there,' I repeated. Whatever that meant.

'Exactly. So if someone starts an argument, you step in and smooth it over.'

'Should I start arguments?' I enquired.

He was horrified. 'Definitely not. That's a sure-fire way to be voted out. You want people on your side. Both the contestants and the viewing public. It's the only way.'

I pursed my lips. 'What about my outfit? I think it's a bit risqué.'

Moonbeam cast a critical eye at the dress. 'It does show rather too much flesh,' he agreed. 'I wouldn't have thought you'd be the one to be set up as the seductive honey pot but,' he shrugged, 'I guess it takes all sorts.'

Plonker. I wasn't going to rise to his backhanded criticism, though, not when I'd finally managed to find a way to ask him about his mother. I touched my neck and assumed a wistful air. 'I just wish they'd let me keep my necklace on. I miss its weight against my skin.'

Moonbeam drew breath, as if to jump back in with some other inane observation. I hurriedly continued before he could. 'I saw your mum was wearing a necklace yesterday. It looked pretty.'

He wrinkled his nose. 'What? Yeah, she has a lot of jewellery.' He rushed into his next sentence. 'So if Barry and the other producers want you to play the part of—'

'Where did she get it from?' I asked, unwilling to let him change the subject. 'I'd love to get one to match.'

'It's one of a kind,' he said, tugging uncomfortably at his sleeve. 'Besides, it's pretty ugly. Anyway, you should—'

Moonbeam was determined to talk about something else. I was equally determined to stay on topic. 'What's inside it?'

'Huh?'

'It looks like a liquid,' I said patiently. 'Mercury or something.'

He tugged at his sleeve again. 'Yeah,' he said unconvincingly, 'that's what it is. Mercury.' He checked his watch. 'Bugger. I'd better go. I promised the boom operators I'd help them out before the opening.' He turned and skedaddled.

I frowned, watching his departure. Moonbeam definitely didn't want to talk about his mother's necklace. I was sure he was lying and knew more than he was letting on. The question was why.

I didn't have the chance to go after him and find out more. Barry leapt into the void Moonbeam had left and dragged me away. 'The other contestants are arriving,' he informed me. 'You need to join them. They've had a couple of weeks to get to know each other, re-member, so you have a lot of catching up to do.'

I lifted an eyebrow. 'Why do you do that? Why do you let them ... us ... meet each other before the show?'

He spoke without thinking. 'People are on their best behaviour when they meet someone else for the first time. Generally it takes a few days for strangers to settle down in each other's company. Add the unfamiliar cameras into the mix, and we'd have the talent tiptoeing around each other for a full week. That doesn't make for good television. It's far better to make sure that everyone already knows who they like and dislike beforehand. It cuts out a lot of the boring stuff.' He glanced at me. 'Of course, you'll be at an advantage. You're the unknown quantity.'

We joined the other contestants, re-dressed in their finery. Harriet shot me an evil look, even though I was certain that she was the one who'd screwed things up by pointing the finger in my direction for her wardrobe change.

'Oh,' I murmured to Barry, 'I wouldn't worry about that. I think I've already made an enemy.'

When Bellows appeared, wearing his ridiculous Halloween costume again, and sniffed imperiously upon spotting me, I knew it wasn't just Harriet I'd have to worry about. The other contestants looked at me curiously. I briefly considered telling them not to worry. I wasn't here to win in order to carve out a career in morning television; I wanted to find the zombie master. Somehow I didn't think that would go far in the reassurement stakes.

The macho guy ambled over, leering in my direction. 'So you're the newbie.' He stuck out his hand. 'I'm Mike.'

I put on my prettiest smile. 'Hi, Mike!' I trilled. For all his muscles, his handshake was surprisingly weak.

'I like your dress,' he told me. 'You stick with me. I'll keep you safe.' He leaned down and lowered his voice. 'I'm an expert at all this magic stuff. Last year I found a spell to hotwire cars. Now I can travel at full speed without the need for any petrol. I'm saving the planet and my money at the same time.'

Mike was obviously an idiot. 'Except that's impossible. You can't mix magic and technology like that.'

He flexed his muscles and grinned at me like I was stupid. 'That's what the Order wants you to think.'

I rolled my eyes. 'It's the truth.'

'She's an Order witch,' Harriet interrupted. 'There's no point saying anything about magic to her.'

Mike stiffened, while the other contestants stared at me. 'You? You're in the Order?'

'No. But I could be if I wanted.'

'So could I.'

No, he couldn't. I didn't need to present him with the entrance exams to know that any magic he possessed wasn't worth the Order's time. Even the lowest and weakest Neophyte would leave this plonker in the dust. 'Sure,' I said. 'Whatever you say.'

Mike glowered at me. 'I do say.'

I noticed that the others were shuffling away from me, as if I'd taint them by simply standing too close.

A weedy guy in a suit spoke up. 'Do you remember Faith in series four?' Various people nodded. 'Well,' he said knowledgeably, 'she was in the Order. She was voted out in the second episode.'

I gritted my teeth. She had *tried* to enter the Order but failed at the first hurdle. Out of the corner of my eye I noticed Bellows smirking and tried to relax. I wasn't here to win the show, I reminded myself. If I wanted to find out anything useful, I had to be more congenial. It would do the investigation no good if everyone refused to speak to me. My movements were going to be curtailed enough now that I was a contestant and not a runner. I had to show Winter that he needed me; I just wished it didn't have to be such hard work.

'The Order didn't want me,' I said in a slightly raised voice. 'They kicked me out. Sure, I've got a bit of magic in me but I bet it's nothing compared to you lot.' I pasted on a wistful expression. 'I'm just here as a last-minute replacement to make up the numbers. I know I'll be voted out quickly. That's okay.'

An older woman, dressed in a painfully tailored power suit, smiled at me. 'Don't say that. If you were in the Order even for a short while you must be able to do some spells. Don't worry about this lot. We're all just nervous.' Mike let out a snort. She ignored him. 'I'm Lou.'

An ally – unless she was only pretending to be on my side so she could shaft me later. Good grief. No wonder I preferred watching *Enchantment* from the safety of my sofa. Being here could drive a person nuts. 'I'm Ivy,' I told her.

She patted my cheek in a motherly fashion. 'You'll be fine, Ivy.'

Trevor Bellows looked away in disgust. He adjusted his hat and cleared his throat. 'You'll have plenty of opportunity to judge each other's abilities soon,' he said, his jowls juddering as he spoke. He still looked rather pale. I fixed my attention on him, examining his tired eyes. Perhaps he really was being targeted by our nasty necromancer. He certainly didn't look like he'd had much sleep last night. 'Remember,' he continued, 'you are only to use magic when we tell you. We can't have you lot shooting off spells and destroying half of the Scottish Highlands in your wake, now can we? I'll be on hand to help you if you need me to. You'll all be perfectly safe. We've even managed to get extra security, just to be sure.'

No wonder the set looked busier than yesterday. I guessed *Enchantment* weren't taking any chances.

Another producer wandered up with a clipboard. She had an earpiece and was obviously listening to something. After a moment or two she nodded before clapping her hands together. 'It's time, people!' She spoke with an odd accent that made her voice rise at the end of each sentence, a strange mixture of peppy American cheerleader and overly excited Australian soap opera star. It should be illegal to expend that much energy while speaking. 'Follow me! We're off to the stage!'

Lou sighed. 'Let's hope nobody dies this time around.'

Amen to that.

Chapter Twelve

Things felt very different now that I knew I was going to be in front of the cameras rather than behind them. As we clustered together, ready to make our debut, I spotted Brutus slinking up and let out a sigh of relief. He might be a contrary cat who seemed to care about little more than food but he'd obviously picked up on the fact that I was feeling a bit nervous and come to provide me with some much-needed moral support. Then he ignored me and made a beeline for Trevor Bellows, snaking round his legs.

Bellows leaned down and absentmindedly scratched Brutus behind the ears. In response, my cat let out a tiny meow. 'You're a clever little thing, aren't you?' Bellows murmured. 'I wonder what you'd say if you could really talk.'

He really didn't want to know. I threw my errant familiar a narrow-eyed glare and turned away, noticing Winter at the far side, scrutinizing all the last-minute preparations. Barry was deep in conversation with another of the producers so I took advantage of the moment to edge over.

'Hey.'

Winter glanced at me and frowned. 'You need to stop talking to me so publicly, Ivy. It's common knowledge that we were once partners but we still need everyone to believe that I came here to keep an eye on you.'

'That was rather clever of me to come up with that, wasn't it?'

He sighed. 'Ivy...'

I reached up on my tiptoes and slapped him in the face.

'What the hell?' He spun towards me.

'Is that enough?' I enquired.

'Now everyone is looking at us!'

'They were looking at us before. They're just not hiding the fact any more.' My eyes danced but I kept a stern frown on my face just for show. Then I raised my voice. 'The Order should have sent some-one else. You shouldn't be here, Adeptus Exemptus. It's a conflict of interest.'

'Don't be too enthusiastic with your protests,' he growled, 'or *Enchantment* will demand someone else takes my place.'

'And the Ipsissimus will ignore them. They can't dictate who is here.' For good measure, I raised my hand to slap him again. This time he was prepared and caught my hand before it connected with his cheek. 'Stop that!'

I leant forward, hoping it looked like I was demanding he release me at once. 'The vial I told you about that's around Belinda Battenapple's neck,' I said, keeping my voice low. 'There's definitely something fishy about it. I quizzed Moonbeam and he couldn't wait to change the subject. It's definitely worth investigating.'

Winter let go of my hand. 'Investigate it then.'

I crossed my arms. 'You're the Order rep around here. I'm just the hired help.'

'They won't let me get close to her,' he muttered. 'I think they're afraid my presence might sully her reputation. If an Order investigator is seen talking to her, word will get out and—'

'And it'll be all over the press.' I wrinkled my nose. 'That's annoying. I guess that yet again I'll just have to do your job for you.'

'I've told you before not to be overly reckless, Ivy.'

Pah. 'I'm not reckless,' I informed him. 'I just don't see why you always have to take the long way round when there are shortcuts.'

'If you get hurt...' His voice trailed off.

I met his eyes. 'What? Would you be upset?'

Winter took a deep breath. 'Of course I would be.'

'Is there a problem here?' Barry shouldered his way between us and glared at Winter as if he'd compromised my honour.

'Everything's fine,' I snapped. 'I just hate having this man around.'

Barry pulled back his shoulders. 'Leave Ivy alone,' he said to Winter. 'She's not with the Order and she's no concern of yours.'

I raised an eyebrow. It was rather sweet of Barry to come to my defence like that. Winter nudged me with his elbow as if in warning, so I did my best to play my part. 'Yeah, Adeptus,' I said. 'I've got nothing to do with you any longer.'

'As long as you're on this television show, Ms Wilde,' Winter said with what I thought was a tad too much sneer even for Barry's benefit, 'then you're my concern. Everyone here is my concern. Magic is not something to be played with like a toy.'

'Oh, I'm well aware of that, Adeptus Exemptus Winter. I have just as much respect for magic as any of you Order geeks do.'

'Geeks?' A line marred Winter's forehead as he bristled. 'If a geek is someone who works hard and has respect for others then, sure, call us that.'

Barry coughed. 'Maybe we should go.'

Both Winter and I ignored him. 'It's always work with you, isn't it?'

'Hard graft is not something to disparage, Ms Wilde.'

'Ooooh.' I flounced. 'Look at you and your big words. And here was me thinking that army intelligence was an oxymoron.'

A muscle throbbed in Winter's jaw. 'I'm a damn sight more intelligent than Tarquin bloody Villeneuve.'

'I know that!' I shot back. 'But given he has the smarts to equal a plank of wood, that's hardly surprising, is it?'

He took a step towards me. 'Is that how you like your men? Weak and stupid so you can run rings around them and wrap them round your little finger? Does it make you feel good to flaunt yourself in their faces and have them pant after you?'

I jabbed my finger in his chest. 'You don't get it, do you? The only person I want panting after me is you and you don't care! All you're interested in is the bloody Order and your latest assignment. When you look at me with those ridiculous blue eyes of yours all I want you to do is—'

Barry grabbed hold of my arm. 'Uh, Ivy,' he interrupted. 'I don't think this is a good idea right now.'

I shook Barry off. Winter stared at me. 'What?' he asked softly. 'What do you want me to do?'

My mouth was suddenly dry. 'I, er, I...'

'This is our sixty-second countdown!' Clipboard Lady yelled. 'Everyone get to your places and shut the hell up!'

Barry took my arm again, all but dragging me back to the group of contestants. Each and every one of them was gazing at me openmouthed. I wasn't interested in them, though; I was only interested in Winter. He was watching me like a hawk, with his expression completely shuttered. Arse.

I couldn't even pinpoint when our play-acting had become real. Or was he still making it all up? It hadn't seemed that way. I thought he was coming around but maybe I was mistaken. Or maybe he was starting to feel a little of what I felt for him. I shook myself. That was silly. We were complete polar opposites. And yet ... he continued to watch me, ignoring the flurries of activity around him.

'Well,' Lou fanned herself. 'That was something. That was something indeed. I don't blame you. He certainly is gorgeous.'

And intelligent. And quick-witted. And sensitive. And ... arse. Arse. Arse. I wondered how badly it would reflect on us if I just ran back over and dragged him away from here so we could talk properly. Screw *Enchantment*.

'Ten seconds!'

Something batted my leg. I looked down to see Brutus sauntering away. I took a deep breath. We were here to stop any more murders and to find out who was disturbing the dead. I shook myself mentally. I had to sort myself out. But Winter was still bloody well staring at me.

Belinda's dulcet tones filled the air. Regardless of why she'd been interrupted yesterday, her script hadn't changed. She stuck word for word to what she'd said last time. 'It's Friday and we are here in the stunning Highlands of Scotland for the most epic, most unique and most special series of *Enchantment* every created. Twelve new contestants are waiting in the wings and all of them have special skills and abilities. All of them want to win the coveted Trophy of Spells. And all of them know that,' she paused for dramatic flourish before she launched into her catchphrase: 'Magic. Is. In. The. Air. Welcome back to *Enchantment*!'

The gaggle of producers herded us closer to the stage. I caught one last flash of Winter's sapphire eyes before I was swallowed up in the crowd of contestants. It was too late to do anything now. Story of my life.

***

Given that the show was pre-recorded I hadn't expected it to be seamless but I wasn't prepared for the stopping and starting that went on. Bellows fluffed his lines on three separate occasions and had to restart. A dark cloud momentarily passed across Belinda's sculpted cheekbones and she had to be re-shot. At one point, Brutus darted across the stage. Considering how heartily Bellows and the rest of the crew laughed, however, I had a feeling that part wouldn't be edited out.

With all the delays, I was convinced that I had plenty of time to sneak away and find Winter again. That was until one of the make-up artists who came up on stage to re-touch Belinda's foundation gave her a small mirror to hold, and she dropped it accidentally. It smashed into umpteen pieces. Surely even Winter wouldn't be able to ignore that kind of omen.

Once all the opening scenes had been covered, the contestants were brought up on stage one by one. Barry's explanation about why they had been given the chance to get to know each other first now made sense. Each of my supposed competitors was on their very best behaviour, offering happy smiles into the cameras and hamming it up for all they were worth. I was fascinated by how well they each fitted into their assigned roles. Maybe the producers were cannier than I'd given them credit for and they really did have amazing insights into each person's character.

I glanced down at my own costume and grimaced. I hoped not.

Mike bounded up onto the stage and flexed his muscles, flashing a toothpaste grin to an almost simpering Belinda. Harriet, who was still taking every opportunity to throw me the evil eye, all but shuffled over when it was her turn. Her shoulders drooped and she spoke in a hushed voice: The Mouse indeed. The trouble was that, in my experience, it was the quiet ones who you had to watch out for.

Rachelle, a beautiful young woman of Haitian descent, swayed her hips and murmured fake voodoo incantations to elicit a gasp. Shoto, the token Asian, spoke of Zen's role in creating powerful magic spells. Lou blushed and told everyone she was just a housewife who'd discovered a talent for magic when she'd burnt some cupcakes in the oven and managed to reverse their dodgy appearance. Although when Belinda prodded her, Lou admitted that they'd still tasted of charred sponge.

I hopped from foot to foot. 'I need to pee,' I told Barry.

'You'll be fine,' he said. 'It's just a nervous reaction. Once you're up there, it'll go away.'

I thought of all the coffee I'd downed before Amy and I left the room that morning. 'Nope. I really do need to pee.'

'There's no time.'

'But...'

Barry rounded on me. 'Listen,' he said. 'I need you to stop being so difficult and get with the programme. Literally. I've never had a contestant of mine in the final and I think you could be the one to do it – if you play your cards right. But all this running off and causing problems isn't going to endear you to anyone. If you want to do well, you need me on your side.'

I blinked at him, astonished. Barry had a lot of hidden depths. 'Good for you,' I told him. I was aware it probably sounded patronising but I meant it. 'I still need to pee though.'

'Tough.' He gave me a little shove. 'You're up.'

My stomach flip-flopped then I sternly told myself to get a hold of things and tripped up the small flight of steps.

'Our twelfth contestant is quite unlike anyone we've had on *Enchantment* before. She's told us that the allure of competing in our special Highlander survival edition was simply too great to pass up,' Belinda beamed.

What? I'd said nothing of the sort. Even so, I did exactly the same as everyone else and put on my best smile. Except smiling so broadly hurt, so I decided that maintaining it would be too much effort and relaxed. I'd go for more of a mysterious Mona Lisa expression instead. It required less energy.

'She used to be a member of the Hallowed Order of Magical Enlightenment, so we are expecting great things from her magic skills! Ladies and gentlemen, I give you Ivy Wilde!'

Reminding myself not to twitch, I nodded at Barry and took my cue, walking onto the stage and greeting Belinda. Even though it was still daytime, the artificial stage lights were bright so it was difficult to see much of anything beyond the stage. Was Winter watching me, along with everyone else?

The others sat bolt upright on the contestants' special chairs, which faced Belinda's, as if having good posture suggested an upright and moral personality. I slouched, leaning back gratefully because the chair was quite comfortable.

'Make yourself at home, Ivy,' Belinda told me.

I hooked both legs over one of the armrests and grinned. 'Okay.'

Belinda laughed, playing the part of congenial host to perfection. 'Is this why you were expelled from the Order, Ivy?'

'Because I got too comfortable?' I shook my head. 'Oh no, Belinda. I was expelled for cheating and assault.'

Her mouth dropped open and she sent a quick sidelong glance towards Armstrong who was watching from the wings on the other side. 'Seriously?'

'Oh yes.' I briefly considered telling her that it was on trumped-up charges but I didn't think that would endear me to the Ipsissimus. Or Winter. Sometimes the truth hurts. I shrugged. 'I was a different person back then. I'm much more mellow now.' I smiled. 'I promise not to deck you.'

She tittered. She was obviously taken aback by my honesty. Either that or Armstrong's digging hadn't uncovered the real reason why I'd been booted out from the Order and I'd genuinely shocked her. It didn't matter; I was fishing for something different to meaningless plaudits from strangers.

I eyed Belinda's neckline and thought I could see a faint bulge where the vial was hidden. I had to take this advantage and get a closer look at it but I wasn't sure how to do it while being filmed from every angle.

'So you must have magical skills which you think you can put to good use in our challenges,' she said. 'Do you think you have an edge on the competition? We have some talented contestants this year, you know.'

I was fully aware of the protocol. I was supposed to say something along the lines of how much I respected my fellow *Enchantment* competitors and how they were going to be difficult to beat. I couldn't be bothered with all that palaver. It was already proving hard to keep track of the web of lies I'd found myself embroiled in; I didn't need to create more by affecting false modesty.

'I can assure you,' I told her, 'that they're no match for me. You see, Belinda, I'm a real witch and I can do real magic. Not the silly tricks that you usually see from *Enchantment* contestants but serious show-winning stuff. If anyone messes with me, they'll be sorry.'

'Those are fighting words.'

My inner fan danced at the glee in her voice. 'It's just the truth.' I leaned in slightly. 'I can give you a demonstration if you like.'

Belinda turned to the camera, giving it a full wattage smile. 'We'd like to see that,' she said with a purr.

Bingo. I pulled myself upright and dropped my hand. I didn't want the cameras to catch my rune – I couldn't give away all my secrets. 'I need you to stand up,' I said. 'If you don't mind.'

'No problem.' She rose gracefully to her feet.

I cast a critical eye up and down her outfit. 'The one thing that has always impressed me about you, Belinda, is how well dressed you are. Didn't you win an award for that last year?'

'I did indeed.'

I tightened my muscles and concentrated. It was vital to get this right because I'd probably only have one chance. I should really be thanking Wardrobe Lady for giving me the idea. 'That tartan really suits you,' I murmured, beginning to move my fingers. 'I bet it would look simply fantastic as a ballgown.'

Belinda cocked her head. 'Do you mean...?' Then she gasped. The tartan skirt she was wearing began to change, dropping down to her feet and billowing out in a meringue-style concoction. I flicked my attention to her top half, transforming her blouse into a low-cut bodice of the same material and removing her scarf. Her décolletage was perhaps a little too risqué but at least now we matched. Even better, the vial around her neck was now visible.

I considered removing it completely but if it did have any magic surrounding it – and that magic was linked to Belinda herself – then its removal could cause chaos. This way was safer. And I'd get a good look at the thing.

'This is amazing!' Belinda gave a twirl. 'I feel like a Scottish princess! You really are a talented witch, Ivy!'

I was indeed. I'd be more talented if I could tell what liquid was inside that little glass bottle. I moved closer to her. 'I just need to make a few adjustments,' I said, with a furrowed brow as if I were trying to work out what was missing.

The vial was hanging on a delicate silver chain and was stoppered with a tiny amount of purple wax. The etching on the outside of the glass appeared to be Chinese characters, so I had no way of knowing what it said. There couldn't be more than three ounces of liquid inside it and, now I was close, I could see that it didn't resemble mercury at all. It was silver and relatively viscous but there were strands of other colours within it.

Distracting my audience, I flicked out another rune and altered Belinda's hairstyle from loose chic to an elaborate chignon. For good measure, I added a tiara on top. 'Now you're Queen Belinda!'

She reached up and touched her hair. 'Wonderful! I need a mirror!'

I winced. She'd already done enough damage with the make-up artist's mirror. The last thing any of us needed was more bad luck to contend with. Even though I knew I'd regret it later because of the energy it required to conjure one up, I created a full-length mirror out of the chair I'd been sitting upon.

While Belinda gasped some more, I angled my head closer to the vial. I could see swirls of black and orange in the silver liquid. They seemed to moving all the time, expanding and contracting within the confines of the glass.

'Beautiful,' Belinda said. She curtsied to her reflection.

I smiled. 'A workman is only as good as her tools.' I glanced at her reflection and focused on the vial, memorising every millimetre of it. This was probably the best chance I would get.

I released the spell and reversed the runes, returning Belinda to her original form before doing the same to the mirror so I could sit down again. They might have been simple spells but they were enough to sap me of what little of my energy remained. All I wanted to do now was curl up and sleep. Okay, that was about all I ever wanted to do. This time, however, I was genuinely liable to doze off while on television. Between bringing down the zombie and all of this malarkey, my body was about ready to throw in the towel and re-sign for good.

Fortunately, Armstrong was clearly concerned about the changing light as the day wore on and motioned to Belinda to wrap things up. She smiled, pointing down at her clothes with an expression of marvel, and thanked me.

I tripped off the stage like the good little contestant I was supposed to be. However, the tight knot of worry I felt at what was in that damn vial was quickly becoming a full-blown panic attack.

Chapter Thirteen

So much time was spent on the initial interviews and Belinda's set pieces that there wasn't chance to sneak off and find Winter. Instead, with the cameras rolling, I was unceremoniously dumped into a team of four: me, Mike the Muscle Man, Harriet the Hater and Lovely Lou. I supposed it could have been worse – but not much.

Retrieving our challenge envelope, Mike ripped it open and started to read. 'Your first task is to survive the wilds. Find yourself shelter for the night and stay safe from the elements. There will be significant disadvantages given to the last team to set up camp.'

Excellent. 'I know where shelter is,' I declared. 'My hotel is about ten miles that way. We just need to hitchhike in that direction and we'll be there in no time.'

Harriet rolled her eyes, while Mike produced a map and waved it at me. 'We've been given several choices,' he said. 'And none of them involves going back to Tomintoul and getting a hotel.'

I couldn't see why not. It was creative. And there'd be a duvet. Not to mention hot running water. I suspected that the choices displayed on the map would be considerably less comfortable.

Ruing the day I'd agreed to do this, which I was very much aware was still today, I peered over his shoulder. Good grief. We'd be up for half the night. And I wasn't forgetting that this was *Enchantment*. There was bound to be some magical stuff to contend with before we could bed down for the night. That was the formula.

'This one.' Mike jabbed his thumb at the nearest marker. 'We pick up now and head straight there. It's the closest.'

He really was an idiot. 'It's up a mountain. It might be the closest but it'll take us longest to get there. We need to be smart about this.'

He stared at my breasts. 'We go there. I've made the decision.'

My eyebrows flew up. He had, had he? 'Look,' I said, 'I'm a taxi driver. I know how to read maps. I do it every day.' I was lying about the last part; I use sat nav. That doesn't mean I can't orienteer myself when I really need to.

'I thought you were a witch. Why would a woman drive a taxi?'

Harriet's lip curled. 'Sure she's a witch but all she can do is bespell clothing.' She sniffed. 'So why she's wearing *that*, goodness only knows.'

She was right here. Except I simply didn't have the energy for an argument, much as I wanted to bop Mike on the nose for being sexist as well as stupid. I pushed back my hair and sighed. 'Please,' I said. 'Don't be plonkers. If we head for the nearest point, it will take hours. This is not as the crow flies. We don't have wings. We still have to get there.' I turned to Lou. 'Help me out here.'

Lou looked like the last thing she wanted to do on our first day was to get into a fight. She gave a helpless smile. 'I'll go with the majority. I have no sense of direction anyway.'

When it was me against Mike, Harriet would choose Mike every time. She'd choose anyone who wasn't me; I'd be on a constant losing streak. I considered my options, glanced at the map once more and made a decision. Reaching out so that one hand touched Mike's arm and the other touched Harriet's, I drew out runes on both their bodies. An almost immediate wave of exhaustion overtook me but it was nothing compared to what happened to them. They yawned in unison before collapsing to the ground.

'Oh my goodness!' Lou shrieked. 'They've passed out! We need a doctor!'

'They're just sleeping,' I said, feeling sour. I'd like to be sleeping too.

Her mouth dropped open. 'Did you do that to them? Did you make them fall asleep?'

'Trust me, it's for their own good.'

Barry, hovering nearby with another producer, seemed concerned. He stepped forward but I held up my palm. 'They're absolutely fine. There's nothing to worry about.'

I watched the cameraman swing his lens towards them. Mike looked kind of cute when he wasn't conscious. I retrieved the map from under his arm. 'Look,' I said to Lou. 'There's a river just round the next bend.'

She still couldn't get over what I'd done to Mike and Harriet. Her jaw worked but she couldn't appear to find any words.

I shrugged. 'All we need to do is to get these two to the river. Then we float all the way down to here.' I pointed to one of the marked locations. 'It's right next to the river itself. Even though it's further away, we can get there much easier than the place Mike wanted to aim for. It'll take us no time.' I fixed my eyes on her. 'Are you with me?'

'Uh...'

'Lou! Come on. If you really think we should tramp up a mountain, I'll wake them up straight away and we can tramp up a mountain together. Trust me though, this way is much better.' Please, Lou. I wasn't up to mountain climbing. Not today.

She swallowed. 'The river seems the best course.'

Praise the heavens. 'Great. I'll take Mike, you take Harriet.' I expended some more energy in spelling away their weight but, even so, I dragged Mike along the ground, scuffing his heels in the process.

Lou, bemused by how easily she could lift Harriet's prone body, slung her over her shoulder fireman-style and caught up with me. 'You really are a proper witch. You're not like the rest of us at all.'

I grunted. I was aware of the camera following my every reaction. This would be easier if it didn't keep getting in my damn way.

'I really wanted to win,' Lou whispered, more to herself than to me.

'So win.'

She jumped, startled. 'I can't compete against you.'

'I'm not here to win,' I said without thinking.

'Then why are you here?'

Arse. 'Er ... I want to test my limits. And...' think, Ivy, think. '...prove to the Order that they were wrong to boot me out.'

'You want to rejoin them?'

Not even if Winter himself stripped naked, prostrated himself on the ground for my delectation and begged. 'No,' I said slowly, seizing any reason I could think of for being stuck in the past and motivated by revenge. 'I just don't want any other witches to go through what I did when I was kicked out. If I can show the Order they were wrong to expel me, they might think twice before doing it to someone else.'

Mike's heel caught on a stone so I tugged at him. There was an ominous sound of ripping fabric as his trousers caught on something. Oops.

'Aren't you afraid?' She hesitated. 'I spoke to Benny a few times. He was a nice guy and to be killed like that...' She shivered.

'Benjamin Alberts? Yeah,' I agreed. 'That was pretty nasty.' And if I had anything to do with it, the person who was responsible would spend the rest of their life behind bars.

'At least we know they caught the bastard who did it.'

'Mmm.' I craned my neck round the last of the trees. 'Do you know why Benjamin went up that mountain in the first place?'

She shrugged unhappily. 'He just wanted some fresh air. That's what he said anyway.' She looked as if she were about to cry. That was the last thing I needed.

I pointed. 'Look. There's the river.'

We walked to the bank and lay down Mike and Harriet's bodies. I gave the river a critical glance. This was summer so it wasn't quite as deep or fast flowing as I'd hoped.

Lou looked around dubiously. 'Is this going to work?'

Spotting a hole in the sandy shore opposite, I felt around inside myself. I probably had enough energy left. Just. I grinned. 'Watch this.'

I sketched out a complex rune, binding together what I knew of Myomancy with my knowledge from experimenting with Brutus. For a moment nothing happened then some of the sand shifted and a small questing nose appeared.

Lou stiffened. 'What is that?'

'Shhh,' I said. 'Don't scare it off.'

The otter emerged fully, whiskers quivering. It wasn't entirely trusting and took several moments to scan the area. For good measure, I added another rune into the mix. Unwilling to deny the call any longer, it swam across.

'Hey buddy,' I said, crouching down beside it.

It squeaked in response. It was kind of cute. Now that Brutus had apparently abandoned me, maybe I'd take on an otter instead of a cat as my new familiar. I wondered whether it could be trained to make tea.

'We need to get down river,' I told it. 'About five miles, give or take. Could you help us out?'

Lou stared at me as if I were crazy. 'Are you having a conversation with a wild animal? Does it even understand what a mile is?'

Probably not but I reckoned it got the gist. It chittered and jerked its head to the right. Whatever that meant.

'Something's up there,' I said softly to Lou. 'Can you go have a look?'

She edged away. I got the impression that she was glad to have a reason to put some distance between us. I shrugged at the otter; I wasn't being that weird, was I? The otter seemed to agree with Lou, however. It blinked at me warily and backed down to the river, obviously keen to leave. I inclined my head and let it go. If I'd felt fresher,

I'd have been tempted to persuade it to pull us all along with some of its otter buddies.

Lou wasn't long. She emerged from behind a tree and scratched her head. 'There's a boat tethered there.'

I clapped my hands. 'Brilliant.'

'We can't take it, Ivy. That would be stealing.'

'We're only borrowing it.'

She shook her head. 'It has a small motor. And there are keys still in the engine. Whoever it belongs to, they're probably coming back. They're going to need it.'

Huh. I tilted my head and listened. There was no one else near here; if there had been, the producers would have already shooed them away. I glanced at the cameraman, whose lens was still trained on my face, and considered.

'It's a set-up.'

Lou squinted at me. 'Pardon?'

'We're in the middle of nowhere. What are the chances that there just happens to be a boat right next to the river that leads us to a camp? And that there are keys in the engine?' I shook my head. 'It's too convenient. They're setting us up. The producers, I mean.'

'Do you really think they'd do that?'

I rolled my eyes at her. This was 'reality' television. Of course they would.

'If that's the case, then we have to leave it.'

'Nope.' I grinned. 'If that's the case then we absolutely have to take it. They're trying to make television. We need to give the viewers something to shout about.'

'We can't steal it!'

I patted her on the back. 'I told you. We're just borrowing it.'

'But...'

'Don't worry, Lou. If anyone complains, I'll take the blame. We can be home and dry in less than an hour if we do this.'

Well, not exactly home as such. But at least somewhere I could finally get some real rest. If there wasn't a nice fluffy pillow at this campsite, heads were going to roll.

***

Our meandering amble was rather pleasant. I wouldn't call it peaceful, since Harriet had begun to snore with such force that the entire structure of the little boat shuddered. The noise she made was akin to a twenty-decibel drill, and I was still irritated that both she and Mike were sleeping while I had to stay awake. All the same, there was immense satisfaction in being on our way and probably far ahead of the other two teams.

Lou remained a bit twitchy at my casual theft of the boat but when no police came screaming out of the woods to clap her in chains – and when the trailing cameramen didn't stop us – she seemed to relax a little. Well, she trailed her hands in the cool water and leaned back, so she couldn't have been feeling too edgy.

A small log cabin had just come into view, with a little flag in the *Enchantment* colours perched on top of its roof, when there was an odd rustling from the bank on our left. I swung my head around, expecting to see another otter or perhaps a bird. Instead what appeared from the undergrowth was a sheep.

It trotted along to the edge of the river and began chewing nonchalantly at a clump of grass. But this wasn't a farmer's field and there were no other sheep in sight. I couldn't prevent myself from stiffening in alarm.

I grabbed hold of the rudder and steered the boat in. It was probably nothing, it was probably just a damn sheep. All the same...

Lou sat up. 'What is it?'

'Scottish wildlife,' I said, with far more cheeriness than I felt.

She glanced over, spotted the sheep and laughed. Then she immediately sobered up. 'You're not going to kill it, are you?'

My worry was overtaken by confusion. 'What? No! Of course not!'

Lou exhaled. 'Oh, good. I thought that you might, you know, want it for dinner. Or something.'

I had no illusions about where my supermarket meat came from but that didn't mean that I wanted it in anything other than a neatly packaged polystyrene packet with cooking instructions included. I was most definitely not in the business of slaughter. Too messy, for one thing. Although given that my stomach chose that moment to grumble rather loudly in between Harriet's snores, I probably appeared prepared to chomp on the poor animal.

Instructing Lou to stay where she was with the others, I jumped out of the boat and walked slowly towards the sheep. It paused from its grassy meal and looked up at me. Then it returned to eating.

I scratched my head. I'd managed to communicate with the otter. I certainly had no problem when it came to talking to Brutus either, even if he did flatly ignore everything I said. How difficult could a sheep be?

I flicked my index finger, ready to draw the rune, but that first movement made me realise that I wouldn't be able to manage it. Exhaustion was seeping into my bones and, rather than being sharp and fluid, even the start of the rune felt sluggish. I muttered a curse under my breath and stared at the sheep instead. It just kept on chewing.

I was hardly an expert in the ways of sheep. As far as I could tell, it looked perfectly normal. And getting jumpy simply because it was roaming around the Highlands, where there were probably a million other sheep doing exactly the same thing, was ridiculous. Probably.

I brushed my hand along its back, marvelling at its coarse wool, then sighed and pushed back my hair. I was jumping at shadows.

Lou called out to me as I went back to the boat. 'What was that about?'

I shrugged. 'Nothing.' She looked like she wanted to press me for more so I hastily got back into the boat. 'Look,' I said unnecessarily. 'Our chateau awaits.'

A smile spread across Lou's face. 'That has to be record timing.'

I beamed. 'Yep. And now we can all get some proper rest.'

Famous last words.

Chapter Fourteen

I woke up Harriet and Mike while Lou tethered the boat. Naturally they were disorientated for a minute or two but it didn't take Mike long to realise what had happened. 'What did you do?' he yelled, his face going an extraordinary shade of puce.

I twirled a stray curl. I could make something up but it was probably just as easy to tell the truth. 'You weren't going to listen to reason. Instead of spending five hours traipsing up a mountain and getting sore and tired, we spent an hour getting here and you're all rested.' I wasn't, of course; I was about dead on my feet but I wasn't going to tell him that.

'Unbelievable,' he muttered. He gestured angrily at the nearest cameraman. 'She can't be allowed to get away with this! There are rules!'

The cameraman didn't react. Mike huffed and glared.

'Complain to your producer later,' I said. 'Let's get inside first.'

Harriet, who hadn't said a word since she'd woken up but who was evidently upset, pulled herself out of the boat and walked up to the hut. She rattled the doorknob. 'It's locked,' she informed us flatly.

Mike growled. 'Let me try.' He joined her, shoving all his weight against the door. It wasn't going to budge.

'There's something here,' Lou called over. She held up an envelope. My heart sank. Great. This would be the supposedly inspired *Enchantment* twist.

Ripping open the envelope, Lou began to read. '*Congratulations. You have found shelter. The problem is that you can't gain access to it until you master the entrance spell. This chalet is warded against intruders. It's up to you and your team to find a way in and complete your first task.*'

I rolled my eyes. Chalet. As if. If this were a chalet, I wanted Swiss chocolate and a hunky ski instructor, not this lot and an empty belly.

'There are some herbs in here,' Lou said. 'And instructions for how to use them.'

'Go on then,' Mike sneered at me. 'You're the expert. Open it up.'

'I can't.' I slumped into a sitting position. 'I'm too tired.' If they had instructions and they could read, they really didn't need me.

His mouth flapped open. Then his eyes hardened. 'Fine. We don't need you anyway. Come on, Harriet. Lou.'

The three of them hunkered down, picking over the herbs and discussing the spell. A few of their words drifted over. What they had to do was so basic that even if there were only one iota of magic between them, they'd manage it.

I dropped backwards with my spine on the ground. It was hard and cold and there was an icky wet patch somewhere near my right thigh but right now I didn't care.

I let my head flop to the side. It really was very pretty around here. The grass was long and there had to be different varieties all growing naturally because the range of shades of green was extraordinary. There were long-stemmed daisies in one patch, and a lone bee buzzing around a clump of thistles. My eyes tiredly tracked its path as it abandoned the spiky plant in favour of something tastier. It flew over a muddy puddle, bypassed the rabbit droppings and the bloodstains, and headed up the slope behind the hut.

I sat bolt upright. Bloodstains?

'It's open!' Mike crowed. He shot me a nasty look. 'No thanks to you.'

I ignored him and scrambled to my feet. Maybe it wasn't blood. Maybe it was something else. I ran over and knelt down, taking care not to touch the dark patch with any part of my body. Bringing my nose down, I sniffed then recoiled. It was definitely blood. Not just

that – it smelled rotten, an almost exact match for the reek from the zombie-thing that Winter had killed only last night.

I sprang up in a panic. 'We have to get out of here.'

The others didn't hear me. They'd already gone into the small hut, although one of the cameramen had stayed behind to film me. I walked right up to him and spoke into the camera. 'It's not safe here. We have to leave now.'

He simply carried on filming. Gritting my teeth, I tried a different approach. 'I need to see Barry now.'

There was a crunch of footsteps on bracken and I turned to see the man himself approaching. Clearly he'd been close by the entire time. 'Good job, Ivy! I'm impressed you made it here so quickly.' He wagged his finger at me. 'You shouldn't steal though. It's very wrong.'

I ignored the twinkle in his eye that told me that I'd been right about the boat being a set up and grabbed him. 'We're in danger!' I shouted. 'There's blood there! It's the same as from the thing that killed Benjamin Alberts! If you don't want any more deaths on this show, you have to get us away from here as quickly as possible!'

Barry's eyes widened. 'Blood? Where?'

I twisted round, pointing at the patch I'd just discovered. 'There! And there was a sheep! Call Winter and get him here now. And get those three away before someone gets hurt!'

Barry darted over and crouched down, following my finger. He seemed to take his time. It was a wonder that the smell didn't put him off. He really was a brave soul.

'Ivy,' he said slowly. 'There's nothing here.'

The other three, who'd heard my yelling, came back outside and stared. 'What's the problem?' Lou asked.

'You need to leave!' I screeched at them. 'You're in danger!'

Lou's hand went to her throat and she looked alarmed. Mike turned several shades paler under his orange tan, while Harriet swallowed and leapt towards the cameraman as if for safety.

'Everyone needs to calm down,' Barry said. 'There's nothing there.' He glanced at me. 'You're seeing things, Ivy.'

'I am not!' I marched over to where he was and looked down. I blinked. He was right. What I'd seen as blood was nothing more than the shadow cast by a nearby bush.

'What?' I shook my head. 'But the smell...' I sniffed. There was nothing other than the rich scent of earthy goodness.

'You're tired. You've done a lot of magic today and you're probably just hallucinating.' Barry's expression was kind. 'We'll get one of the medics to check you over.'

'There was a sheep as well,' I protested. 'Lou saw it. She knows.'

The older woman shrugged. 'It was just a sheep.'

'But...'

Barry put his arm round me. 'Don't worry. We'll get you looked over and get you some rest and then you'll be right as rain.'

I stared dumbly at him. 'I was so sure....'

'You're letting your imagination run away with you. The person who hurt Benny is dead, Ivy. There's nothing to worry about.'

It was the dead part that frightened me. I ran my hands through my hair. 'Maybe I should lie down,' I said shakily.

'That sounds like a good idea.' He patted my cheek soothingly.

An engine rumbled towards us from the nearby dirt road. One of the show's doctors jumped out, followed closely by Belinda and Bellows. When I spotted Winter in the back, his blue eyes fixed on mine, a wash of relief came over me. At least someone was here who knew what they were doing.

The cameraman kept filming while the doctor pulled me over to one side. He checked my blood pressure and looked into my eyes. Belinda watched with a concerned expression. 'Can you tell us what the problem is?' she finally asked, when it appeared that he had finished his ministrations.

'She's exhausted,' the doctor pronounced. He raised his eyebrows in what I could only presume was admonishment. 'Lay off the unnecessary magic spells and you'll be fine.'

I mumbled an agreement. It didn't make sense. I'd tired myself out on more than one occasion by going overboard with spells but I'd never hallucinated before. And the spells I'd conducted today hadn't been all that elaborate, even if there had been more of them than I was used to doing. I'd been up half the night being attacked by a zombie up a mountain, though, so there was that.

'Can she continue on as a contestant?' Bellows enquired.

'I don't see why not,' the doctor replied.

I could swear Bellows looked disappointed. I glanced over at him. 'No cat?'

He pursed his lips. 'It's run off somewhere. It'll be back. It knows it's onto a good thing with me.'

I only just managed to stop myself snorting. Catching Winter's eye as he finally got out of the car, I muttered something about a call of nature and struggled up to find a handy bush to hide behind. Fortunately Winter got the message and followed, albeit at a discreet distance. Going to the loo seemed to be about the only chance I'd have to avoid being filmed.

I walked as far I dared, realising my legs were remarkably shaky. The others' voices drifted into the background. They'd be preoccupied for a while discussing my condition, so I reckoned we had a bit of time.

I halted and turned, waiting for Winter to catch up to me. It didn't take long. He might not have been running but he was still striding towards me with the speed of an Olympic walker.

'Are you alright?' he asked, as soon as he reached me. He took hold of me as if I were about to collapse, grasping me by the shoulders and gazing into my eyes.

I passed a hand over my face. 'I think so.' I shook myself. 'I don't know. I was so sure that what I saw was blood.' I bit my lip. 'Do you think I was hallucinating as well? Am I just tired?'

'Has it happened before?'

'No.' I paused. 'Well, I might not know if it has happened before. I don't think so. Is your magic telling you anything?'

His expression was alight with concern. 'Something's not right. I can't quite put my finger on what it is, but there's definitely something different.' Something akin to anger flashed in his eyes. 'There's more to this than exhaustion.'

I swallowed. That didn't sound good.

'Has anyone given you anything strange to eat or drink?'

I scratched my head. 'No. Everything I've had has been from the canteen. I had coffee this morning with Amy but she drank it too.'

'Could she have slipped something into your drink?'

It was highly unlikely. I grimaced. 'I doubt it, though right now it feels like anything's possible.'

'I'll check this Amy out. If she's done anything to you, given you something to drink which is spiked or brushed some kind of herb mixture against you which has hurt you, then I'll make sure she never sees the light of day again.' His voice was low but I was taken aback by his vehemence. I'd never seen Winter so irate. He kept clenching and unclenching his fists as if he wanted to punch something. I watched him, half fascinated, half concerned. Then his words trickled through.

'Wait,' I said slowly. 'I did touch something.'

He stilled. 'What?'

'Belinda's vial. When I was on stage, I changed her clothes so I could get a better look at it.'

'I saw. You're lucky you got away with that. It looked highly suspect to me.'

'That's because you knew what I was up to. Everyone else was watching Belinda,' I said dismissively. 'Anyway, I touched her vial. Not the contents but my skin definitely brushed against the outer glass.'

'Plenty of poisons and herblore spells work through touch.' His expression shifted. 'Did you manage to work out what was inside it?'

I shook my head. 'No. Just that it's some kind of silvery liquid with orange and black threads moving around inside it.'

Winter's eyes grew sharp. 'Moving independently?'

'As far as I could tell.'

He nodded grimly. 'Okay. I'll see if I can get hold of the rushes for today and we can use them to get a closer look. There were plenty of cameras pointed at the stage. One of them must have a decent shot of the vial. If we can get a good picture, together with your description, someone back in Oxford is bound to know what she's keeping so close to her chest.'

'Why would a fêted celebrity want to raise the dead?'

Winter gave me a long look. 'Why would anyone?'

Indeed. 'I should get back. If I'm too long, they'll send someone after me.'

'Good,' he growled. 'They should be looking after you better. Drink lots of water. If there is anything untoward going on here, that will help to flush it out of your system.'

'Am I going to be alright?'

'As far as I can tell.' He tilted his head. 'You'll still be annoying though. And your hair will still do that weird thing where it sticks out at the side like...'

I thumped his arm. 'You can stop that now.'

Winter grinned briefly before sobering up. 'I won't let anything happen to you, Ivy. I promise you that.'

I licked my lips. All of a sudden I felt very hot. It was probably another side-effect. 'You know,' I told him, looking serious, 'if this isn't poison, and if I really am just tired, then it's clear that work of any sort is very bad for my health.'

Winter leaned forward and brushed his lips feather-light against my temple. 'If you say so, darling.'

I pulled back and looked at him. 'Rafe...'

'I know.' The blue depths of his eyes turned a shade darker. 'We need to have a proper conversation. Not about magic or dead people rising from their graves but about us.' He licked his lips. 'This isn't the time though.' His hand touched my cheek. 'You said you liked me.'

'I do.' Even with the weariness permeating every bone in my body, it took almost everything I had not to jump on him then and there. He was right though; this really wasn't the time. 'When all this is over...'

He nodded. 'We'll talk.'

Barry's voice drifted over from down by the cabin. 'Ivy? Is everything alright?'

'It's fine.' I offered Winter a crooked smile. 'I'll talk to you again soon.' I held up my pinkie towards him.

He stared at it. 'Is something wrong with your finger?'

'Pinkie promise!'

His brow furrowed. 'Huh?'

'Never mind.' I reached up on my tiptoes and kissed his cheek. Then a wave of dizziness overtook me and I swayed. 'I really do need to lie down.'

Winter took my arm and helped me stumble back down the slope. I should have felt rage or worry or something like that. All I felt, however, was brimful of delight.

***

I couldn't have said with any certainty how long I was out for. When I woke up, birds were already tweeting the dawn chorus and light was streaming in through the cracks in the timber frame of the cabin. Harriet was snoring just as loudly as she had on the boat yesterday and, as far as I could tell, both Mike and Lou were also still out for the count. For a long moment, I revelled in the chance to finally stretch out and doze. Unfortunately the pressure in my bladder wouldn't permit me to stay in that position for long.

Groaning, I stretched and got up before wandering outside and greeting the latest cameraman, who was lounging on a rock nearby, with a grunt and an admonition not to follow me. I curved back round the cabin in the same direction as I'd taken to talk to Winter the day before, pausing briefly at my hallucinated bloodstain. It was still just a shadow. Not blood. I breathed out; with any luck, I was now completely back to normal.

I hunkered down behind a bush for a pee then, just as I was standing up, I heard a rustle and heavy footsteps plodding towards me. Alarmed – and suddenly wondering whether this was really happening – I straightened up. Hallucination or not, I'd meet it head on. My magic reserves were back to normal so, even if this were another damn zombie, I reckoned I could manage.

There was a heavy sigh followed by a curse. Then the familiar face of Gareth, the farm helper who'd found what was left of Benjamin Alberts, came into view.

I dropped my hands and broke into a smile. 'Gareth! How are you?'

He froze, obviously startled to see me. 'What ... what are you doing here?'

I gestured towards the cabin. 'Filming.'

He relaxed slightly although his lip still curled. 'I might have guessed. I skirted round the perimeter and avoided the security guards but I thought all the action was taking place further downstream. There were a lot of cameras there.'

Another team had probably set up camp down that way. 'There are a lot of us about,' I told him cheerfully. 'Why are you sneaking past security to get here anyway?'

'I'm not sneaking. All Scottish lands give right of way. It's not illegal for me to be here.'

I held up my hands. 'I wasn't trying to suggest it was.'

He seemed slightly mollified. 'I've lost another sheep,' he said. 'My...' he hesitated '...my mum is getting pissed off. I thought I saw tracks leading down this way but now I'm not so sure.' He glared at me. 'All your lot have muddied everything.'

Given he'd already told me that he wasn't much of a tracker, I doubted it would have made much difference. All the same, I tried to look apologetic. 'I saw a sheep over the other side of the river yesterday. It was on its own.' It was probably not a good idea to tell him I'd decided it was an evil omen. Gareth was sensitive enough as it was, without thinking he might end up falling across another dead body.

He cursed under his breath. 'Bloody creature.' He paused. 'Thank you.'

I curtsied. 'You're welcome.' He gave me a half smile in response.

I looked him over. I didn't know him well but he certainly appeared healthier than the last time I'd seen him. Maybe those gym workouts had helped after all. I grinned to myself. Nah. Not a chance. It was more likely that the counselling sessions I'd helped arrange had done the trick. It might have only been a couple of days but spilling out your heart to a stranger could have a remarkable effect. It really did help to offload.

'You look better,' I told him.

'I feel better,' he admitted. 'Thank you for your help. It's made a difference.'

I beamed at him. 'Good.'

He shoved his hands into his pockets. 'I should get off,' he muttered. 'Your lot must be at the cabin, right?'

'Right.'

He wrinkled his nose. 'I'll cross the river further upstream.'

That was probably a good idea. I was about to wave him off when another thought occurred to me. 'Actually, Gareth,' I said, 'do you happen to have a phone on you?'

'Yeah. Why?'

I tilted my head and did my best to smile sweetly. 'Do you think I could borrow it? Just for a moment?'

'Where's your one?'

'I've been promoted to contestant. I'm not allowed any communication with the outside world.'

Gareth raised his eyebrows. 'What are we doing right now then?'

'You're not supposed to be here.'

He considered this. 'True.' He reached into his pocket and tossed me his mobile. 'There you go.'

I grinned my thanks and quickly put in Iqbal's number. My scholarly friend had better bloody answer. It took several rings and when Iqbal finally did pick up, he sounded particularly unfriendly. 'Who is this?'

'Ivy of course!'

He breathed out. 'Oh. I've been trying to get hold of you for ages. This isn't your number.'

'Nope.' I remained cheery. 'I've borrowed someone else's phone. Is everything alright with you? You sound kind of ... antsy.'

'My supervisor's after me,' he said morosely. 'He keeps threatening to pull my funding unless I show him some evidence of what I've done so far.'

I winced. 'Idle threats?'

'Alas no. I think he's serious this time.'

'I'd offer to help,' I said, 'but I'm not sure I'd be much use to you. If there's anything I can do though, let me know.'

'Oh, I will, don't worry.' He sighed. 'Anyway, I suppose you're calling because you want to know what I've found out about that vial.'

'Yep. It's not easy for me to call these days so I've got to take every opportunity I can.'

'Sounds intriguing.'

I snorted. 'More like hard work. The real world seems to be encroaching on both our lives.'

'We should form a commune and live in the wilderness where no one can bother us.'

I looked around. The wilderness didn't offer much in the way of creature comforts. One day in and what I wouldn't give for some quilted toilet roll... 'Somehow I think that would be even more like hard work.'

'You're probably right.' At least Iqbal sounded a bit happier now. 'Anyhow, who did you say was wearing that vial?'

'Belinda Battenapple.' At my answer, Gareth's head jerked up. Maybe he was more interested in the celebrity goings-on of *Enchantment* than he made out. 'I've seen it close up this time.' I described it in more detail for Iqbal.

When I'd finished, he hissed through his teeth. 'Well,' he said, 'that answers one question.'

'What?'

'There was a good chance it was a decorative piece. I found reference to some necklaces which the Victorians used that contained mercury and were supposed to ward off evil spirits.'

Intriguing. I put a lot of credence into superstitions, especially some of the more obscure ones. 'Did they work?'

I could almost hear his shrug. 'Damned if I know.'

'But you don't think this one is decorative?'

'Not the way you've described it now.'

I waited for Iqbal to continue but there was silence on the other end of the phone. 'Iqqy?'

'Look, I might be wrong,' he said finally. 'But this is what some of my research uncovered.'

Instantly wary, my fingers curled tighter round the phone. 'Go on.'

'It draws death.'

I quashed down my sudden nausea. 'Draws death?'

Gareth looked even more interested. I gave him a tight smile and walked away, turning my back to stop him eavesdropping further. He didn't need to hear this.

'Yes. That's why the different coloured threads you saw keep moving all the time. It's constantly working. It's like a well of magic which even a non-witch can use.'

I swallowed. 'What does drawing death actually mean?' Somehow I doubted it was akin to Picasso scribbling a picture.

'I was hoping you would know. I found three separate references to it, none of which were in English so my translation might be a little murky. One was Latin, one French and one Hindi. Each one roughly seems to mean the same thing – drawing death or pulling death in. It could be that Belinda Battenapple doesn't know what she's wearing. Or maybe she's got some kind of suicidal impulse. It's not even clear from what I've read that I'm on the right track – it could be something entirely different and completely innocuous. It might mean nothing, Ivy.'

Or it might mean that she's dabbling in necromancy. It seemed bizarre to think that she could have been responsible for what happened to Benjamin Alberts. If the murder was down to her, she was still wearing the vial now. Whatever her plans were, they weren't finished yet.

'That's not good,' I said.

Iqbal registered my concern. 'Are you in danger?'

I thought of my strange hallucinations. It didn't appear so. If touching the vial caused them, then they were purely accidental. Except everyone – including Belinda – now knew that I'd been seeing things. If she'd laid a trap around the vial to catch anyone who took too close an interest in it, she might well be on to me.

I nibbled my lip. 'I don't know,' I said eventually. 'Probably not.'

'*Probably* not? I don't like the sound of that, Ivy. Maybe it's time you left Winter to sort this out for himself.'

I smiled at the mention of Winter. 'He'd be lost without me.' I paused. 'Besides, he's promised to make sure I'm safe.'

'Has he now?' A faintly teasing note entered Iqbal's voice. 'Is he going to wrap his big arms around you?'

With any luck. 'I should go,' I said hastily. 'I've borrowed this phone.' I could hear voices from down by the cabin. If I didn't get back soon, there would be cameras after me trying to find out what I was up to.

'Fair enough.' Iqbal returned to serious mode. 'But even if you do have Winter to protect you, keep a lookout. I don't think my supervisor would believe me if I told him my best friend had died again and I had to go to the funeral instead of writing my next section.'

Wait a minute. 'Have you told him I've died before? As well as your grandmother?'

'Got to go Ivy! Bye!' He hung up.

I rolled my eyes and returned the phone to Gareth, murmuring a thank you. It was definite now: Belinda Battenapple had just become the prime suspect.

Chapter Fifteen

When I got back to the cabin, I ignored the fact that Barry had reappeared and was throwing me suspicious looks at my prolonged absence. The others were up and ready. Harriet was clutching an envelope and looking more animated than I'd ever seen her. 'We have our first challenge!' she cried.

Despite the gravity of all that was going on, I still felt a small thrill ripple through me. This might be the new improved Highland Survival edition, but *Enchantment* still followed a set course. Teams. Tasks. Challenges. Voting. And the challenges were where it was really at. They almost always involved magic in some form or another and were completed by pairs or individuals. The winner was automatically protected from being voted out. Everyone else, regardless of their team, then decided who deserved to go.

The genius of it was that if you tried hard and won, you were safe. If you tried hard and only *almost* won, there was a great big target on your back. As the teams changed between every challenge, however, it wasn't always wise to get rid of the strongest contestants because you might want them on your side for the next round. Everything was a gamble. But, hey, so is life. Besides, this was the one time when I could be sure that everyone was present – not just the contestants and Armstrong and Trevor Bellows. Belinda would be there too. And Winter.

At that moment, I wasn't sure what pleased me more. Did I want a torrid love affair or did I want to catch an evil murderer? Both, of course, but given the choice between the two it was a tough call.

We were transported upstream, past the spot where Lou and I had 'borrowed' the boat, and on until the river became too narrow to navigate. There was no further sign of Gareth so I assumed that, despite his assertions regarding rights of way, he'd decided the safest way to retrieve yet another lost sheep was to avoid the camera crews and anyone related to *Enchantment*. Frankly, those animals seemed considerably more trouble than they were worth.

For my own part, I took advantage of the journey to work on my people skills. I sat at the front, next to Harriet. If I could bring her round to my side, my life would get a whole lot easier. I'd probably find it easy to inveigle my way back into Mike's good books simply by flashing some more cleavage at him, but I couldn't bring myself to do it. I still have some standards, even if they were slipping considerably with all this work I kept having to do.

'Listen,' I said. Harriet turned her head away, as if resolving not to look in my direction. 'I didn't mean to get you into trouble when I altered your clothes. I was just trying to help you out.' I pointed down at my ridiculous garb. 'I paid the price. That woman definitely got her own back on me.'

Harriet sniffed. I supposed it was better than complete silence.

'And about the putting you to sleep thing yesterday? I probably shouldn't have done it but it worked out well in the end, right? We weren't the last team to arrive because we didn't receive any extra disadvantages. I know if we'd gone for the shelter that Mike wanted, it would have taken us hours.'

'He is a bit of a knucklehead,' she admitted. Hurray! I was getting somewhere. 'But not as moronic as you for doing so much magic that you began seeing things.'

Arse. 'That's never happened to me before,' I said, 'but you're right. Hopefully this challenge won't involve much energy. I wonder what Trevor Bellows has devised for us.'

Her lip curled. 'Assuming he has the time in between everything else.' The disdain in her voice, not to mention her expression, immediately piqued my curiosity.

'What do you mean?'

Harriet raised a sarcastic eyebrow as if it were patently obvious what she was talking about, but I was still drawing a blank. 'Oh. I keep forgetting you weren't here at the start,' she dismissed, before turning away once more.

I ground my teeth. Bellows might not be my immediate focus but that didn't mean I was going to forget about him. It was still possible that the bloody pentagram in his trailer was a warning designed solely for him. Winter hadn't yet discovered any hidden meanings or the purpose behind the pentagram, but it remained pertinent.

'Yeah,' I said, doing my best to chivvy her along and encourage her to open up more. 'I feel like I really missed out. I love a bit of gossip, though. What's Bellows been up to?'

Harriet kept her eyes averted. 'I'm no tattle-tale.'

Oh, for goodness' sake. She'd already brought up this little titbit so pretending to be close-lipped now was pointless. But it was clear that she would refuse to say anything else about the matter. I'd just have to find someone else to fill me in.

Unfortunately, there wasn't time to move to the back of the boat and question Lou. It was already pulling into the side and I could see crowds of people gathered in a grassy field to the right. We were ushered off before being directed towards our positions. I tried to edge back slightly to engage Lou in conversation but I received an angry hiss from Barry. I'd have ignored him but for the fact that one of the medics ambled over to check I wasn't still going loopy from too much magic. This whole investigation would be a damn sight easier if people didn't keep getting in my way.

Various bits of equipment were being checked over. As far as I could tell, the producers had set up some kind of open-air torture for us involving ropes, climbing frames and mud. I wondered whether the government knew that a reality television show was flouting the Geneva Convention.

I submitted to the medic's ministrations while eyeing the obstacle course with trepidation. Maybe I could plead illness. 'Actually,' I said, 'I'm still feeling a bit weak. I think I should sit this one out.'

He frowned at me. 'You seem fine.'

'This isn't the sort of medical problem you usually deal with. This one is magic related so, although I might look alright on the surface, there could any manner of problems going on inside me.' I leaned in a bit closer. 'Spells are dangerous.'

'Mm-hmm.' He turned his head and motioned to someone in the crowd. When I realised it was Trevor Bellows, I couldn't resist another peek at Harriet but she was deep in conversation with Lou and Mike. Something about faking an argument so the other contestants wouldn't think any worrisome alliances were being formed. I rolled my eyes.

Bellows, with his pretentious purple robe flapping around his ankles, strode over. 'What seems to be the problem?' He pulled up his sleeves, which was a pointless effort because they were so baggy they immediately fell back down round his wrists again. 'If it is within my powers to help then I shall.'

The medic pointed at me. Barry, apparently sensing that something was up, also came over. This was a lot of attention considering all I was trying to do was weasel my way out of the challenge. 'This one says she's still feeling ill and wants to sit out the challenge.'

Bellows' mouth twitched. I instantly got the impression that he'd be absolutely thrilled if I didn't participate. 'The wellbeing of our contestants is paramount!'

Tell that to Benjamin Alberts. I gave Bellows a weak smile. 'I don't want to be any trouble but I don't want to collapse mid-challenge either.'

From the corner of my eye I spotted Winter look up from a conversation with Mazza. There was a frown on his face as if he knew exactly what I was up to. I glanced away hurriedly.

'Well,' Bellows said, 'if you're not up to it, it's essential that you don't take part. We can get you on a train and back to civilisation in no time.'

Arse. 'I'll probably be okay by tomorrow...'

He shook his head. 'Oh no. We want to make sure you don't do yourself serious injury, so we'll have to withdraw you from the show. Of course,' he added with a smile, 'we don't permit anyone to hang around the set if they have no reason to be there.'

Without realising it, I'd played right into his hands. The smarmy bugger was smarter than I'd given him credit for. 'I'll soldier on,' I said.

Barry looked anxious. 'I think that would be best.'

'Anything for my lovely producer.'

'We can't have you getting sick,' Bellows interjected.

'I'm fine, Trevor,' I told him. 'I'll be brave for the sake of *Enchantment*.'

Something like annoyance flashed in his eyes. 'You're such a trooper.' He turned on his heel and stalked off.

'He really doesn't like me very much,' I murmured.

Barry chuckled. 'Is it any surprise? You can do the sort of magic he can only dream of. And you're not in the Order so he can't dismiss you. You're competition for our Trev and he knows it. He's on the outs as it is, and if everyone else thought about it they'd realise you could replace him.'

'I'm a contestant,' I protested.

'If you win the show, or even if you do well, there'll be a contract in your hands the next morning. Trevor Bellows is old school. Viewers enjoy seeing some fresh blood.'

I considered this, finally feeling some sympathy for Bellows. It couldn't be easy thinking that there were incomers on all sides trying to steal your job from under you. Although surely he must have made enough money by now to sit back on his laurels and enjoy all that a quiet life had to offer.

I watched as he walked from group to group, his wide sleeves flapping every time he waved at someone and tried to get their attention. Poor guy. Then Brutus pitched up out of nowhere and rubbed himself against Bellows' legs. Nah. Bellows deserved everything he got.

'I'm not here because I want to work for *Enchantment*,' I said to Barry.

He glanced at me appraisingly. 'I can't work out why you're here at all.' He jerked his head at Winter, who was examining a sheet of paper with a furrowed brow. 'Unless it's because of him.'

'He's here because of me, not the other way around.' I had to stick with the narrative.

Barry snorted. 'Yeah, right. No matter what we've been told, the Order is obviously still concerned that there will be more murders. There are witches all over Tomintoul.'

I let out a slow breath. 'Do you think there *are* going to be more murders?' It was unlikely, but Barry might have insights that the rest of us didn't. 'I have enough on my plate to worry about without getting killed too.'

'You're perfectly safe,' he dismissed. 'You heard Belinda. All that had nothing to do with *Enchantment*.'

'But...'

'You know, the other three in your team are planning to get you voted out if you don't win. Lou is leading the charge. I heard her talking about it.'

I frowned. Something about the way he said that didn't ring true. 'Are you hoping that I'll confront her on camera and that fireworks will ensue?' I enquired.

His eyes widened. 'Of course not! I would never do such a thing. You can absolutely trust me, Ivy. I'm on your side. All the way.' He punched his chest for effect.

His protests were far too vociferous to be anything other than lies. Good grief, there was a lot to have to try and keep track of.

Witches like Tarquin, with their wheeling and dealing to inveigle their way into better positions, had nothing on reality television.

'Mmm.' I watched Bellows and Brutus approach Armstrong, who was directing a group of cameramen to get ready for the challenge. 'What's the deal with Trevor? What else has he been up to?'

'What do you mean?'

I shrugged. 'Harriet suggested he was busy with ... other things.'

Barry's cheeks flushed. That was interesting. 'I don't know what you're talking about.' He checked his watch. 'We're starting in less than thirty minutes. The other two teams will be here shortly. You should prepare. Warm up or ... something.'

Or something, indeed. He turned and walked away, pretending to look occupied.

Nibbling my lip, I wove my way through the crew towards Winter. He looked up, watching as I approached.

'Hey.'

His eyes softened. 'Hey.'

We smiled at each other for an all-too-brief moment. Then I shook myself and drew him aside, quickly filling him in on all I'd learnt about Belinda and her mysterious vial.

Winter's expression darkened. 'We need to find out what it is. It might be time to bring her in for questioning.'

'Won't that tip our hand?'

He rubbed his cheek. 'There's been no sight or sound of anything untoward since the blood in Bellows' trailer. Either our necromancer has gone to ground or something else is being prepared. Something bigger and nastier than we've already seen. We need to prevent any more deaths from occurring.'

We both turned in Belinda's direction. She was sitting in a chair with a make-up artist dabbing at her face with some kind of powder. 'She's hard as nails,' I said. 'And all the evidence so far points in her direction. But there's no motive and I find it hard to believe she could be capable of such a thing.'

'Because you're a fan?'

I shrugged. 'Yeah, maybe.' I sighed. 'You should never meet your heroes. They only ever disappoint.'

'And here was me thinking I was your hero.' Winter's tone was light.

I turned and met his eyes. 'You are.'

'Do I disappoint you?'

I didn't smile this time. 'Never.'

He edged a bit closer and I caught a whiff of spicy aftershave. Winter didn't often bother wearing it – was he trying to impress me? It was certainly working.

'You look like you're feeling better,' he murmured.

'I am. Whatever caused that hallucination yesterday must have been mild.'

'You still need to be careful, Ivy,' he cautioned. 'You might be being targeted.'

'I might be. But it might not be anything to do with our necromancer. Bellows, for example, can't wait for me to get booted off.'

A gleam lit Winter's eyes. 'He knows you're better than him.'

I grinned. 'Yeah.' I thought about what Harriet had said. 'There's more going on with Trevor Bellows than we know. He's been up to something else besides all the show stuff.'

Winter agreed. 'When you lot are off filming this challenge, I plan to take advantage of the chance to investigate both him and Belinda. I only came to see if you were alright. As soon as I get the chance, I'm heading back to the main set to sneak into their trailers.'

'Raphael Winter!' I said, with a mock gasp. 'Are you really going to enter someone's domain without a warrant? How shocking!'

'Someone's dead,' he reminded me. A muscle throbbed in his jaw. 'And someone tried to hurt you yesterday.'

Barry started waving at me. 'Ivy! Get over here! We're starting!'

I sighed. This contestant malarkey was becoming irritating. 'Time to go. I'll try to get hold of Belinda's vial so we can find out for sure whether she's involved. It'll be better if she doesn't know what we're up to just yet. If she is our necromancer then she has a hell of a lot of power. We don't want it unleashed unless we're sure we can contain it.'

Winter smiled. 'I'm glad to see you're being sensible for once.'

'I'm sure it won't last. Not unless there are more necromancers around. Anything to do with dead bodies scares the bejesus out of me.' I shivered.

'Be careful.'

I gave him a hard look. 'You too.' I stretched up on my tiptoes. 'I can't have my hero getting into trouble for breaking and entering,' I whispered in his ear.

Both corners of Winter's mouth crooked up.

Chapter Sixteen

We were walked through the challenge by Morris Armstrong, along-side our producers. The other two teams of contestants looked con-siderably worse for wear; the last team to arrive sported weary ex-pressions and several bruises. When I caught one of them muttering about how sore her legs were after marching up a mountain, I al-lowed myself a satisfied smirk. Unfortunately Mike was too busy flexing to hear her.

Previous challenges on *Enchantment* had been guided by loca-tion and this was no different. To begin with, there was the excruci-ating obstacle course to complete. Armstrong pointed out the rope swings, a precarious-looking balance beam and the marshy mud pit. Once those had been traversed, we were supposed to assemble a Celtic knot to unlock a box and reveal a magic wand. When the wand was pointed at the finish line, with the not-so-immortal words of '*Enchantment* commands you', our names would be revealed in puffs of multi-coloured smoke.

'Of course,' Armstrong said with a knowing wink, 'there are lay-ers of magic built into this challenge which will not be revealed to you beforehand.'

I nodded, unsurprised. It was typical for there to be few magical demands put on contestants in the early stages for the simple reason that few of us could perform any spells of consequence. However, the show was called *Enchantment*; there had to be magic of some form or another to satisfy the watching public.

I didn't really rate my chances of winning. I wasn't fit and I knew that it would take me far longer than anyone else to get across the obstacles. Even Lou would probably be faster. And it didn't seem particularly wise to exert my own magical abilities too far after the events of yesterday. Despite both my and Winter's suspicions that my exhausted hallucinations had been caused by something nefarious, I couldn't discard the idea that I'd simply cast too many spells. I had to be careful. After all, who knew when another real zombie would appear?

Taking up our allotted places, I glanced down the line. The others' expressions ran from grimly determined to absolute glee. I sighed. Then a camera was thrust in my face and Barry, staying well out of shot, addressed me. 'How are you feeling about this, Ivy?' he enquired.

I knew the protocol. I had to answer in full sentences to make it appear as if I'd not been prompted to speak. I considered the fact that I was never going to win or save myself from the upcoming vote and spoke carefully.

'I'm feeling terrified,' I confessed, widening my eyes for emphasis and speaking loudly so that the other contestants could hear. I looked down at myself. 'I'm not really built for athletics and some of those obstacles look almost insurmountable.'

It clearly wasn't the answer Barry was looking for. He frowned slightly and nudged me some more. 'There must be some spells you have up your sleeve that will help you to compete with some of the more sporty contestants.'

I spotted Mike giving me a sidelong glance, apparently waiting to hear my answer. No prizes for guessing what he was thinking. From his body language he was raring to go – and he seemed absolutely convinced that he was going to win.

I let out a tinkle of laughter. I couldn't have sounded more fake if I'd set off in a spaceship named *The Majestic Untruth* on course for the Fraudulent Galaxy. 'I'm not an accomplished Order witch. The only spells I can perform are mere tricks and sleights of hand.' I pasted on a rueful expression. 'Maybe if I could sprout myself a pair of wings, I could soar over the obstacles. Unfortunately, I don't think that's likely to happen.'

Out of the corner of my eye, I noticed Mazza run over to Belinda. She was standing to one side, talking into a mobile phone while her hair was being teased out and fluffed up by an attendant.

Mazza handed Belinda a piece of paper that she perused with pursed lips before dismissing him. Even when he walked away his expression remained like that of an eager puppy. He looked even brighter when Amy crossed his path as she dashed off in the other direction on someone else's bidding. Just watching her made me feel tired. Yeah, I might have an obstacle course to get over but things could always be worse.

I flicked my attention back to Belinda. Unsurprisingly, there was no sign of the vial but I had no doubt that it was still round her neck. I wondered how badly it would go if I rugby-tackled her to the ground in order to snatch it from her. It'd probably be carnage. In a magic-less fight, I reckoned the primped and preened presenter would beat me hands down. It was just as well I had oodles of magic at my disposal. All I had to do was to come up with the right plan.

'Ivy!' Barry barked.

I glanced at him, belatedly realising that he must have been asking me questions in a bid to get me to say something interesting – or incriminating – for the ever-rolling cameras. 'Sorry. Could you repeat that?'

He scrunched up his face in irritation before carefully smoothing his features. He was going to have to work on his acting skills if he wanted to get me to believe anything that came out of his mouth.

Dropping his voice to a whisper so the others couldn't hear him, he leaned towards me conspiratorially, although he still managed to keep away from the camera lens. 'Don't tell anyone you heard it from me,' he said, 'but one of the other teams has decided that you're their strongest competition. To stop you from winning, they're going to try to bring you down, probably during the obstacle course. They want to make sure you're voted out first.'

Yeah, yeah. I pushed back my hair. 'Barry, I know you want to see me do more spells but you saw what happened yesterday. I have to be careful not to overdo it.' It sounded like the perfect excuse for not trying very hard. I'd hallucinate every day of the week if it meant I didn't have to put in too much effort.

'The medics have cleared you. You wouldn't be here if you weren't good to go,' he sniffed. 'And it would be so shameful if you were booted out first. Just think what all those Order witches who are watching would say.'

I rolled my eyes. 'Barry, honey. I know what you're doing and it's not going to work. This would be a whole lot easier if you'd just tell the truth when you spoke to me. I can sniff out a lie at a hundred paces. '

Instantly he seemed interested. 'Because of magic?'

'No. Because most people aren't very good liars.' I sighed. 'I know you want to make good television because it makes you look better. But you have to know I'm not going to beat the others. You can fabricate as many stories as you like about what you've overheard but it's not going to make a difference. If this relationship is ever going to work, we need to reach a mutual understanding.'

Barry's eyes shifted as he weighed up my words. 'Fine,' he said eventually. 'You want the truth, you'll get it. You were brought in to replace the contestant who we had lined to be the bitch.'

'So I heard.'

'We don't have anyone else who's nasty enough to draw the viewers' anger. We need someone to be an object of hatred.'

Finally he was being honest. I gave him an approving nod, followed by a frown. 'If I'm horrible, or if I do something during this challenge to piss off the others, then I'll definitely be voted out first.' While in theory that wouldn't be a bad thing, I wouldn't get anywhere with my investigations if I were forced to leave the set.

'We need someone nasty. If you're not going to use magic, then be evil. I'll make sure you stay in for at least the next few rounds.'

'You can do that?'

He looked down the line. 'The rest of this lot are much easier to manipulate than you.'

I didn't think that was true. The contestants often seemed superfluous to what the producers wanted and the shenanigans they were aiming for, but that didn't mean they were stupid. In fact, I reckoned they were smart enough to see which way the wind was blowing and act accordingly. After all, keep the crew on your side and you would probably be allowed to stick around for longer.

Moonbeam sidled up. 'What's up, partners?'

Barry scowled but, given Moonbeam's ancestry, he stopped short of telling him to piss off – at least in so many words. 'We're having a quiet chat,' he said. 'Me and Ivy. You should go and make sure that Morris has everything he needs.'

Moonbeam pretended not to hear him. 'It looked like you were discussing strategy.' He glanced at me. 'I thought I was going to be your tactical expert.'

'You are,' I soothed. Ignoring Barry's glare, I told him what Barry and I had been talking about.

Moonbeam scratched his chin thoughtfully. 'You won't win if you're the bitch.'

'Maybe I'm not looking to win. Maybe I just want to get to the later stages.' If Winter and I hadn't found our necromancer before filming was over, we'd never find him. I flicked another look at Belinda. Or her.

'Then it's a good plan.'

I raised an eyebrow. 'That was decisive. You were telling me before not to start arguments.'

'That was when I thought you were in this to win. Now I know it's the grand prize you're after.'

'Eh?'

Moonbeam grinned. 'Longer lasting fame.'

Good grief. That was most definitely not what I wanted. It sounded like hard work to me; I preferred a quiet life. All the same, I smiled back at him and bobbed my head towards Barry. 'Then I shall do as you request.' I paused. 'Ask me those questions again.'

Barry's face filled with delight and he wasted no time. 'How are you feeling about this, Ivy?'

I bared my teeth. 'I feel great. This obstacle course looks hard and I'm not very sporty, but have you seen what the rest of this lot look like? Besides, if any of them seem to be getting ahead of me, I might cast a spell and trip them up. They'll fall flat on their faces and I'll stroll through the finish line as the winner. Piece. Of. Cake.'

Moonbeam smiled in approval. Barry was almost giddy. 'That was brilliant.' He glanced at Armstrong, who was tapping his foot and looking irritated. 'I should leave you now.' He winked at me. 'Good luck.'

Armstrong beckoned Belinda and, with an imperious flick of her hair, she strolled up and took her place directly in front of the obstacle course. 'Here we are, at the gateway of our very first challenge! The winner receives automatic immunity from the vote. Everyone else will be fair game.' As she continued, I blocked out her voice and focused on how I could find out what her vial was really about. There had to be a way. 'On your marks,' Belinda beamed. 'Get set... Go!'

Everyone hurtled towards the first obstacle with extraordinary speed. I let them all pass then ambled forward. I was conserving my strength. As Belinda burbled away about who was in the lead, I took my time reaching the net and crouching down to get underneath it.

'And Mike has already cleared the first obstacle while Ivy has only just reached it!' Belinda yelled.

Good for Mike. I hunkered down and began to shimmy through. Even with my glacial pace, this was hard work. The net snagged on my daft corset several times and, unwilling to expose more flesh than was absolutely necessary, I took my time freeing myself. By the time I scrambled out the other side, at least three of the others could barely be seen. I shrugged and moved up to the rope swing. This could work.

Picking up speed, I flung myself towards it, snagging it with one hand. I let myself swing out. Then, in a moment of panic and with the rope burning the skin on my palm, I released it, dropped to the ground and rolled with a loud groan.

I did my best to look hurt and squeezed my eyes shut. Then I opened the left one just a crack and peeked. Morris Armstrong waved to stop the proceedings and in less than a heartbeat a medic, Belinda and several cameras were surrounding me.

'Ivy!' Belinda said, her voice the epitome of concern. 'What's happened? Are you alright?'

No. I needed her to lean over so I could grab that damn vial. I groaned. 'My back,' I said in a strained voice.

'Don't move,' the medic instructed. 'We'll look you over and make sure you're alright.'

Trevor Bellows appeared from out of nowhere. 'This is the second time this contestant has been out for the count. I think it's time we withdrew her from the competition.' He paused for a beat. 'For her own safety, of course.'

I struggled up to my elbows. 'I think I'm okay.' I pressed one hand against my ribcage. 'It really hurts here, though.'

Belinda leaned close enough for my plan to work but there were too many cameras. I couldn't see any angle from which I could perform the rune I needed and not get caught. I grimaced. Well, so much for that idea. If I wanted to steal Belinda's vial without her noticing, I'd have to do it off camera. That was a pain in the arse.

Gasping, and trying to appear winded, I gently pushed away the medic and got to my feet. 'I'm fine,' I said. 'I can do this.'

Barry looked concerned. Even Belinda's concern seemed genuine. It belatedly occurred to me that I couldn't do this kind of thing again. With one contestant dead, *Enchantment* couldn't take any chances with our wellbeing. They really would pull me from the show, whether I was their much-needed nasty contestant or not.

Thinking quickly, I babbled out a reasonable excuse. 'I've been hexed!'

Everyone blinked in shock.

'Hexed?' Belinda tried to frown but her forehead couldn't wrinkle naturally. Botox? 'What do you mean?'

'I had it,' I said with defiance. 'I had the rope in my hands and then I felt a shooting pain which only magic could create. One of the other contestants has bespelled me because I'm such strong competition.' Even to my own ears I sounded ridiculous.

I saw Armstrong open his mouth to speak but Barry sidled over and murmured something in his ear. The director's expression cleared and he gave me a happy thumbs-up. Yes, this was all part of an act. Just not for the reason he thought.

'I'll get my own back on whoever did this,' I said, with an added snarl. 'No one hexes Ivy Wilde and gets away with it.' I applauded myself mentally; I'd make an excellent panto villain.

I followed up my words of dire consequence with a glare, flinging a narrowed-eye look at the other contestants. The truth was that they were all too far away to see what I was doing but it didn't matter. The camera picked it all up and I managed to soothe the last of the crew's worried expressions, as well as fulfilling my brief. 'I'm good to go again,' I said. 'I won't be beaten!'

I threw my arms around in an extra flourish and almost smacked Bellows' face in the process. His expression hardened. 'I have to insist—'

'I'm fine,' I interrupted. 'Never felt better.' I jumped up and down as if to prove it. Immediately I regretted it; I still had three-quarters of the obstacle course to complete.

'Everyone else has been kept in the position they were when you fell,' Belinda said.

I nodded, catching sight of an irate-looking Harriet perched precariously on top of a high bar with her hands fluttering in the air. Oops.

'I'll blow the whistle and you'll begin again. If you're sure?'

'I'm sure.'

'Excellent.'

I breathed in deeply and, a moment later, we were off again. Rather than merely strolling, I tried a bit harder this time around. Coming last after my faked collapse might not reflect well on me.

The trouble was that I had a lot of ground to make up and the obstacle course was incredibly hard. It didn't help that when I reached the top of the bar where Harriet had been forced to stop, the first of the magic waves hit me. No wonder she'd looked so annoyed. Someone, possibly Bellows, had conjured up a host of flying lizards. They were insubstantial and, when one flew directly at my face and its tail grazed my skin, I realised that they more illusion than anything else. It didn't mean that they weren't bloody annoying at this height.

I clambered down, making a beeline for the mud pit. At the far end, three other contestants were still struggling to pull themselves out. As I edged forwards, a flaming streak of fire whooshed in my direction. It wasn't magically induced, however; the fire came from canisters rigged at shoulder height along the side of the pit. Sneaky. What was the betting that they would be hidden from the camera's view to make it appear as if more spells were being cast? It didn't really matter. The fire was obviously working to a schedule. Flames of death. Beats of three. Flames of death. Beats of three. Even I could manage to escape this part.

The mud pit might be a different matter, although I vaguely re-membered watching a science experiment on television involving a swimming pool and custard. At the time my focus had been on the poor sod who had to clean up the mess afterwards. However, there was something to be said for being a couch potato; that show might stand me in good stead now.

I decided to make a run for it. Counting under my breath I dashed across, picking up speed when I hit the mud to avoid sinking into it. It worked. The momentum – and something to do with the laws of physics – kept me going. I scampered across the surface, springing happily onto solid ground on the other side. That was how to do it.

I let out a crow of exultation then, remembering my promise to Barry, swivelled round to the three contestants who were still stuck and shouted, 'In your face!' It was mean and nasty and I felt more than a trickle of guilt but I needed to make sure I wasn't thrown off the show.

Panting hard, and under no illusion about what Winter would say about my lack of fitness if he saw me now, I completed the last few obstacles. I was almost ready to collapse but I still had a way to go. I jogged forward, weaving in and out of the trees which I was sure had been placed there just to annoy me. I could see the Celtic-knot puzzle up ahead. Then a root came up out of nowhere and I went fly-ing. Arse.

Heaving myself up and spitting out a mouthful of dirt, I ignored the cameras that were zooming in on my exasperated face and wiped my eyes. As I blinked away flecks of muck, something flitted across my peripheral vision. I half-turned, just in time to see something shoot behind one of the larger trees fifty metres or so away. It could have been an animal – but what it looked like was a human being with long straggly hair moving around on all fours.

I froze. Did I really just see that? I spun round towards the cameras but they were all pointed at me. Engaging the cameramen in conversation would be useless. First of all, they were under orders not to communicate; second, I reckoned I'd used up any goodwill I had with them. Another mutter about a hallucination and I'd be out on my ear.

Swallowing hard and trying to stay calm, I glanced back warily. There was no sign of any potential zombie. I edged to my right and peered round, catching a flash of dark clothing. Then there was a loud heaving grunt, not dissimilar to what I imagined a death rattle would sound like.

I raised my hands, ready to perform whatever defensive or offensive runes were required, when there was a ragged whoop from behind me. The zombie, if that's what it was, rustled in alarm. I heard a single pant, like a breath, then the thing crashed away through the undergrowth. The three contestants who'd been stuck in the mud pit were oblivious. As they passed me, they continued to whoop, holding hands and beaming with muddy delight.

Rachelle, who was closest to me, turned in my direction. 'This is what happens when you work together and when you're nice to others,' she sniped.

My jaw worked uselessly. Whatever I'd seen had already gone. The river was in that direction so maybe the bloody thing would drown. I could only hope.

'Be as nice as you want,' I shot back to them as they skipped away in front of me. 'But just remember that only one person can win!'

They ignored me. I twisted away and stared back through the undergrowth. If this really was another undead necromantic being, I needed Winter and I needed him now.

Chapter Seventeen

In the end I came last, a very bedraggled last at that. The rest of the contestants clapped politely as my name, quite literally, went up in smoke. Then Belinda stepped forward and pointed at Harriet as the winner.

Despite my fear about what I may or may not have seen, I was surprised. She must have come ahead in the puzzle section. I raised my hands to clap then caught Barry frowning at me. I dropped my arms and pouted instead. Being mean was rather hard work.

The only saving grace was that we were given an hour's break before voting. I knew that I'd be free from the cameras because, on screen, the transition between the challenge and the voting happened instantaneously. All the producers made a beeline for their contestants. No doubt this 'break' was to make sure that everyone voted the way they were supposed to.

'Ivy!' Barry stretched his arms out expansively. 'Bad luck.'

I shrugged. 'Whatever. I have to go.'

'Huh?'

'You want to talk strategy for the voting, right?'

'Of course. What else is there?'

Bloodthirsty zombies lurking in the trees less than half a mile from here. 'You'd be surprised,' I murmured. 'But either I'll be voted out or I won't be. Nothing else I do will make a difference now.'

'Ivy...'

'I have to go.' I paused for a beat. 'I've got my period.'

As expected, Barry blanched and backed off. I stalked away from him, my posture ramrod straight to ensure he didn't come after me. Now all I had to do was hope that Winter had returned from his snooping.

Ignoring the crew members busying themselves rigging up the voting area, I swept along as if I knew exactly what I was doing.

I couldn't see Winter anywhere. Moonbeam, however, was coming straight towards me so I veered away and moved into the trees. I didn't dare go far; after all, there might be a damn zombie lurking there. All the same, the last thing I needed now was to be drawn into yet another chat with Belinda's plotting son.

Keeping to the fringes of the small wood, I looked desperately for Winter's familiar form. I was so busy searching for him that I almost tripped up again. This time it wasn't on a pesky tree root, however; it was Brutus.

'What gives?' I growled. 'You abandon me as soon as I get here and now you're trying to kill me?'

My cat yawned and began to wash himself. I scowled. I didn't have time for this.

'Magic man,' Brutus said as I started to turn away.

I looked back. 'You mean Bellows? Your new owner?'

I received a scathing look in response. Clearly, Brutus didn't believe anyone owned him. In that, of course, he was absolutely correct. 'Fish.'

I raised my hands helplessly. 'Am I supposed to understand what that means?'

Brutus licked his lips. Given that he wasn't using his usual refrain to demand food, I suddenly understood. 'Oh. He gives you fish.'

'Good fish.' His whiskers quivered. 'Give fish.'

I gazed at him in exasperation. 'Do I look like I'm carrying a string of mackerel with me? Some familiar you are. You're supposed to aid me in my magic quests, not piss off at the first chance of a deluxe meal.'

If Brutus could have shrugged, he probably would have. 'Magic man no magic.'

Yeah, I probably wasn't surprised at that. All the same, I wanted to double-check. 'You're sure?' At least if Bellows possessed no real magical abilities, he could be struck off the list of necromancer suspects. That meant there were only about a hundred thousand people left to investigate if I included everyone in the town, all the outlying villages and the cast and crew involved in *Enchantment*. The way things were going right now, I had to take every success.

Brutus sniffed, as if he wouldn't deign to answer. It was fine for him to repeat the same things over and over unnecessarily but when I asked him to do it for me, he took the hump. Contrary cat.

'Bad man.'

I froze. 'Trevor Bellows is a bad man?'

Brutus yawned again. Then he turned his head to the right. There was a rustle in the trees. The zombie. It had to have come back. I swallowed hard and flicked a warning glance at my cat. 'Get back,' I warned. 'This could be bad.'

There was another rustle and Winter appeared. I exhaled loudly in relief. He stared at me. 'What's wrong? You look as white as a sheet.'

I opened my mouth to answer but Brutus got in there first. 'Bad man,' he said.

For a fleeting moment, Winter looked hurt. 'Me?'

Brutus sighed and stood up, walking away with his tail waving violently in the air as if he couldn't bear to be near either of us.

'I think he meant Bellows,' I said.

Winter's mouth flattened into a grim line. 'Then he's right. Trevor Bellows is a very bad man indeed.' He gave me a look filled with meaning that I couldn't interpret then reached into his jacket and withdrew a small manila envelope. 'Here,' he said.

The expression on his face and the tone of his voice made me take the proffered envelope with considerable trepidation. Winter put his hands into his pockets and looked away whilst I slid out the contents and examined them. It was a series of glossy photographs, obviously taken in sequence.

I flipped through them, with the odd sensation that the last lingering vestiges of my childhood were being shattered in one swoop. I didn't make it through all of them. Seeing the first few, of Belinda Battenapple in compromising positions involving nudity and a range of objects, including ropes, blindfolds and a lurid pink ball gag, I'd seen enough.

I breathed out. 'Well.'

The tips of Winter's ears were red. He was obviously embarrassed. He coughed awkwardly. 'I didn't take it but there was also an envelope stuffed full of cash and a note.'

'What did it say?'

He sighed. '*You've got what you wanted.*'

I absorbed this. 'So you think that Trevor Bellows has been blackmailing Belinda?'

'That's certainly what it looks like.'

'Do you think he took the photos? Or did he come by them through other means?'

'I don't know. But we do need to speak to Bellows at his earliest convenience.'

I shook my head, as much in dismay as in a bid to get the images of Belinda out of my mind. 'It's horrid,' I said, 'and he's clearly a bastard. But that doesn't mean he had anything to do with dead bodies rising up from the ground. You should pass this on to the police and let them deal with it. It's out of our remit.'

Winter grimaced. 'It's a strange world when you're the one suggesting we do things by the book. Unfortunately I came by these during an illegal search. The police will have their hands tied. Unless Belinda herself makes a complaint, they can't act.'

I cast my mind back, thinking of all the times I'd seen Belinda and Bellows together. 'I've not noticed anything that suggests she despises him or that she's scared of him. Truthfully, most of the time he seems completely beneath her attention. She's the star and he's just the hired help.'

'This is assault, Ivy.'

I bit my lip. 'Yeah,' I said quietly. 'I know.'

I heaved in a breath and told him about my failed efforts to steal Belinda's vial from right under her nose – literally – followed by what I thought I'd seen in the woods. At my mention of another zombie-like creature, Winter stiffened. 'You're sure?'

I shrugged helplessly. 'Given my recent hallucinatory episode, how can I be? I wasn't alone and nobody else noticed anything. There's still security all over the place. Even though this area is larger than the main set so they're spread thinner, you'd think one of them would have seen something if there had been something to see.' I pushed back my hair. But then Gareth had managed to sidle through without being spotted and without any great difficulty.

Winter rubbed his chin and dug out his phone. 'This is Winter,' he barked, as someone answered. 'You need to check out the grave-yard. Find out whether any other graves have been disturbed. Every-one not at the graveyard needs to get to the current location where *Enchantment* is filming. There has been another possible sighting. If there is another exanimate body out there, we need to find it.' There was a pause. 'I don't care. This is a priority.' He hung up.

'You have a less than charming phone manner,' I said.

Winter rolled his eyes. 'Do you want to call them back and ask them about the weather? Find out if they're comfortable and getting enough sleep?'

I grinned. 'No, I'm good. It wasn't a criticism. More like an ob-servation.'

'Well those witches tasked with investigating the town could do with some criticism,' he huffed. 'They seem to spending more time in the pub than doing any work. Apparently the most they've uncov-ered is that a couple of hundred years ago a family with very strong magical powers moved into the area. We already knew that. Until they can uncover something that's not ancient history, their presence is nothing more than a waste of time.'

I patted his arm. 'There, there. To be fair, we've not uncovered a whole lot either and we've been here for days. We've got access to everything on set and we're still floundering.'

Winter grimaced. 'Okay,' he said. 'Let's stop floundering and start swimming. Rather than confronting Bellows, let's go and talk to Belinda. We'll find out what on earth that thing is around her neck and ask her what Bellows is up to at the same time.'

'You think she's more likely to be honest if we're trying to help her as well as accuse her?'

Winter raised a shoulder in a half-hearted response. 'If there is another zombie then we don't have much choice. If it reaches a populated area there will be carnage.'

'Maybe you were right and we should have confronted her earlier.'

'No. The more evidence we have the better. If she denied everything, she'd know we suspected her and we wouldn't have any reason to detain her. This way we have an another angle.' He sighed. 'Even if it doesn't feel right using it.'

I knew exactly what he meant. Belinda was a victim of Bellows, no matter how you looked at it. But if the necromancer was performing magic again, we had to act. It had got to the point where we had to rule Belinda Battenapple out or in for good before more people were killed.

I glanced down at the photos. In every one, she was wearing the vial. She might not have had on a stitch of clothing but she clearly wasn't about to abandon her death-drawing necklace, even for this.

We started walking back again. Before we reached the edge of the trees, I turned to Winter. 'There is one good thing to come out of all this,' I said.

He frowned. 'What's that?'

I didn't smile. 'Now you're calling them zombies as well.'

Winter didn't argue.

***

In an ideal world, we could have marched straight over to Belinda and pulled her away for questioning. Instead, there was the small matter of the vote. At least both Belinda and I would be in the same space so she couldn't hide herself away and avoid us. As soon as this last part of filming was over, Winter and I would both ensure that we got her alone and in a quiet spot.

I eyed her while Armstrong barked out orders involving technical stuff I didn't have a hope of understanding. She didn't look like an evil necromancer – but she didn't look harried or upset like the victim of blackmailing either. This was a woman who spent her entire life in front of the cameras. I might have told Barry that most people weren't good liars but I reckoned that someone like Belinda had it down pat. And perhaps calling what she did lying was a bit unfair. She presented an image to her adoring public – that was part of her job.

I joined the other contestants. Lou looked at me questioningly. 'Where have you been?'

'Just clearing my head,' I said airily.

She frowned at me. Yeah, I wasn't a great liar either.

Armstrong came up and gave us a critical once-over. He pointed to Rachelle at the back and someone darted over and adjusted her hair. Then he frowned at Mike, who hastily undid two of his shirt buttons to reveal his chest hair. Only when he was completely happy with everyone's appearance did Armstrong speak.

'This is a vital moment! This is your first chance to say what you really think about your fellow contestants. It's not the time to be shy or retiring. It's not the time to bite your tongue. We expect you to let rip with exactly what you think. Have you got that?' There was an indistinct murmur of agreement. 'I said,' he bellowed, 'have you got that?'

'Yes.' We dutifully bobbed our heads.

Armstrong didn't appear appeased. 'This is the greatest show on television,' he said, his dour expression entirely at odds with his words. 'You are incredibly lucky to be here. Do not waste it! Regret only what you do, not what you don't do!'

I was starting to see why he'd been chosen as *Enchantment*'s new director. For all his cheesy lines and erratic mood swings, he possessed a great deal of charisma. If it weren't for a certain blue-eyed witch standing not a million miles away from here, I might even have been tempted.

The murkier the investigation got, the clearer my feelings towards my erstwhile partner became. I shot Winter a sidelong glance to where he was standing by Mazza and Moonbeam. He was watching me with a shuttered expression but when I gave him a tiny wave he returned it with a tiny smile. Butterflies flipped in the pit of my belly. Even the prospect of being part of an *Enchantment* vote couldn't beat what Raphael Winter did to my emotions.

We were counted down then directed out. One by one, we trooped into the clearing where a semicircle of cauldrons had been placed. Our names were written on the near side. I took up position behind mine and peered into the contents. It was a gloopy neon sludge, designed to show up on camera. I beamed. This was always my favourite part of the show.

Belinda strolled down the pathway, lanterns blazing into life as she passed them. Again, it wasn't magic providing their power but basic technology. I'd always suspected as much; having my suspicions confirmed now I wasn't viewing everything through a television screen was rather disappointing.

'Welcome,' Belinda said. 'This is the very first vote-off for this series and we know it's going to be an exciting one. All twelve contestants have had the chance to get to know each other's strengths and weaknesses. Some relationships will snap under the strain of tonight's events while others will grow and blossom into friendships for life. *Enchantment* isn't just about the magic that surrounds us. It's about the magic within us.'

Under any other circumstances, I'd have vomited in my mouth. Instead, I bounced around on the balls of my feet in delight. Just for the next five minutes, I was prepared to put aside all the worries and fears I had about the undead and the unsavoury. *Enchantment* was worth it.

'Each of you,' Belinda said, addressing us, 'has a cauldron in front of you. For now your cauldrons are safe but if you are voted out, they will be tipped over and the magic inside will cease to exist. Your names will be drawn at random. State clearly who you wish to see voted out and what your reasons are.'

This was where the magic really happened. Depending on when a contestant's name was drawn could change the course of the entire game. I'd seen episodes where it went right down to the wire, with equal votes cast for different people. I'd also seen episodes where the first vote decided who the unhappy victim would be. As Armstrong directed the cameras into a sweeping shot of the whole area, I cracked my knuckles in preparation.

Belinda delved into her velvet drawstring bag, withdrawing one slip of paper. 'The first contestant to vote is Harriet.'

At least three cameras swung towards her. The others focused on the rest of us, ready to capture the expression of the first unlucky target.

Harriet took a deep breath. 'I've thought about this a lot,' she said, her voice quavering only just slightly. 'I have clashed with Ivy and she has done several things of which I disapprove.' I'd have tried to look contrite but I was playing the role of evil contestant. Rolling my eyes, I clicked my tongue and folded my arms as if she were being completely ridiculous. 'However,' Harriet continued, 'I have come to realise that she is not a bad person. She can still see the error of her ways and I'm happy to help her do that.'

I raised my eyebrows. Harriet was painting herself as some kind of saint. It shouldn't have annoyed me, she was playing a part as much as I was, but it still irritated me.

'The person I would like to vote off,' she said, while everyone else held their breath, 'is ...'

Harriet never got the chance to finish. From somewhere to the left there was a loud shout. Armstrong leapt to his feet, a furious expression on his face. 'Who the hell is that?' he yelled. 'Who is interrupting our shooting?'

There were more shouts. I jumped in front of my cauldron while Winter started to sprint towards the sound. Before he even reached the trees, a nightmarish creature sprang out, crashing into him and knocking him to the ground.

If I thought the monster man who had attacked us up on the hill was gruesome, then I'd been naïve. The straggly hair told me this was the same creature I thought I'd seen in the trees during the challenge. Now I could also see his face I felt ill. He'd obviously been much further down the decomposition process than the previous zombie. There were scarcely any scraps of flesh clinging to his bones; in fact, half of his skull was pure bone. The other half was writhing with maggots. A single worm slithered out of his eye socket.

I swallowed down my horror, let out a cry and raised my hands. I was going to send this damn thing back to kingdom come where it belonged.

Screams tore the air and people scattered in all directions. I held my ground and flicked my fingers, twisting my right index finger into a figure of eight and using my pinkie for added impact. Whether the zombie sensed what I was doing or not, it wheeled round and barrelled towards me. That was fine. I only needed two more seconds. I rotated my wrist – then something slammed into me, knocking me down and interrupting the rune.

For one horrifying moment, I thought there was more than one undead bastard. Then Mike's arms went round me, pinning me in place. 'Don't worry, Ivy. I'll save you.'

The bloody plonker. I wriggled underneath him in a vain attempt to free myself as security guards streamed in from all the directions. Some were carrying tasers but I doubted they would help. This was a corpse, after all; electricity would increase its strength and speed, not decrease it.

'Let me go!' I screamed.

Mike looked down at me with a confused expression. I twisted round so I was on my back and thrust my hands upwards to shove him off while turning my head to see where the zombie was. Why wasn't it on us yet? At the speed it had been going...

I gasped in horror. With Mike's intervention, it had abandoned its sprint towards me in favour of focusing on the one other person who was standing alone. Frozen in shock and seemingly unable even to scream, Belinda only managed to blink once and hold up her hands. Then the thing was on her.

Blood sprayed out in all directions, arcing into the air before splattering on the hard ground as the thing bit Belinda's neck with its teeth and ripped at her flesh with its claws. Fingernails, I thought dully. Not claws. That used to be a human being.

'Oh my God.' Mike's entire body was quivering. He gave me a wide-eyed look of horror then sprang up and bolted away, as streams of red-robed witches finally appeared from all directions.

Working as one, the Order witches raised their hands and cast out a combined rune. The zombie was flung backwards from Belinda, her blood staining every inch of its body and features. With nothing to support her any longer, Belinda collapsed. Moonbeam pelted towards her.

The zombie, grappling with the invisible magic forces that were being flung at it, caught sight of Moonbeam and made for him. Again, the witches' magic pushed him back.

'You need to stop it moving!' I screamed. 'Make ice and trap its legs!'

I had no idea whether they heard me or not. I was already scrambling towards Moonbeam. He fell by Belinda's side, his fingers pressing against the red-stained skin of her neck. The blood just kept on coming.

Focusing on the immediate danger, I flung out my hands again towards the zombie. It groaned as another barrage of magic hit it from behind. Its knees gave way, the joints making an audible pop – but it wasn't finished. Using only its hands, it scrabbled forward, mindlessly doing whatever it could to get back to its meal.

Without Winter right next to me, I couldn't draw water and make ice as quickly as we'd managed during our previous undead encounter. Fire would be fastest – and riskiest. Pulling as much oxygen into my lungs as I could, I threw out a double-handed flame rune. Within an instant, the zombie lit up, the remnants of its clothes alight. As the acrid scent of charring flesh and burning hair filled the air, I ran straight for it. I was short and unfit but, if I snagged it in just the right spot, this might work.

Using all the momentum I could gather, I knocked into its shoulder, forcing it away from its path towards Moonbeam and his mother. Then I followed up with an immediate wind rune, flattening it completely to the ground and holding it there. At least, that was, until magic slammed into my body as well as the zombie's. Pain flashed through me and it felt like my very bones were breaking. I heard Winter's strangled yell then my knees gave way.

The red-robed witches advanced, finally gaining on the zombie and adding more flames to my fire while ensuring that it didn't move towards anyone else and the fire was contained. I fell all the way down, using the last of my strength to roll away while keeping my body from the heat. It was about all I could manage to do. The pain was excruciating.

I coughed and choked, squinting back at Moonbeam and Belinda. My vision swam; I was either going to throw up or pass out. Maybe both. For one strange moment, I thought I saw Tarquin sprint up towards them and lunge downwards, grab something and smash it under his heel. Then Winter was on me, gathering me up in his arms as my consciousness finally gave way to blessed release.

Chapter Eighteen

It was the raised voices that I heard first. Through the fugue of pain and semi-consciousness, I could make out Winter. Curiously, his voice was shaking with fury. 'You could have killed her!'

'We're very sorry. She was in the way of the spell and—'

'Any idiot could have avoided her! You call yourselves witches? You're not fit to be in Arcane Branch if you can't perform simple runes to hit a damn zombie!'

'Uh, Adeptus Exemptus, it wasn't really a zombie. It was an animated—'

Winter interrupted them again. 'I know damn well what it was!'

I groaned, opened my eyes and looked around. As far as I could tell, I was lying on a narrow camp bed in one of the *Enchantment* trailers. It was tempting to close my eyes again and rest but then I remembered what had just happened and felt sick instead.

Jerking upwards with a violent movement that made me feel even worse, I searched around desperately for a container. I only just grabbed a plant pot in time before I threw up. Most of the vomit landed inside but some spattered the leaves of what had been a pretty bonsai. I regarded it morosely. Very Zen.

'Ivy!' Winter appeared from the depths of the trailer, rushed over and knelt down beside me. 'How are you feeling?'

I pointed to the plant. 'Not great,' I said weakly. Then I burst into tears.

Sheer panic flitted across Winter's face before he drew me into a loose hug. 'It's alright,' he murmured. 'You're alright.'

I hiccupped. 'It was my fault. Belinda's dead because of me. I saw that thing in the woods earlier and I didn't tell anyone. I was too afraid they'd think I was crazy. If I'd said something maybe she'd still be okay.'

He pulled back and smoothed my hair away from my face. 'Shhh. Everything's fine. Belinda is fine. The only person who got seriously hurt was you. And that,' he said in a hard tone, 'was because we have too many incompetent witches in Arcane Branch.'

'It wasn't their fault.' I sniffed. 'I was in their way.' I wiped my nose with the back of my hand and stared into his eyes. 'How can Belinda be alright? That thing ripped out her throat.'

'That's another story. For now, you need to rest.'

He reached into his jacket and pulled out a monogrammed linen handkerchief. I wasn't in the slightest bit surprised that he was old school enough to carry one. I took it gratefully and blew my nose into it then I offered it back to him. A ghost of a smile crossed his face and he shook his head. 'Keep it.'

I sniffed again. 'You don't want my snot?'

'Not particularly.'

I twisted the handkerchief into a ball, my fingers clutching it for dear life. 'Are you lying to me? Is Belinda really okay?'

Winter smiled. 'She's really okay.'

'And the zombie?'

'It's been taken care of.'

'Do we know who the necromancer is? I mean, it's obviously not Belinda Battenapple, is it?'

'No.' He sighed. 'And no, we don't know who's raising the dead either.' He cupped my face in his hands. 'Stop worrying about it. You should lie down and rest. I'll stay here with you.' His eyes searched mine as if he still wasn't convinced that I wasn't dying. 'You took a really nasty hit, Ivy.'

Clearly being smacked by a devastating spell designed to bring down a creature of the undead had caused some seriously adverse effects because I shook my head and stood up, wobbling ever so slightly. 'I've never felt better,' I said, lying through my teeth. 'Now explain to me what happened with Belinda. How on earth is she still alive?'

Winter's response was soft but his expression was intense. 'You already know. According to Villeneuve anyway. He finagled his way up here. It's probably just as well he did or the outcome would have been very different.'

I blinked. 'Tarquin? What on earth does he have to do with anything?'

'He said you already knew. That he'd told you all about it.' Winter paused. 'In fact, he told us that you had given him your blessing.'

I hissed through my teeth. My vapid, idiotic excuse for an ex-boyfriend still wouldn't hesitate to blame me for everything from the Salem witch trials to the ever-diminishing size of extra-large chocolate bars. 'Bloody plonker.'

Winter watched me carefully. 'He said it was the night the Ipsissimus and I came to your block of flats. That he'd told you all about it in the back of your taxi. I knew he had to be lying though.' He smiled at me.

'Of course he's lying! How could he have anything to do with Belinda Battenapple? And if I'd known about it, why wouldn't I have...' My voice trailed off. Oh.

'Ivy?'

I bit my lip. Arse. 'Actually,' I said, suddenly unable to meet Winter's gaze any longer, 'he did tell me something that night. I just don't know what it was.'

Unsurprisingly, Winter looked confused.

I squeezed my eyes shut. 'I set up a spell to block him out. He wanted to talk and I knew he wouldn't shut up so I put up a barrier in order to avoid listening to him. I only released it when we got home. He did ask me if I thought he'd done the right thing and I said yes.' I shrugged and groaned at the same time. 'I didn't know what on earth he was talking about.' I opened one eye to risk a glance. Winter's expression was studiously bland. I winced. 'What has he done?'

'He went to school with Moonbeam, some expensive private place in the Lake District. They kept in touch from time to time over the years. Moonbeam went to Villeneuve to ask for help.'

I almost dreaded to ask. But I had to. 'What kind of help?'

'Moonbeam's mother, Belinda Battenapple, has had quite a lot of surgery over the years.'

'She's ill?'

Winter half-smiled. 'No. I mean plastic surgery. But things were, uh, advancing to the point where the surgery wasn't doing what she needed it to do. Moonbeam turned to Villeneuve for help and Villeneuve cast a spell for his old friend.'

'The vial,' I breathed. I slapped myself on the forehead. What an idiot. I'd spent all this time trying to work out what was in it when I should have known all along.

Winter nodded. 'The vial. It was indeed a death-drawing spell. But death drawing in the sense that it kept Belinda looking young and fresh. Villeneuve added to it and improved it from time to time but he increased its power to the point where, if it were destroyed, it'd never be renewed. Now that she's not wearing it, well, let's say that her appearance is somewhat ... altered.' He gave me a wry glance. 'By smashing the vial and releasing the entire spell at once, your boyfriend saved her life. That will go some way towards mitigating the trouble he's in for creating a vanity spell off the books in the first place.'

'He's not my boyfriend.'

Winter met my eyes. 'I know.'

From outside the trailer there was a sudden scratching sound. I leapt half out of my skin. Winter, almost as alarmed as I was, opened the window and peered down. A heartbeat later, Brutus jumped inside. When he saw me, I like to think that he relaxed slightly.

'Good?' he enquired.

I gave him a small smile. 'Good.'

His tail went up and he sauntered over, rubbing his head against my legs. 'Good.' There was a pause. 'Food?'

I rolled my eyes. 'No.' I glanced at both Brutus and Winter. 'So we still have a necromancer to find. What about Bellows?'

Winter's mouth flattened into a grim line. 'He's being questioned as we speak. So far I don't believe he's admitted to anything. He's a bastard, to be sure but I don't think he has the power to pull off raising the dead.'

I sighed. 'No. Neither do I.'

Brutus raised his head. A moment later there was knock on the partition wall and the Ipsissimus stuck his head round, a tentative smile on his face. 'How's the patient?'

Somewhat taken aback that the Order Head had made the journey all the way up here, I stared at him dumbly for a second before answering. 'Er ... good. I'm okay.'

'Pleased to hear it. You had us worried there for a second.'

I eyed him sceptically. Was that worry because I'd been knocked out by his own witches and he was concerned about the ramifications? After all, the whole episode had probably been caught on camera.

'I won't press charges,' I said, only half-jokingly.

The Ipsissimus's smile grew then he glanced at Winter. 'Perhaps you should go and check on Morris Armstrong. He seems convinced that the show can still go on.' He wrinkled his nose. 'Obviously that's ridiculous.'

'I think someone else can handle Armstrong,' Winter replied. 'I'll stay here and make sure Ivy's alright.'

'I'm alright,' I protested. 'I keep telling you.'

'Go and speak to him,' the Ipsissimus repeated, this time in a firmer tone of voice that clearly brooked no argument.

I thought that Winter was still preparing to refuse him and I doubted that would go down well on his CV. There really was no need for him to stay around, as much as I wanted him to. I reached out and touched his arm. 'It's fine, Rafe. Go.'

Winter gazed at me for a long moment before eventually nodding, albeit with considerable reluctance. He hesitated then dipped his head, his lips brushing against mine. 'Don't do anything foolish, Ivy.'

I tilted my head up and kissed him back with more feeling. Winter's mouth opened in surprise and I took full advantage as the pain still running through my body was replaced by a different kind of ache. He tasted of minty toothpaste and masculinity. Yeah, I knew how ridiculous that sounded, but as my senses swam I had no other words to describe it.

There was a cough. Winter pulled away and glanced at the Ipsissimus who was studiously avoiding looking in our direction.

'I should go.'

'Yes, Adeptus. You should.'

Winter threw me one last long look filled with meaning and left. The Ipsissimus stuck his head out the door and barked at the rest of the witches, whoever they were, to leave also. Only when he was sure they were gone did he look back at me.

'What gives?' I asked. I really didn't have a good feeling about this. The man had a burning desire to talk to me alone so, whatever it was, it was bound to be important. And no doubt something I didn't want to hear.

'Can your familiar be trusted?'

Still at my feet, Brutus let out a small growl.

'Of course.'

They eyed each other for a long moment. Surprisingly, it was Brutus who backed down, stalking out of the room with his whiskers quivering.

'I'll get straight to the point, Ms Wilde.'

It was about time someone did. I refrained from speaking and simply watched him. He sighed heavily and sat down.

'We've not had a necromancer show their face for almost a hundred years. Frankly, I find it hard to believe that anyone could be stupid enough to think that raising the dead is a good idea. But,' he shrugged, 'here we are.'

Something occurred to me. 'You knew all along, didn't you?' I said in wonder. 'When you sent Winter and me here, you knew it was a necromancer.'

'I suspected. I didn't know for sure. And, regardless of his praise for you, you are not here because Adeptus Exemptus Winter wanted you.'

I felt my body tense. 'Go on.'

'It is imperative that the necromancer is stopped. Unfortunately, from what we understand, that is easier said than done. Philip Maidmont, the librarian who I'm sure you remember, has been diligently at work trying to discover the best course. There is only one method detailed in the Cypher Manuscripts and it is not going to be easy.'

I snorted. 'Tell me something I don't know.'

The Ipsissimus didn't smile. 'Fair enough. Necromancy is a powerful art. It can consume the user, adapting and changing almost at will to suit its own needs. Not for nothing is it considered the blackest magic. Once its power is released, it is nigh on impossible to rein it in.'

Frowning, I tilted my head. 'But it can be done, surely? How was it halted last time?'

'The Great Kanto Earthquake.'

Huh? A faint smile crossed the Ipsissimus's face at my obvious confusion. 'Tokyo, 1923. It started with one necromancer and it ended with a death toll of more than 140,000 people. Not to mention the near destruction of an entire capital city.'

I sucked in a breath. 'Oh. That's ... bad.' I was horribly aware of how much of an understatement my words were.

'Indeed. While we are blessed that our little hell raiser, whoever they may be, has decided to undertake their evil work in a rural setting, we can still expect considerable damage. Necromancy feeds on itself,' he explained. 'It thrives on death and it is a demanding mistress.'

I paced over to the window and glanced out. The *Enchantment* set was like a ghost town. Mazza ambled from one side to the other with a sad expression on his face. I couldn't see another soul, no matter how badly Morris Armstrong might want filming to continue.

'Keep going,' I said grimly. I turned back to the Ipsissimus. 'There's a reason you're telling me all this and not Winter, so you might as well let me know what it is.'

For one fleeting breath, I thought he looked guilty. Then he raised his chin and met my gaze head-on. 'Indeed. Either the necromancer must be killed before he grows too strong, or the magic must be halted before it can overtake him. Maidmont thinks he has found a way to neutralize the power. There is an incantation which, if performed by a highly capable witch, is likely to stop the magic in its tracks. I believe you possess that capacity.'

'What's the catch?' Because there was always a catch. Always.

At least the Ipsissimus didn't beat around the bush. 'The side-effects of doing such a thing are catastrophic. As far as we can tell, the witch who performs the incantation will be forced to absorb the necromantic magic themselves. In all likelihood, it will destroy them, body and soul.'

Now we were at the crux of the matter. 'You want me to do this. You want me to sacrifice myself.'

His answer was simple. 'Yes.' He paused. 'I am sorry. I do like you, Ms Wilde, despite what has gone on in the past. It is a shame that you are not in the Order. I think you could have done great things.'

He met my gaze. 'Of course, if you can kill this rogue witch in time then the incantation may not be required.'

I swallowed. Killing another human being wasn't usually in my daily planner. Not that there was ever anything in my daily planner. But if it meant stopping the loss of life on a grand scale, there really wasn't any choice to make. Unfortunately the same went for the incantation. If it were the choice between destroying myself and destroying half of Scotland, I'd have to step up to the proverbial plate.

I didn't bother suggesting that Winter should do it. He possessed just as much magic as I did, but he was in the Order and I wasn't. I was expendable. That might have rankled if it weren't Winter. I would do this for him. I wouldn't be able to live with myself otherwise.

'How will we know?' I asked quietly. 'How will we know whether there's still time to neutralize the magic?'

'He has already raised two undead creatures. If a third one is brought from its grave then it's too late. But it takes time to maintain that kind of energy, especially between the first few raisings. There may be a day's grace.'

Except a day wasn't very long at all. And the Ipsissimus didn't sound very convincing. 'You don't think it's likely. You think it's already too late.'

'I do.'

I sighed. 'In truth, we might not know if there's been a third raising, even if we find the necromancer.'

'It's death magic,' the Ipsissimus said. 'If you can find the bastard in question, spill some of their blood and it remains red in colour, his or her death will be all that's required. If their blood is tinged with black then it's too late. If you can't get close enough to draw blood...'

'Then the incantation should be performed anyway,' I finished. The risk would just be too great not to. I didn't like the odds of coming through this unscathed.

He knitted his hands together. 'I am glad you see what must be done.' His expression didn't change. 'I need to know if you can do this, Ms Wilde.'

I laughed humourlessly. 'What's the choice?'

'Other than Adeptus Winter? Me.' He gestured at himself. 'I'm the only other witch in the vicinity with the capability. The other Third Levels who can do it are making their way here with all due haste, but I don't think they'll arrive in time.' His voice was filled with frustration. 'We're in the middle of nowhere.'

He sat down heavily. 'Raphael Winter has it in him to be Ipsissimus one day and he will be a damn good one. He has both the integrity and the ability. But that day is not today. I'm not convinced that there are any Third Level witches who could manage it either.'

I understood what he wasn't saying. 'If you do it and you die in the process, the Order will be thrown into chaos. Things are unstable enough as it is.'

He sighed. 'Yes. Maybe in a year or two we will have made enough inroads into changing our laws and structures to manage my ... abdication. However, I am deeply concerned about what would happen without a strong and ethical successor already in place. After what happened with Adeptus Diall and Price, the next Ipsissimus must be appointed with great caution.'

I nodded. The Ipsissimus wasn't simply worried about his own skin. I'd already experienced first hand what problems a bunch of ambitious Order witches could create. The wrong person in charge could set the whole place alight – and not in a good way. Those witches needed a strong hand and, despite what had gone on in the past, I did believe the man in front of me was that person.

I pushed back my hair. 'I can do this,' I told him. 'I *will* do this.'

The Ipsissimus reached over and took my hands. 'I believe you. It might not come to your sacrifice—'

'But if it does, I know what to do. Give me the incantation.'

He released his hold on me and reached inside his coat, drawing out a rolled-up scroll. He handed it over without a word; he was sensible enough not to express his thanks. I wasn't a martyr just yet. I took the scroll from him and stuffed it down my dress. The paper was itchy against my skin but at least the leather corset was enough to manage to conceal the bulge.

'I need to find the other Order witches. We're going to try to triangulate our magic to see if we can locate any power surges in the area. It's a long shot but we have to try something.' The Ipsissimus passed a hand over his eyes. 'This is so fucked up.'

Startled by his swearing, I flashed him a smile. 'Hey, it'll be fine. We'll find out who the necromancer is and turn them into a corpse long before I need this. No problemo.'

He didn't smile back. 'I'm counting on you.' He paused. 'We all are.'

Chapter Nineteen

I gave myself a moment after the Ipsissimus left and then, telling myself that it was only because I had to save the world, I made my way outside. Both Brutus and Winter were there, seemingly in the middle of some kind of argument.

'She needs peace, Brutus. She needs to sleep.'

'Food.'

'I'll get you food. Just let me check on Ivy and then I'll find you some tuna or something.'

Brutus yawned and raised a paw in my direction. 'Food.'

I shrugged at him. 'I don't have any. I'd suggest you go to your new friend for some but I suppose he's still being interrogated.'

Winter turned in surprise then gave an irritated frown when he saw me. 'You need to lie down. I can handle the investigation.'

I smiled at him. 'I'm not going to let you steal all the glory, buster. Not after all this work.'

He wasn't appeased by my light-hearted answer. 'I won't have you collapsing on me, Ivy. You look bloody awful.'

'Well, thank you very much.'

He gritted his teeth. 'It's not a criticism.'

I crossed my arms. 'It sounded like it.' I couldn't let Winter bundle me back off to bed. Not now. 'You keep complaining that I'm too lazy. Now I'm taking action and you're still complaining. I can't win.'

He drew in a breath as if unsure of himself. 'I'm worried about you.'

I waved an airy hand around, hoping I didn't look as nauseous or exhausted as I felt. 'I'm absolutely fine.' I pulled my shoulders back. 'We can't hang around. We have to find who's behind this.'

Winter's eyes narrowed. 'You must have hit your head. This definitely isn't the Ivy Wilde I know.' I let out a fake laugh, which only served to increase Winter's suspicions. 'What's going on, Ivy? What exactly did the Ipsissimus want?'

I had a ready-made answer – and one which I was sure would prevent Winter from probing further. 'He asked me to join the Order. Said that I'd done enough to prove myself and that I'd be welcomed in with open arms. I wouldn't even have to begin at Neophyte again.'

He stared. 'And you want to do this? I thought you were determined not to go near the Order with a barge pole.'

'I am. And that's exactly what I told him. He said that if I helped you find the necromancer and put a stop to his crimes, he would leave me in peace.'

Of course there was no logic to what I'd just said. That was why I reckoned it would work. If I came up with a more rational reason for not hiding under a duvet when I'd been given permission to do just that, Winter would continue to question what I was doing. Instead, he'd spend so much time puzzling about it that he'd stop asking.

Just in case, I rushed ahead. 'We need to go and speak to Bellows. If Belinda and her vial have been ruled out, he's the only other person who's got any reason to be dodgy.' My mouth flattened into a grim line. 'And from those photos, he's dodgy as hell.' I swung a side look at Winter. 'Has Belinda said anything about them?'

He was silent for a moment, as if he still wanted to ask more about the Ipsissimus and my reasons for springing up from my sick bed. Fortunately, his inner investigator took over. 'Our focus was on the vial. The photos, distasteful as they are, don't seem pertinent to necromancy.'

'No,' I agreed. 'But they are pertinent to being a bastard.' I still didn't think Bellows was the bastard witch we were looking for but there were few other options at this point. 'Where's Tarquin?'

Winter stilled. 'Why?'

'He's obviously good friends with Moonbeam. I imagine he has insights into all this which we can only guess at.'

Winter was only slightly appeased. 'Unless he's gone with the others, Tarquin's probably around here somewhere. Many witches are. They're using tracking spells to see if they can work out where the zombie came from.' His expression was grim. 'Not to mention making sure there aren't any more of the damn things anywhere.'

I frowned. 'Gone where with the others? What others?'

'Other than Armstrong, everyone else in the crew has been shipped back to Tomintoul. No matter what Armstrong wants, it's pretty certain that *Enchantment* is finished.'

'Rampaging zombies are just a bit too much even for reality television?'

'It appears so.'

I sniffed. After what had happened to Benjamin Alberts, they were lucky that no one else had died. Yet. All the same, it was a bit of a shame that my television career was probably over before it had barely started. I wondered if they'd use the footage of me after I died saving the world. I shouldn't have played the bitchy role like Barry wanted me to; post-mortem montages of yours truly would be much more effective if I looked like I was a nice person. Oh well.

Then a thought struck me. 'Wait a minute,' I said slowly. 'Everyone involved with *Enchantment* apart from Armstrong is back in Tomintoul?'

'Yes.'

'Then why did I see Mazza strolling around when I looked out of the window?'

Winter's blue eyes darkened. 'The runner?'

I nodded, feeling the sudden chill fingers of dread tap down my spine.

'Where was he?' There was a sudden urgent edge to Winter's voice.

I tried to think. Pointing to the side, I drew an imaginary line. 'He was walking from there over to there.'

A muscle throbbed in Winter's cheek. 'There are supposed to be Order witches guarding the entire perimeter. How the hell did he manage to avoid them?'

'Let's apportion blame later, shall we? We need to find out where he is.' My tone hardened. 'Right now.' I took off in the direction where I'd seen Mazza and almost immediately regretted moving so quickly. My head swam and I was forced to take several shallow breaths to avoid passing out.

'Ivy...'

'I'm fine.'

Brutus shot out in front of us, scampering across the clearing at full speed. I blinked. I'd never seen him run before, not since he was a kitten anyway. I exchanged a quick glance with Winter and then took off after my cat with my fingers crossed. I was going to look mightily stupid if he'd just decided to chase after a woodland mouse.

Fortunately, Winter also seemed to believe that Brutus was onto something. In less than a few heartbeats he overtook me, sprinting towards the tree line. I quashed my trepidation at the thought that the shy runner was out there with a zombie just waiting to chomp on him, and tried to keep up. Not surprisingly, I couldn't. I slowed down in an effort to reserve some energy – not to mention to avoid throwing up – and did what I could to keep Winter in sight. At least the river was over in that direction so there was a natural barrier.

Winter had just disappeared behind a tree when I heard a strangled shout. Muttering a curse, I picked up speed again, reaching him – and Mazza – just in time. Winter had grabbed the kid by the throat and was holding him at arm's length whilst Brutus hissed repeatedly.

'Is it you?' Winter demanded. 'Is it you raising the dead?'

Mazza's eyes bulged. 'What? No! I didn't have anything to do with that!'

I eyed him. He seemed more scared than anything else. But was that scared because he'd finally been found out or because he was being falsely accused? It was imperative we learned the truth.

'Let him go, Rafe,' I said softly.

Winter glared then did as I asked, releasing his grip. Mazza staggered backwards and rubbed his neck vigorously. 'What's wrong with you?' he croaked.

I stepped forward. 'We're looking for a very dangerous person, Mazza. Someone who might not even realise how much of a danger they are. All the other crew members are back in town. Why are you still here?'

He mumbled something under his breath.

I leaned forward, ignoring Winter's bristling fury. 'I didn't catch that. Say it again.'

'Amy.'

I squinted. 'Pardon?'

'Amy lost her necklace out here. I was looking for it.'

Winter was incredulous. 'After the carnage that happened here, you thought you'd come back to look for some girl's stupid necklace?'

I put my hand on his arm. 'Did she ask you to come and do this?'

Mazza wouldn't meet my eyes. 'No.'

'How did she lose it?'

He shrugged. He was growing redder and redder by the second. 'Dunno.'

'How did you get back here from Tomintoul?'

'I never left. I didn't get on the bus.' For all his embarrassment and awkwardness, he was being remarkably recalcitrant.

Winter folded his arms across his chest. 'You're lying.'

'Wh – what?' Mazza stammered. 'I'm not! Amy lost her necklace and I want to find it for her.'

'He is sweet on her,' I remarked.

The glow on Mazza's cheeks intensified. 'She's a nice person!' he said, as if daring me to argue with him.

'Yes, she is. But you're still lying about something, Mazza.'

He glared at me. 'I'm not.'

I tapped my foot impatiently. There really wasn't time for this. Whatever he was doing out here, there was next to no chance it had anything to do with zombies. Maybe he was just looking for Amy's necklace in a bid to impress her. Stranger things had happened.

Brutus, sensing my irritation, jumped up and sauntered over. He circled round Mazza like a predator, sniffing as he went. Then he sat back on his haunches and washed his face. 'Blood,' he said.

Mazza screeched, 'That cat just spoke!'

I ignored him and focused on Brutus. 'Blood? You're sure?'

Brutus continued to wash himself as if he'd already given us every possible answer we could want.

A dangerous smile lit Winter's lips. 'Where's the blood from, Mazza?' he asked silkily. He sounded far scarier now that his voice was low than he had when he'd been shouting.

'I... I...' Mazza's eyes darted from side to side as if he were expecting someone to appear and rescue him. Just to be sure, I glanced around as well. The Ipsissimus had said we had at least a day before we could expect another zombie but that didn't mean the impossible couldn't still happen. When there wasn't even the faintest rustle of leaves, I relaxed.

'Spit it out, Mazza,' I said tiredly, 'or I'll get Winter here to turn you into a toadstool.'

His eyes went even wider. 'You can do that?'

'Oh,' Winter purred, 'I can do that and more. I'm a highly trained Order witch, Mazza. There are no limits to my magic.'

At those words I opened my mouth but Winter nudged me in the ribs. Yeah, okay. This wasn't the time to point out that the limits to his magic included finding out who was raising the dead or getting Mazza to tell the truth.

Mazza's entire body seemed to droop. 'It's not what you think,' he said.

It never was. 'Go on.'

'It's not human blood.'

I glanced at Brutus. He didn't twitch so I reckoned Mazza wasn't lying on that part. I tilted up my chin and stared at him. 'Sheep blood?'

Mazza shrunk even further into himself. 'Yes,' he whispered. 'I thought I'd washed it all off.'

He hadn't been counting on Brutus. What most people don't realise is that cats have a better sense of smell than bloodhounds. Yet again, our investigation seemed to involve white fluffy animals with less sense than lemmings. A deep unease filtered through me.

'Where did the sheep come from? How did you kill it?' The second question was particularly pertinent. If Mazza had used magic to rip life from the animal, that magic could have been used in turn to feed necromancy. As the Ipsissimus suggested, the truth of the matter lay in blood.

Mazza looked horrified. 'It wasn't my fault!'

I gazed at him in disgust while Winter inched forward, his eyes the colour of glacier ice. 'Oh, I see,' he said, his voice dripping with sarcasm. 'You *accidentally* killed it.'

'No!' he burst out. 'I just found it! It was already dying. I didn't do anything to it apart from...' He halted abruptly.

'Apart from what, Mazza? What did you do?'

He flapped his arms and began to babble. 'Nothing! I didn't mean to! I mean, I did mean to but only because he's such a prick! No one would listen to me and I wanted to scare him off and make him stop, and when the herbs didn't work I had to do something. I couldn't just let him get away with that kind of thing!'

Winter shot me a glance and, interpreting the look, I nodded and put a hand on Mazza's shoulder. He was visibly trembling. 'Slow down,' I told him. 'And tell us from the start.'

He sucked in a ragged breath. 'He wouldn't leave her alone. He was using his position to get exactly what he wanted.'

There could only be one woman he was referring to. 'You mean Amy.'

He nodded vigorously. 'She told him no but he wouldn't listen. I had to do something.'

'Who are we talking about?'

He looked at me as if I were dense. 'Trevor Bellows, of course. He goes after all the woman. Barry told me he was always the same but no one did anything about it because Belinda wanted to keep him around.' He shrugged helplessly. 'He's been on *Enchantment* since the beginning. He's got power and money and status and any time anything happened, it just got hushed up.'

My mouth was dry. 'I need you to be explicit, Mazza. What was he doing? What did he do to Amy?' She'd never given any indication that anything was wrong. But then, if she were scared of him she probably wouldn't have. I cursed myself. She'd been my room-mate, even if only for a couple of nights. How could I not have noticed that something was up?

'He wanted her to sleep with him. He said that if she didn't he'd get her fired.'

I sensed Winter's rage. His fists clenched and his body went rigid. I was right there with him but I had to stay in control. I had to find out what Mazza had done and if he was the person we were looking for.

'So what did you do?' I asked. I spoke softly because if I tried anything above a whisper I had the feeling it would sound like a strangled scream of fury.

'I wanted to protect her. If I could stop him, I thought maybe I could find something that would keep her safe. This is my second series with *Enchantment*. Last time one of the contestants sprinkled some herbs around their beds to keep them safe at night. I thought I could do the same.'

I frowned. 'I don't remember that.'

'Nothing happened. He sprinkled the herbs and then slept like a baby. It didn't make the cut.'

I sighed. 'So you thought it was an effective protection spell?'

'Yes. I copied exactly what he did except in larger quantities.'

'Let me guess,' Winter said through gritted teeth. 'Mandrake, cinquefoil and prickly ash bark.'

Mazza blinked. 'How did you know?'

'We found it all around the first set.'

'Oh.' Mazza deflated even further. 'It didn't work anyway.'

'Funny that,' Winter muttered.

'I'm not a witch. I don't have any magic at all.' He ran a hand through his hair. 'But I thought that if I did what he had done, then it might be okay.' He threw Winter an accusing look. 'At least I tried!'

I offered a soothing nod. 'You did.' I gave him a moment's pause to gather himself together then my voice hardened. 'But this still doesn't explain the scent of blood.'

'Bellows wouldn't stop what he was doing. I had to take action. I thought if I could scare him I could make him stop. I was going to saw through his staff so that it snapped when he put his weight on it but I knew that wouldn't be enough. I didn't have a clue what to do. Until I found the sheep.'

'Where was it?'

Mazza obviously didn't want to answer. He scuffed the ground with his toe and demurred. 'It doesn't really matter.'

I leaned forward until I was almost nose to nose with him. 'We'll decide what matters. Where did you find the sheep?'

'By the cemetery,' he mumbled. He pulled away from me.

I didn't move. He could only mean the one at the bottom of Dead Man's Hill. 'Before or after Benjamin Alberts was killed?'

'After,' he whispered. 'Armstrong wanted me to go and scout out the area. He wanted to do a challenge amongst the graves. You know, to make it spooky or something. He didn't want anyone to know because he thought they might be annoyed that he was still thinking about using that place after what happened. I found the sheep there. I don't know what had happened to it. It was lying on its side and there was a wound in its stomach. Maybe a wild animal had got to it. I was going to get a vet but my phone kept cutting out. Bad reception or something. I knew that by the time I got to town and found someone it would probably be too late. With all that blood all over the place I just...' His voice dropped and he hung his head. 'I collected as much of the blood as I could and then I hit the sheep over the head and put it out of its misery.'

I felt a bit ill – and it wasn't just because I was still recovering from being hit by a zombie-targeted spell.

'You used the blood to paint Bellows' trailer.'

He nodded. 'When he went to make-up, I snuck in through the back window. After what happened to Benjamin, I didn't want anyone to think someone else had died so I put some sheep wool onto the fence so they'd know it wasn't human blood. I was going to leave more wool inside but there wasn't time. I was only going to draw the pentagram but I panicked when the door opened. I thought that Bellows had returned. When I looked at him, I knew I was staring at the face of pure evil. His eyes turned bright green, like some kind of crazed monster. He had horns growing out of his head.'

Mazza's voice dropped to a horrified whisper. 'Horns.' He shook himself. 'As soon as he saw me, he attacked. The blood went everywhere. I hit him over the head and ran. The next thing I knew, Marcus was coming out of the trailer and screaming.' Mazza looked confused. 'I don't know where he came from or what happened to Bellows. He looked normal the next time I saw him.' His eyes were wide. 'But he's the devil.'

Mazza obviously meant that last part literally. Okaaaay. Winter opened his mouth to ask another question but I already had everything I needed and I forestalled him. 'You do realise what you did was wrong?'

Mazza looked away. 'Yes,' he mumbled unconvincingly.

'Mazza, you killed a defenceless animal instead of getting help for it.'

'It was dying anyway.'

'Unless you're a trained veterinarian, you don't know that. You tried to use magical herbs, which could have had any number of dire consequences on any or all of the crew members. And that's without even getting into what you did in Bellows' trailer.'

'He attacked me! He turned into a monster! Besides, it worked. He stopped going after Amy. He stopped harassing all the female crew members. I stopped him from doing all that because I scared him when no one else was going to do anything!'

Brutus let out what could only be described as a loud snort. I'd almost forgotten he was there. I raised an eyebrow in his direction and he pouted.

'Was that you?' I enquired. 'Did you stop Trevor Bellows from harassing Amy?'

'I am cat.'

I stared at him. Apparently that was all the answer I was going to get. I suppose Brutus felt he'd made his point.

'What?' Mazza shrieked. 'The cat didn't do a thing! I stopped Bellows. Alright, he tried it on again last night when he was out here before the vote. He grabbed Amy and that's when she lost her necklace. But she said he let her go before he did anything. He was obviously scared what would happen if he continued. I made him feel like that. No one else.' He thumped his chest. 'Me.'

Brutus snorted again. He picked himself up and walked a few metres away, pawing at the ground. Then he dipped his head for a brief moment before looking up with a quiet purr – and a delicate gold necklace dangling from his mouth.

'Good job, Bruty baby.'

'It was me!' Mazza said, continuing to protest. 'I'm the hero! Not a bloody cat!'

Winter rolled his eyes. 'Grow up.'

'We need to find Trevor Bellows,' I told him. 'Everything seems to centre around him.'

Winter's brow furrowed. 'But...'

'Let's just see what he has to say.'

He nodded. 'Fine.' He walked over and hooked his arm through mine. 'Let me help you. I've borrowed that bike again. We'll be back in Tomintoul in no time.'

I smiled weakly. 'Great.'

Brutus ran lightly over to us, springing up onto my shoulders and coiling his tail round my neck.

'You could have told me what was going on,' I scolded him.

'Food.'

Yeah, yeah.

'Hey!' Mazza shouted. 'What about me? I need a lift back to Tomintoul as well.'

Both Winter and I ignored him and carried on walking. I was pretty certain, however, that Brutus stuck out his tongue.

Chapter Twenty

I let Winter drive the bike while I took the opportunity to lean against his back. It was slightly uncomfortable with Brutus wedged between us but it might have been the only opportunity I was going to get to be close to Winter again.

When we reached the edge of the town, I tapped him on the shoulder to make him pull up. He flipped his visor and peered at me. His sapphire eyes were soft and concerned and, just for a beat, I doubted myself. All I really wanted to do was stay by his side.

'I don't feel well,' I said.

His concern turned to alarm. 'What is it?'

I shook my head. 'I don't know. The after-effects of that spell are still hitting me really hard. I feel woozy. I think I might pass out.' I looked away. 'Maybe you were right and I should have stayed in the trailer until I felt completely better.'

'I'll drop you back at your hotel.'

I tried a weak protest. 'But we need to talk to Bellows and find out what he knows and what else he's been up to. It's vitally important.'

'I'll do that,' he declared decisively. 'You should rest.'

There was a sinking sensation in the pit of my stomach, even though this was exactly what I wanted. 'Okay.'

We continued a bit further until we reached the Hook and Eye. It was dark although it was barely ten o'clock. The inn and its environs seemed remarkably quiet considering how many of the crew were staying there. I guessed none of them felt like partying after seeing Belinda Battenapple almost die at the jaws of a rotting zombie.

I slid off the bike, released my hold on Brutus, took off my helmet then gestured at Winter to do the same. 'Thank you for doing this, Rafe,' I said.

'It's my job. I'm the one who dragged you into this in the first place.'

'I'm glad you did.' I reached up and touched his cheek. His hand covered mine. 'We've still not had that chat yet.'

He gave me a small crooked smile. 'There will be time later when you're feeling better.'

Mmm. 'I want you to know,' I said aloud, 'that I've fallen for you. About as hard as it's possible for anyone to fall. You're still the most irritating man I know. You still spend too much time working. You need to learn the value of kicking back and relaxing.'

He grinned at me. 'Maybe you can teach me how to do that.'

I didn't smile back. 'Maybe.'

'When Bellows is brought to justice and we find out whether he's the necromancer or not, you'll feel the same kind of satisfaction I do at a job done well.' He leaned into me. 'We make a pretty good team.'

I closed my eyes tightly. 'We do.' I put my arms round his neck and kissed him. He groaned slightly, pulling me further against him. I could have stayed like that forever.

Winter's arms tightened round me, his mouth left mine and he trailed kisses along my jawline. 'You were embarrassed,' he said. 'In fact, you were more than embarrassed. You were horrified.'

I frowned at him, not sure what he meant.

'The morning after, when we woke up together,' he explained. 'I wanted to give you a way out so I said we should forget it ever happened. But I'll never be able to forget it.'

'Me neither.' I took a deep breath. 'And I wasn't horrified. I was a bit shocked to start off with but when I woke up properly I knew it was one of the best nights of my life.' I was lying. It was *the* best night of my life. I touched Winter's cheek.

'You're the laziest person I've ever met, Ivy Wilde,' he whispered in my ear. 'You're also the smartest, most beautiful and most wonderful person I've ever met. I don't think I'm in love with you, I *know*

I'm in love with you. We have nothing in common but I don't think that matters. You're always there in my thoughts. Always.'

Tears pricked at the back of my eyes. I was being selfish. I should be telling him that we weren't meant to be together, that it would never work. At least that way he'd find it easier to move on if this went down the way the Ipsissimus thought it would. But I couldn't do that. I genuinely didn't think I was capable of it. I wanted him to know the truth about how I felt, if nothing else.

'I better go and get some sleep,' I said softly. 'You don't need to see me up. I need to maintain some sense of decorum.'

He smiled. 'I'd never associate you with decorum, Ivy.'

'It's virtually my middle name.'

He tucked a loose curl behind my ear. 'I'll come and check on you first thing in the morning,' he promised. 'If there's anything you need in the meantime, don't hesitate to call me. Trevor Bellows can wait. He's not going anywhere.'

Unable to trust my voice, I simply nodded. Then I turned on my heel and went inside the main door, aware that Winter was watching me go. I held my breath until I heard the bike's engine rev and tear off again down the road. Only when I was sure he'd gone did I get to work.

I strode through the narrow corridor to reach the hotel bar. Fortunately, it wasn't entirely deserted. Making a beeline for the group at the back, who were all nursing their drinks and looking glum, I did my best to smile and appear happy. This wasn't the time to exude anything other than brilliant confidence.

'Ivy!' Barry got to his feet as I approached. 'I'm so glad you're alright!'

I stretched out my arms expansively. 'You can't keep a good witch down.' It was probably just as well I wasn't a good witch.

'Come and join us.'

'Actually,' I said, 'I'm pretty busy. I just need a few favours.' I glanced at Amy. 'Have you lost anything recently?' I enquired.

Her fingers briefly touched her collarbone. 'My necklace. I lost it, er...'

'When Trevor Bellows tried to assault you?'

She blinked rapidly, her cheeks colouring and her eyes filling with dismay. Well, now I knew that Mazza definitely hadn't been lying.

'That should not have been allowed to happen,' I admonished Barry.

'I ... I ... didn't know.'

Amy shot him a look. Obviously he had known. He'd probably been as scared for his job as she had been but that didn't make his silence right – but it did make it more understandable. Slightly.

I forced my anger to a simmer to avoid it spilling over. 'We're going to make this right for you, Amy,' I told her. Something in my expression must have convinced her I was telling the truth because she bit her lip and nodded.

I flicked my attention to Moonbeam. 'How's your mother?'

His nose wrinkled. 'Furious. That vial was about the only thing keeping her sane. Now that it's gone and she looks her age...' His voice trailed off.

'Just how old is she?' My question had no bearing on anything important; I was simply curious.

He shook his head. 'If you want to avoid being knocked unconscious again, you wouldn't ask.' He sighed. 'Tarquin has told me that even if he could, he's been forbidden from giving her another spell. I don't know what we're going to do.'

'Is *Enchantment* going to continue?'

Barry's shoulders drooped. 'That's the million-dollar question. Certainly not this series. Not now. Preparations are already underway to ship this lot of contestants home. The only silver lining is that they've all signed binding non-disclosure agreements.' He raised his eyebrows meaningfully at me as he said this. I shrugged. I was probably going to be a corpse in a few hours so what did it matter? I'd tell the devil if I saw him. I doubted he'd care.

'Give me your car keys,' I said, without further preamble.

Barry reached into his pocket, automatically doing as I'd instructed. Then he paused. 'Hang on. Why should I do that?'

'Because you were my producer, Barry. You were supposed to be looking out for me and I almost died.' That was something of an exaggeration but I needed transport.

'Are you going to give them back?'

'Sure.' I couldn't have sounded less convincing.

Amy nudged Barry and he exhaled resignedly. 'Fine. Here you go.'

'Great. I need my phone back too.'

'It's in our room with the rest of your things,' Amy said. 'I took them all back after...' She swallowed.

'Thanks. One final thing – has anyone seen Armstrong?'

Moonbeam let out a humourless smirk. 'He got back just before you did. You walked right by him.' He pointed over to the bar.

I followed his finger. Slumped in the corner was the familiar figure of *Enchantment*'s director. He no longer looked despotic or even fully conscious. The best word I could think of to describe him was crumpled. I'd have felt some sympathy for him if I could have found the time.

'Thanks,' I muttered, pocketing the keys. 'I'm going out for a few hours. Amy, if I'm not back by the time dawn breaks, call this number.' I scribbled down the Ipsissimus's direct line onto a napkin. 'Tell him I've disappeared, then all of you need to get as far away from here as possible.'

Even Moonbeam seemed to register how serious my tone was. 'Why? What's going to happen?'

'Nothing you need to worry about yet. But tomorrow morning...'

He drained his pint and stood up. 'Screw that. I'm collecting my mother and we're getting out of here.' He stalked out.

'Don't worry, Ivy,' Amy said softly. 'I can do that for you.'

I smiled my thanks and walked over to Armstrong. 'Hello buddy!' I chirped.

He didn't even look up. 'What do you want?'

'Don't be like that. I'm your superspy, remember?'

He raised his eyes balefully. 'You never gave me any useful intel at all.'

'Well, that was hardly my fault.' I nodded at the barman. 'I'll have a vodka,' I said. 'This gentleman is paying.'

'Make that two,' Armstrong grunted.

Hmm. He already looked well on his way to the Land of Toilet Hugging as it was. I'd better make this quick. 'You told me when we started that this area was chosen because of historical links to magic. I need to know what exactly.'

'What does it matter now?'

'It's important, Morris.'

He scanned my face. 'It was a family. Apparently there were several witches. Things didn't go well for them and most were burned at the stake.' He made a vague attempt at looking apologetic. 'Those were the times.'

'Which times exactly?'

'Around the turn of the nineteenth century.'

It seemed almost inconceivable that their magical bloodline had continued since then without anyone noticing but I had to be sure. I swallowed. I really didn't want to know the answer but I had to ask – everything hinged on it. 'What was their name?'

'McAllan.'

The barman set out the drinks in front of us. With shaking hands, I reached down and picked up the first one, downing it in one with barely a shudder. Then I took the second glass and did the same. Armstrong just frowned.

'I've got to go,' I told him. 'Pack your bags. It's time to get out of Dodge.'

Without waiting for a reaction, I spun on my heel just in time to see Tarquin enter. He strutted in, his shoulders back and his head held high. The few crew members dotted around, including Barry and Amy, gave him a ragged round of applause. I rolled my eyes.

'Tarquin!' I called. I strode over and barred his way before he could start massaging his own ego with his adoring public.

He grinned. 'Hey, Ivy.' He bowed dramatically. 'You're welcome.'

I stared at him. 'For what?'

'Saving the day, of course.'

Never mind that all he'd done was smash a glass vial whilst others tried to deal with the real issue of the zombie. Or that his little spell had sent our investigation wildly off track. I forced a smile and did what I could to get him to listen. 'Pay attention,' I barked. 'I have to go out. Winter is at the police station talking to Trevor Bellows. You need to get yourself there.'

He frowned at me and flipped back his hair. 'I think I've done enough for today. I was going to have a drink and relax. Adeptus Exemptus Winter can look after Bellows.'

I gritted my teeth. 'Bellows isn't the real villain. He *is* a villain but he's not the one threatening the stability of Scotland.'

'Huh?'

Somehow, it didn't surprise me that Tarquin was out of the loop. 'Just get to Winter. Make sure he stays there and doesn't come looking for me. This is hugely important, Tarq.' I needed some way to make sure he did as I asked; I couldn't afford for Winter to come after me. 'There's no one else here I trust to do this. Are you clever enough to keep Winter in one place?'

Tarquin drew himself up. 'What? Of course I am! If I'm clever enough to create a spell to keep ageing at bay, I can certainly hold one Arcane Branch investigator back. Ha! It would be a piece of cake.'

I pushed up onto my tiptoes. 'Are you sure? Winter is pretty canny...'

Tarquin rolled his eyes. 'He is no match for the might of the Tarq. I'll do it now.' He turned on his heel and exited while I let out a breath. He'd been easier to manipulate than I expected. My challenge had at least ensured that he'd not asked why I needed Winter to stay with Bellows. As long as my sapphire-eyed soulmate didn't come near me, everything would be fine. Probably.

I darted up to the room I shared with Amy, quickly changing into warmer clothes – because it's important to be snug when you're facing certain death – then I grabbed my phone and left again. There was just one other thing to take care of.

'Brutus!' There was a faint rustle from some bushes to my right but nothing else. 'Brutus, this is urgent. I wouldn't interrupt your night-time stalking if it weren't.'

I heard another rustle and then the cat in question appeared with a poor mouse hanging from his mouth. I gave him a frown and he opened his jaws, letting the creature to escape.

'I wish you wouldn't do that.'

He gave me a look filled with feline ferocity. 'Food.'

'Try the hotel kitchen.' I crouched down and scratched his ears. 'I need you to listen first, though. I'm going out to find Gareth McAllan. I'm certain he's the necromancer. It's not very likely that I'll come back.'

For once, Brutus appeared to listen. I took a deep breath. 'I'm sorry,' I said, meaning it wholeheartedly. 'It sucks for you. Wait in my room. Winter will show up in the morning and then you can go with him. He's a good guy and I'm sure he'll let you hang out. Besides, you like his familiar, don't you? Princess Parma Periwinkle? You'll get to spend more time with her after I'm gone.'

A flood of unshed tears rose up in my throat. 'You'll be fine. Just do what Winter tells you and everything will work out. I love you to pieces, you miserable bugger, and I'm so happy to have known you.'

Brutus blinked. 'You go? Where?'

'I'll try Gareth's farm. If that fails, he'll probably be at the cemetery.' Preparing for his next raising. I shuddered.

Brutus sniffed and head-butted my hand. Then he turned round and sauntered away. If I were honest, I had hoped for a little more.

Rubbing my eyes, and trying not to feel too hurt, I stood up. Using the remote control key, I located Barry's car and strode purposefully over to it. Everything was starting to add up – and not in a good way.

I'd been blinded by the events on set at *Enchantment* and the extraordinary Oscar-winning acting skills of Gareth McAllan. I knew it was strange that sheep seemed to figure so heavily, even though up here they outnumbered humans by about twenty to one. My hallucination happened after I'd touched the sheep out by the river; Mazza's hallucination happened after he'd killed the sheep on Dead Man's Hill. The sheep really were bewitched. Just not in a way I'd considered. Maybe they figured into the spell for bringing the dead back to life. I had no idea. But where there were sheep, there was also Gareth.

He had obviously slipped by the Order when they looked into his family. By his own admission, the police had considered him as a suspect. And he was the one to find Benjamin Alberts. I was reminded of the old schoolyard rhyme – he who smelled it, dealt it. Except in this case, we were talking about something far worse than wind.

I'd been wholeheartedly hoodwinked. Gareth was the culprit; he was the necromancer. Now all I had to do was find him and pray I didn't end up dead. But if that was what it would take, I'd accept the risk.

The only silver lining was that Winter was safely out of the way and focused on Bellows. He wouldn't try any heroics to take my place. He wouldn't get hurt. He wouldn't even know until it was too late.

I massaged my neck and got behind the wheel, the interior light illuminating the inside of Barry's car. As I started up the engine, I found the contact number I needed.

'Hello! You have reached Julia's voicemail. Leave a message and I'll get back to you as soon as possible.'

Arse. 'Julia, it's Ivy. I know there's patient confidentiality and all that stuff to deal with but I need you to confirm something for me. I'm seriously concerned about Gareth McAllan, the man you referred to another psychiatrist for me. I think he's a danger both to himself and others. Any insight your friend could give me would be useful. If you hear this message in the next hour then call me straight away. If you're listening to this in the morning, well, don't worry.'

There wasn't really much else to say. I hung up. It was time to face the enemy.

Chapter Twenty-One

It took longer to find the main farmhouse than I thought it would. I circled round the area several times before I finally spotted the narrow lane leading up to it. Passing a few fields, each one containing the shadows of more sheep than I dared to count, I drove up and parked right in front of the door. It seemed sensible to have a quick getaway should I need one.

I took a deep breath, pulled my shoulders back and got out. My fingers were twitching to perform as many defensive runes as I could while I had the chance. I reminded myself that I might need to conserve my energy and simply played possible scenarios in my head so I was prepared. Then I knocked loudly on the door. Waiting outside wasn't my usual modus operandi but I was trying to be cautious for once in my life.

A harassed looking woman with a lined face, who I reckoned was in her forties, answered. I couldn't see any resemblance to Gareth but she still looked oddly familiar. Maybe she just had one of those faces.

Without smiling, I introduced myself and got to the point. 'I need to see Gareth. Now.'

'Gareth?' Her face scrunched up as if she didn't have the faintest idea who I was talking about. 'What do you want him for? Do you know what time it is?'

'It's an emergency.' And then, because I thought it might help, I added, 'I'm a good friend of his.'

Her lip curled. 'He's got friends?'

'If you could just tell him I'm here...'

'He's not in.' She made to close the door but I wedged my foot in to stop her.

'Where is he?'

'One of the sheep has run off. Again. He's gone after it. Fool boy can't keep them in one place.' She seemed to take perverse pleasure in his failures. All the same, my blood chilled.

'Where did he go?' I asked urgently. 'Which direction?'

'How the hell should I know?' She rolled her eyes. 'Now piss off.'

This time she succeeded in shoving my foot out and closing the door. Wincing in pain, I drew back and stared at it. I could use magic to force it open but, despite the woman's sour, unfriendly manner, I sensed she was telling the truth about Gareth – at least as far as she understood it. Somehow I doubted he was really searching for another errant sheep; in fact, I'd lay money on him using deepest darkest necromancy right at this very moment. If I were going to stop him, I'd have to move my plump arse faster than it was designed to go.

With heart-attack inducing speed, I accelerated back down the lane towards Dead Man's Hill. Maybe they would rename it Dead Ivy Hill after this; that wouldn't be fair on Benjamin Alberts, or any of the souls resting in the cemetery, but it sounded good. The more I focused on idiotic vanities, the less terrified I felt. That had to count for something.

I wasn't foolish enough to drive up the same track where Winter and I had gone previously on the bike. I parked as close to the graveyard entrance as I could and sprinted through the heavy gates, ignoring the ominous shape of the mountain looming over me. The one small mercy was that the cemetery was at the bottom of the damn hill rather than the top. All the same, I was panting by the time I reached the first of the gravestones.

I doubled over, trying desperately to catch my breath and imagining Winter in my ear snarking at me for not doing anything to keep fit. That was when I heard footsteps.

Staying low, I edged round the neatly manicured pathway. There was a slight rise over to the right – and there was definitely a figure walking towards it, silhouetted against the night sky and with hands in pockets and slumped shoulders. I scanned round. This was no zombie; neither were there any other signs of nightmarish creatures. All the same, I half expected to hear Vincent Price's voice booming about darkness falling across the land. Somehow I didn't think I was going to be treated to an impromptu *Thriller* dance.

I decided that the element of surprise was the best thing going for me. Taking my time, I moved forward following a circuitous route to where the figure, presumably Gareth, was standing. He still hadn't seen me. That was good.

I licked my lips and swallowed, wishing my tongue didn't feel quite so furry. I should have had a last supper. Even condemned criminals got that much.

A gust of wind blew my hair, plastering it across my face and temporarily obscuring my sight. At the same time, an owl hooted. My fear increased; as far as harbingers of death and disaster went, that was one of the best. Winter might scoff at my superstitions but look at what had happened to Belinda after smashing that mirror.

I drew in a ragged breath. There was nothing wrong with being scared; that was only natural. It didn't mean I should turn away and run. Nobody visited a graveyard in the dead of night unless they were kids on a dare or they were planning something evil. Gareth might be young but he was no kid – and as the few clouds obscuring the moon passed, his face was momentarily illuminated. He'd stopped moving and was standing stock still, staring down at one of the graves.

The intelligent thing would have been to cast a rune to knock him dead right there and then. I might never have drawn one to cause immediate death before but that didn't mean I didn't know how. But I was no stone-cold killer, more's the pity; I couldn't strike him down without giving him the chance to speak first. I'd probably end up regretting it but I needed to be sure.

I wasn't going to give him the opportunity to attack me, however. I wasn't completely stupid.

I skirted round until I had a clear line of sight. As I watched, he withdrew one hand from his pocket and ran it through his hair. A strangled whisper drifted over. 'You little idiot.'

Rather than trying to decipher who he was talking about, I prepared. If I could do this while drawing blood at the same time, I would know how far I'd need to take this. A double-handed rune to bring him down, swiftly followed by a second to cut would do the trick.

I bit down hard on my tongue, tasting my own blood. It was now or never. I raised my hands. A half second later, my phone rang.

Gareth whipped round. He took a few running steps towards me, his eyes squinting as he tried to see who and where I was. I fumbled for the bloody phone, doing everything I could to silence it whilst staying in the shadows. As it mercifully stopped ringing, Gareth shouted, 'Alistair?'

Eh? Who the bejesus was Alistair? I frowned, flummoxed. Did Gareth have a partner? Were there two necromancers instead of one? Horror poured through me. I could stop one but I doubted I'd have any chance against two. There wasn't any further time to waste.

Knocked off my equilibrium, I breathed in and cast the runes I'd originally intended. The ground shook, a localised disturbance directly under his feet. Gareth fell forwards onto his hands and knees. As my phone started ringing again, I jabbed out the second rune, turning the very air molecules against him and slicing open his cheek. Gareth cried out, one sharp howl of pain. I had to trust in my magic. It was too dark to see whether I'd actually drawn blood.

I dragged myself forward. The combination of the spells I'd cast, along with the last vestiges of the spell that had slammed into me earlier, was taking its toll. I felt mind-numbingly exhausted.

'Sleep when you're dead,' I muttered to myself. Not my normal catchphrase, of course, but given that I might soon be in that state, it seemed apt.

Ignoring the incessant ringing of the phone, I reached Gareth, my hands extended and more than ready both to defend myself and finish him.

He arced his head up towards me, pain mingled with something indecipherable in his eyes. Whoever he'd been expecting, it wasn't me. His mouth dropped open. 'Ivy?'

I kept my distance on the off-chance that he might try something. 'Why, Gareth? Why did you do it? Was it the power?'

He stared at me. 'Wh – what?'

For good measure – and because I had to ensure that Gareth didn't get up again – I cast my the next rune, pinning his body flat to the ground. If he'd been an Order witch, he probably could have countered it. Fortunately for me, death magic appeared to be rather limiting. With my safety assured – for now – I stepped closer to him as my phone rang off again once more.

'Who's Alistair? Is this your partner in crime?' I knelt down to get a better look at his face. I'd definitely managed to draw blood but it was still too dark to tell how much, beyond the fact that it was wet and dribbling down his cheek. 'Tell me where he is.'

Gareth's jaw worked uselessly. He was trying to talk – even I could tell that – but my last spell must have hit him harder than I'd realised. Either that or he'd already set the next raising in motion and he was exhausted from the effort.

With one eye on him, I scanned round anxiously. There was police tape around one grave, a mound of earth next to a gaping hole and the name emblazoned on the headstone was Mark Fulwright, rest in peace. Then I spotted more police tape a metre away around one of the graves on the next row. Swallowing, I took a step over to see. Scott McGuthrie.

Wrinkling my nose, I focused on Gareth. 'Why these two?' I asked. 'Why did you raise these two men as zombies?'

'Unghhh.'

Arse. I wanted answers. Unfortunately Gareth was in no position to give them. 'Unghhh,' he repeated, his eyes flicking to the right.

I followed his gaze, finally noticing that the untouched grave next to Mark Fulwright and in front of Scott McGuthrie belonged to someone who had once been Morag McAllan. Born 1761. Died 1799.

Suppressing a chill, I closed my eyes momentarily. In terms of necromancy, Gareth was a baby. He'd been aiming for Morag, one of his direct ancestors; instead he'd brought up two strangers whose only crime was being buried next to her. The catalogue of mistakes that had brought both of us to this point was staggering. I slumped down beside him.

'You fucked up,' I told him frankly. I leaned over, holding my breath as I slid my index finger along the blood on his cheek and held it up to the moonlight to get a better look. 'So did I.' I sighed and reached for my phone once again. 'You don't really have any idea about what you've unleashed, do you? No matter what your blood reveals, you're a dead man. There's no other option. Necromancy is too powerful and too uncontrollable. The only thing that remains to be seen is whether I'll be joining you.'

Gareth's expression was clouded with confusion. I turned on my phone to use its light and breathed out. His blood was a pure, beautiful red. That meant there was only one thing left to do.

'I've been so focused on my own impending doom,' I told him sadly, 'that I've not really thought about what it'll be like to end the life of another human being. If there were any other choice, I wouldn't do it. If you hadn't been such a damn good liar and hadn't managed to take things so far already, maybe there would have been another way out. But by raising two dead bodies, you've abused too much necromantic magic, Gareth. Whatever your reasons were, there's no way to contain what you've done now other than by killing you. I really, truly am sorry. I'll make it as swift and painless as I can.'

The confusion in Gareth's eyes was rapidly changing to terror. 'Unnnnngh!'

I ran a hand through my hair. I could do this. I *had* to do this. If I wasn't going to get a full explanation from Gareth then I'd have to deal with that. But there was one answer I had to get first.

'Blink once for yes and twice for no. Is this Alistair working with you?'

'Puh-lease,' drawled a voice behind me. 'I wouldn't work with that loony loser.'

And then something hit me on the back of the head and everything went dark.

Chapter Twenty Two

When I came to, it wasn't just the pain from my head where I'd been hit that was pulsing through me. I was hogtied, my ankles and wrists bound together, and the chafing of the rope, not to mention the uncomfortable position and the hard, damp ground, did not make for a happy Ivy. I was also incredibly disorientated. My vision swam and I had to shake my head to try and see properly. All that did was to make me even more dizzy.

As I gradually returned to full consciousness, panic and fear rushed through me. It wasn't a trickle, it was more like a deluge. It was still dark so I couldn't have been unconscious for long but it was long enough. I was in deep trouble.

Twisting around, I tried desperately to see what was going on. There were heavy grunts and mutters off to my right. To my left, there was another body. I craned my neck and spotted Gareth, trussed up just like I was. His eyes were on me, warning reflected in their depths. It was too late: my captor had already realised I was awake.

'Stop that,' he yelled. 'Or I'll hit you again!'

I blinked, focusing on his face. When I saw who it was, my mouth dropped open in astonishment.

'Yeah,' he sneered. 'You remember me. Well, I remember you too. And I don't like being treated like a fool.' He reached into his pocket and pulled out a crumpled packet, drawing out a cigarette and lighting it, his boyish features momentarily illuminated. 'You're not going to set these fags on fire,' he told me with a snort. 'You're not going to do anything.'

I stared at the teenager, the one who'd told me where to find Gareth when he was in the gym. It didn't make any sense. Neither did the fact that I'd been bested by a damn kid. So much for my supposed magical talent.

'Alistair?' I asked.

His lip curled. 'Yeah. You didn't really think that gormless Gareth was behind all this, did you? He's useless.' For good measure, he kicked Gareth's legs. The force he used was considerable and Gareth's sharp moan of pain attested to its violence.

I didn't understand. My gaze swung from Alistair to Gareth and back again. 'But...'

Interpreting my confusion for what it was, Alistair laughed. It was a humourless sound but I didn't think I imagined the tremble in it. 'Calls himself a McAllan. But he's not really. Tell her what you really are.'

Gareth mumbled to himself.

'Speak up,' Alistair yelled, his fury growing. I realised that this wasn't teenage angst expressing itself in a particularly ugly manner. The necromancy he'd already conjured up was taking root within him. Veins were bulging across his forehead and his eyes had a peculiar glazed look. How on earth had he managed to slip through the net? But I already knew the answer – he was a kid. The Order and the police wouldn't have given him a second thought. I doubted he'd even been interviewed.

'I was adopted,' Gareth said, his voice still barely above a whisper.

'His mother didn't want him. Ain't that right? Even when you were a baby she knew that you'd turn out to be nothing. Gave you up the first chance she got.'

I glanced at Gareth. 'You're brothers?'

Alistair answered for him. 'We are *not* brothers. The only reason Mum and Dad didn't get rid of him when I came along is that they felt sorry for him.' There was another long-drawn-out snort. 'He's a waste of space.'

Bloody hell. This was like a gender-swapped Cinderella. I wondered if my role was supposed to be that of the Fairy Godmother. Somehow I didn't think glass slippers and a pretty gown would do the trick.

'I should be grateful to him. If it wasn't for him, I would never have learned what I'm really capable of.' Alistair paused and gazed down at his hands. 'I can do amazing things. I *will* do amazing things.'

'Alistair, what you're doing is highly dangerous,' I said, shifting round and trying to get into a position where I could wriggle out of my bonds, or at least move my hands enough to cast a rune. 'The magic you're using comes at a high cost.'

'You're just jealous. When did any other witch manage to talk to the dead? When did anyone else do what I can do? At first it was just a bit of fun. I found an old book with her name in it.' He pointed towards the grave. 'And spells for stealing sheep. You've no idea how much fun it was watching him running around the countryside after those stupid creatures. Got him out of my way as well.' Alistair smiled in smug self-satisfaction. 'And he got the blame for losing them.'

I felt sick. This was what happened when magic appeared without the Order around to keep it in check and to make sure it wasn't abused. What had begun as a few cruel pranks had escalated into something entirely different. No one expected someone like Alistair suddenly to show magical talent, despite his ancestry. He'd kept it quiet and been able to use it for his own vindictive ends.

'Then you switched things up, didn't you?' I said, doing what I could to keep him talking so he was focused on himself rather than me. Bit by bit, I was managing to free my fingers. My right pinkie was loose but what I really needed were both thumbs. Right now they were bound tightly against my palms. I just needed a bit of wiggle room and I'd be able to get both Gareth and myself out of this. 'You used some kind of herblore on the sheep to cause hallucinations.'

Gareth started and stared at me but Alistair let out a crow of delight. 'You noticed?' He crouched beside me, an eager expression on his face that revealed his youth. 'What did you see? What happened? Was it really trippy?'

Deciding that he'd be disappointed if I told him it was just a bloodstain, and hoping that happy Alistair was more controllable than unhappy Alistair, I used Mazza's tale and embellished it further. 'I saw the devil,' I said, my eyes wide as if to convey my horror. One of my middle fingers slipped out of the bindings. I was almost there. 'He had horns and glowing green eyes and he tried to attack me with blood. I thought I was drowning. There was so much blood.'

A distant, wistful expression crossed Alistair's face. 'Blood. It took me a while to realise how important it could be. Old Morag's book kept going on about it. She didn't call it blood, though, she used the word *ichor*. At first I didn't pay it any attention. But then I got curious.' He smiled. 'Google is a wonderful thing. With *ichor*, I can do whatever I want. I've used sheep up until now but that's where I think I've been going wrong. Sheep's blood isn't good enough. Human blood will be much better. I was going to use Gareth's. I won't take too much. I won't kill him.' He paused, desperation leaking into his voice. 'I don't want to hurt anyone. I just want the magic that Morag can teach me.'

He looked at me. 'You're a witch. Your blood will be stronger than his. I can use it and this time I will succeed. It will be Morag herself I bring up, not those others. Then she can teach me more about who I really am and what I'm capable of.'

Given how long old Morag had been in the ground, I doubted she'd be teaching anyone anything other than how to run away very, very fast.

Thinking quickly, I looked Alistair directly in the eyes and tried to convince him that what he was doing wouldn't work. At the same time, I shifted round with small jerky movements. I'd almost freed my thumbs but they wouldn't do me any good if I started cramping up after being tied like this. I had to be ready to attack.

'Blood won't help. You know that the first body you raised killed someone. By doing what you did, you caused the death of an innocent man.'

'That wasn't my fault! He shouldn't have been up here!'

Ignoring Alistair's desperate attempt to blame his victim, I persisted. 'His name was Benjamin Alberts. He had his whole life ahead of him and your actions meant he died alone and in pain. It was a brutal way to go. Gareth will tell you that.'

'I've got more control now! That won't happen again.'

I shook my head. 'No, Alistair. You have less control now, not more. You're an inch away from the magic taking you over completely. You'll destroy yourself in the process. You were talking about blood. What colour is yours?'

Alistair's eyes were shifting from left to right. I could see from the expression in them that he wasn't going to believe me. He didn't *want* to believe me. 'Red, of course.'

'Are you sure?' I pressed. 'Because I wasn't lying when I said that necromancy was dangerous. If your blood has even the faintest tinge of black then it's already too late. The power you've unleashed will destroy half this land. Not just me and Gareth, but your parents. The town of Tomintoul and everyone around it. You're releasing hell, Alistair. You need to stop.'

What I didn't mention was that whether his blood was black or not, it was the end of the road for him. I doubted that would go down well.

Alistair spun round with a flounce. The momentary freedom from his gaze was exactly what I needed. With one last jerk, I managed to get not only my thumbs but also my fingers free enough to perform the rune I required. In three heartbeats, my bonds were loose enough for me to escape fully.

I remained cautious, however, and stayed in place so that Alistair wouldn't get suspicious and attack. He already had necromancy to his name; there was no telling what other magical abilities he could boast of. I was determined not to give him the chance.

When he turned back to face me, he was holding a long-bladed knife. There was a bleat and I realised that a few graves away there was a tied-up sheep: Alistair's Plan A before Gareth and I had foolishly presented ourselves. He brandished the knife and for one horrified second I thought he was going to plunge it into one of us. Then he lifted it up and sliced the back of his own hand, blood immediately welling up along the cut. He held his hand aloft.

'See?' he declared. I peered through the gloom and relief washed through me. Alistair's blood looked as natural as mine. The necromantic magic hadn't taken him over just yet. There was still time. 'This is proof that you're lying. My blood is as red as yours. But it's yours that will be spilt this night.'

Not if I had anything to do with it. Unable to waste any more time and regardless of the consequences, I raised my hands and threw out an attack rune. This one was designed to take no prisoners.

Alistair let out a high-pitched cry, one hand going immediately to his throat as his windpipe closed off. He dropped the knife and it fell to the ground with a dull thud. If I'd thought he was going to give up because he couldn't breathe, however, I was sorely mistaken. Still scrabbling to breathe, he ducked his head and barrelled towards me just as I got up to my feet.

Despite my best efforts to avoid cramp, I was wobbly enough to sway and half collapse on one knee, allowing Alistair the time he needed to smack into my chest and knock me down on top of Gareth. I couldn't maintain my hold on the magic and Alistair's breath was released. He spun round for another attack but his magic was too clumsy.

I flung out a ward rune, creating a protective barrier around both Gareth and me. Alistair rammed into it but he didn't know of any way to break it down apart from brute force. It held, shimmering in the night air.

He let out a curse and spat. Then he turned once more and walked over to the knife. He picked it up, his finger touching the tip of the blade as if to test it.

'Ivy,' Gareth said in a strained voice.

'Shhh.' My attention was on Alistair. When he made a beeline for the sheep, I hissed and dropped the ward. I stalked forward, throwing a rune out behind me to loosen Gareth's bonds. 'Leave the animal alone, Alistair.'

The sheep bleated, as if it knew what was coming.

'Everything else is ready,' he muttered. 'I just need the blood and the words and then I can set Morag free.'

'Morag is at peace,' I told him. 'She's no longer there. What lies beneath that headstone is just a shell.' In fact, surely she was nothing more than bones by this point. Even if he did bring back to claw her upwards, I reckoned her skeleton would collapse before it took a single step. At that point, though, it wasn't Morag's corpse that worried me it was what would happen with Alistair's magic if he succeeded.

Alistair started to mutter as the night itself filled with his power. It was so strong I could almost taste it. It was now or never.

There was a faint whoosh of air on my nape and Gareth burst forward. He tackled Alistair and they both fell to the ground. I darted forward to grab the knife but they rolled away from me, grunting – and then the entire area was bathed in bright light. What the hell?

Both Alistair and Gareth froze, as startled by the light as I was. A voice boomed out and I spotted several shadowy figures towards the end of the line of graves. 'Keep going! Don't stop because we're here!'

Morris Armstrong. And not just him: there was a cameraman, pointing the lens in our direction, and the white faces of both Barry and Amy staring at us.

'This is not a damned television show!' I yelled.

'You're right!' Armstrong called back. 'This is better!' I heard him mutter an aside to Barry '*Enchantment* might be down the toilet but with this kind of footage our careers aren't over. Not by a long shot.'

I briefly closed my eyes. This was all my fault; this was what I got for trying to warn them what was happening. The idiots had probably put their numbskull brains together to discuss what I'd told them and decided to track Barry's car. I'd have thought Amy would have known better. Their interference was the last thing any of us needed.

Fortunately Gareth recovered quickly. Taking full advantage of Alistair's shock, he lunged desperately for his hand and wrestled the knife from him. Gripping it tightly, he sprang to his feet and backed away. 'You don't need to do this, Alistair. You don't want to do this.'

I walked up to Gareth's side. 'Give me the knife.'

'An hour ago you were going to kill me, Ivy.' He didn't look in my direction.

'I'm sorry.' My words fell hollow. 'There wasn't any choice.'

'So you're going to kill Al instead? He's just a kid.'

I reached over and took the knife from him, relieved that he let it go. 'Just a kid who's bullied you. Who was prepared to kill you. Who has hurt your sheep.'

'He's a teenager.'

'That doesn't excuse him.'

Gareth's voice dropped to a whisper. 'There's still hope for him. He's only fifteen.'

I passed a hand across my eyes. Gareth was right: Alistair *was* just a kid. Who was I to pass judgment on him? I'd done things I wasn't proud of when I was that age. I defied anyone to put their hand on their heart and say they'd been teenage angels. But what Alistair was doing was different to a few childish shenanigans. This wasn't a bit of graffiti or drinking alcohol or breaking a window.

'I don't need you to stand up for me,' Alistair yelled at Gareth.

'He's a child, Ivy.'

I sighed.

Gareth persisted. 'Our parents haven't been any kinder to him than they were to me. He's desperate to prove himself and he wants attention. He's not evil.'

I had my doubts about that. I stared at Alistair, looking past the furious bravado. Immature eyes looked back at me with a mixture of fear and defiance.

'Give him a chance,' Gareth urged.

'It's not as simple as that,' I whispered. I knew what I had to do.

'Ivy...'

I raised my hand to hush him. Alistair was on the edge of being consumed by the magic he'd unleashed but his blood was still red. He'd not gone so far that his death wouldn't contain the power. If he'd pushed ahead with trying to raise Granny Morag it would have been too late but he'd not managed it. And he couldn't have known what horror his actions would have created. Except ... he knew what had happened to Benjamin Alberts. *His* zombie had done that. A man had died as a result of this child, whether he'd intended that death or not.

I pulled out the incantation scroll from under my shirt and un-furled it. Then I glanced at Gareth. 'You need to promise me that you'll get him help. That you'll do everything in your power to stop him from using magic without appropriate supervision.'

'I will.'

'He can't stop me!' Alistair shouted. 'No one can stop me!'

'I promise, Ivy,' Gareth said, ignoring his brother's rant. 'I'll speak to the Order first thing in the morning and we'll get him what he needs. He's an angry young man but I know his heart is good.'

I still wasn't convinced but I knew I couldn't kill him. I couldn't kill a kid. 'If he hurts anyone else, with or without magic...'

'He won't.'

'Ask for Raphael Winter. He has the patience of a saint. If anyone can help Alistair then he can.' I took a deep breath. And then I started to read. '*Per potestas penes me iubes me in magica.*'

'What is she doing?' Alistair screeched. 'What is that witch doing?'

'*Et tollet a vobis eo quod habetis.*' Goosebumps rose up along the length of my body.

Morris Armstrong nudged Barry in the ribs. He coughed in response and opened his mouth. 'Ivy!' He started forward then, when Alistair flung an irate look in his direction, seemed to think better of it and fell back again. 'Can you tell us what you're doing? What kind of spell is this?'

'*Ego relinquam vos...*' My heart rate increased just as Alistair clutched at his own chest.

'What are you doing?' Gareth shouted. 'You're hurting him!' He grabbed hold of my arm but I shoved him away.

'*...et irrumabo magicae...*'

Alistair let out a high-pitched scream. My knees trembled as my veins filled with power. I could feel it surging through me. Everything else around me dimmed and there was a dull roar in my ears. I sensed Gareth yelling again and Armstrong, Barry and Amy shouting. I dismissed them all. I was almost done.

'*...intrinsecus cava erat.*' The scroll fell from my hand. Magic thrummed through me and I felt my body being lifted upwards. I stretched out arms as far as they could go. Dying wasn't as bad as I thought it would be. In fact, with the euphoria that was coursing through me and increasing, I could have started to enjoy it. Of course, that was exactly when the pain started.

My little toe tingled. Then it hurt. It wasn't like a stubbing your toe kind of pain, it was more like the pain that would make me saw my entire foot off just to get it to stop. My mouth opened in a silent scream as the pain began to move, travelling up my leg and spreading up and up and up. I was on an all-encompassing rollercoaster ride of screeching, mind-numbing physical anguish. It ripped through my body and my muscles jerked impossibly in every direction. My heart was beating so fast it felt like it would burst out of my chest.

From beyond Armstrong and his little group, I thought I saw Winter sprinting towards us through the gloom and the graves like a demon on speed. Hallucination or otherwise, I still managed to smile. That man really ought to learn the pleasures of a slow stroll.

'I love you,' I whispered.

'Goodness,' said the disembodied head of Benjamin Alberts' floating next to me. 'And we've only just met.'

For a very long time after that, I was aware of nothing else at all.

Epilogue

Bellows was shaking. It might have been with anger or it might have been with fear. Either way, Winter didn't really care. 'You abused your position to take advantage of several younger women. You assaulted them.'

'Nobody said no!'

'Oh, I think we'll find they did.' Winter leaned forward. 'You tout yourself as a magical consultant. You pass yourself off as a witch. That means we can try you under Order jurisdiction, rather than the normal courts.' He allowed himself a small smile. 'Our methods and punishments are somewhat ... harsher.'

Bellows blinked and paled. 'I'm not in the Order! I'm not even a witch! I barely have any magic at all!'

'That's not what you tell everyone.'

'I'm lying!'

Winter knitted his fingers together in satisfaction. 'Indeed you are.' He eyed Bellows. 'Why are you using necromancy?'

'What?'

'You're raising the dead, Trevor. You're responsible for at least one death.'

Bellows bolted to his feet. 'I bloody well am not! Okay, I blackmailed Belinda. Okay, I might have seduced some of the crew members. But I have never tried to raise a corpse!'

Winter's eyebrows shot up. 'Seduced? Is that what you're calling sexual assault?'

Bellows began to bluster and babble. Winter would have stayed to listen but frankly he'd had more than enough. Trevor Bellows was a bastard and he deserved to be locked up for a very long time but Winter knew that when he'd denied the necromancy, he'd been telling the truth. Bellows' alarm was genuine.

Winter wasn't surprised. Regardless of what Ivy had suggested, the sleazy supposed witch simply didn't have the magic to pull off those kinds of spells. He stood up and walked out while Bellows continued to talk. Plonker, as Ivy would say.

Out in the corridor, a familiar floppy-haired witch pushed himself off the wall and bounded forward. 'Adeptus Exemptus Winter! How's the interrogation going?'

Winter glared at Tarquin Villeneuve. 'Fine.' He pushed past him. Dawn wasn't far off and he could do with a few hours' sleep before he went to check on Ivy. The last thing he needed was this idiot getting in his way.

'Wait! There's something I have to tell you!'

Winter rolled his eyes and halted, reluctantly turning round. 'What?'

'I made that vial. The one Belinda Battenapple had round her neck.'

'I know. So what?'

Villeneuve was nonplussed. 'Well, my talent is obvious. I think I would be an excellent candidate for Arcane Branch. In fact, I have a few ideas for questions you should ask Mr Bellows.'

'Good for you. But Arcane Branch is full. I suggest you put your ... talents to use elsewhere.'

Villeneuve thrust out an arm to stop him from moving away. Winter stared at it in astonishment. 'What on earth do you think you're doing?'

'You need to listen to me, Adeptus. I don't know what Ivy has said about me but I can assure you that I have nothing but integrity and...'

Winter sighed. 'Shut up.'

Villeneuve gave him a knowing wink. 'You like her, don't you?'

Winter growled, 'What are you wittering on about?'

'Ivy.' Villeneuve smiled, flashing white, even teeth. 'I can understand it. She does have a certain allure, doesn't she? And I can tell you from personal experience that blondes definitely do have more fun.'

Winter bunched up his fists. Unfortunately, Villeneuve wasn't done and clapped him on the back as if they were the best of friends.

'I'm prepared to step out of your way and let you have her. It's the least I can do for an Adeptus Exemptus like yourself. Of course,' he added, 'I wouldn't expect anything in return. You wouldn't have to put in a good word for me at Arcane Branch. Not that it wouldn't be welcome but I believe in hard work and earning the position I deserve.'

Any second now, Villeneuve would receive exactly the position he deserved. 'You will step out of the way,' Winter demanded in a tone that would have sent almost anyone else – Ivy included – running for cover.

'Sure. Anyone with half a brain can see how much you like her. It's the way your eyes follow her when you think she's not looking.' Villeneuve's smile changed to a smirk, as if suggesting that something lascivious went through Winter's mind every time Ivy appeared.

'Maybe,' Winter said through his rising anger, 'Ivy would like to decide for herself. Maybe I don't need you to step out of the way and neither does she.'

'Whoa, chillax, Adeptus! It was just a suggestion.'

Chillax? Was that even a word? Winter had never been prone to violence but he was itching to wipe the smile off Villeneuve's face. He took a deep breath, counted to three, then turned and started to walk away again.

'Did you ask Trevor Bellows about the spells he's been practising in between filming?' Villeneuve called.

Goddamnit. Winter stopped. This time he didn't waste his time turning. 'What spells?'

'You should ask him. All I know is that he's been punching above his weight and trying things he should know better than to attempt. He's still in the interrogation room. The police won't mind if you speak to him again.'

Something was going on here – and Winter didn't think it had anything to do with Trevor Bellows. He decided he'd shake the truth out of Ivy's stupid ex-boyfriend and damn the consequences.

'Meow.'

He glanced over. Brutus had appeared in an open window to the left and was peering at Winter with an uncharacteristic wide-eyed stare.

Abandoning Villeneuve, Winter strode over. 'What is it? Is it Ivy? Is she alright?'

Villeneuve chuckled. 'You're not expecting the cat to answer, are you?'

'Man,' Brutus said. 'Go.'

'Go where? The hotel?' Terror coursed through Winter's veins.

Villeneuve stared. 'Did you throw your voice, Adeptus?'

Brutus gave him a withering look and returned his attention to Winter. 'Ivy is positioning herself in severe and immediate jeopardy. She has departed the hotel in order to locate some local human named Gareth and is under the impression that she will not return from this encounter. One might suggest that you leave this place post haste and go to her aid.'

Shit, shit, shit. 'Where exactly did she go, Brutus?'

'A farm. I believe the name is McAllan? If she does not discover her quarry there, she believes he will be at the cemetery. She departed over an hour ago. You must hurry.'

Brutus was still talking when Winter sprinted for the door. Villeneuve started to shout, 'Wait! You can't go! Ivy doesn't want you to!' There was a pause. 'Ouch! You've pierced through my damn flesh! You bloody cat, what did you do that for?'

Winter burst outside just as his phone started to ring. Thinking it might be Ivy, he answered it.

'This is Iqbal,' Ivy's friend burst out in a rush. 'Something's wrong. We keep trying to get hold of Ivy. She left a message asking about someone named Gareth. His counsellor is a friend of my ex and ... never mind. She called me because Ivy's not picking up. She said that Gareth's a good guy but she's worried about his family. There's a brother. Stepbrother or adopted brother or something like that. I don't know. Adeptus, you have to get to Ivy now. I think something's happening. I think...'

'I'm on my way,' Winter ground out. 'I'm on my way now.' He ran even faster.

***

Every time he reached a red light, Winter flicked a rune out towards it and changed it to green. He'd never normally condone such behaviour even in an emergency but this was different. Ivy was different. When he got hold of her, he'd throttle her. Then he'd hug her and kiss her. After that he might tie her up to ensure she never did anything like this again.

He told himself that the reason his hands were shaking was because of the adrenaline. If he recognised his fear for her he'd be a mess – and incapable of doing anything to help her. But Brutus had genuinely been worried. Winter drew in a ragged breath.

Locating the farm, and ignoring the dirt that flew up around the bike's wheels, he forced it up the narrow lane to the farmhouse at speed. He reminded himself that panic never helped anyone then he leapt from the seat without bothering to turn off the engine and hammered on the door. 'Open up!'

When the door didn't open immediately, Winter raised one leg and kicked it. There was a crash of splintering wood and he stalked inside. 'Ivy! Where the hell are you? Ivy!'

From out of nowhere a woman appeared and Winter's body tensed.

She brandished a shotgun in his direction. 'Get out of my house.' She raised the muzzle.

Winter's hand snapped forward and he yanked the weapon out of her grasp. 'Where is she?' he demanded. 'Where is Ivy Wilde?'

The woman's eyes were as wide as saucers. 'I don't know who you mean,' she stammered. 'No one lives here by that name. It's just me, my husband and our two boys – Alistair and Gareth.'

Gareth. Winter hissed through his teeth. 'Where is he? Where is Gareth?' He took a step towards her.

The woman obviously felt threatened because she stepped back and he could see her trembling. 'He went out after a sheep. It got lost. A woman came round looking for him. Blonde with crazy hair and crazier eyes. She...' Her voice faltered slightly at Winter's look. 'She went after him. She said he was a good friend of hers.'

'Where's your husband?'

She swallowed. 'In the pub.'

'And your other son? Alistair?'

'I ... I ... don't know. Out with his pals, maybe.'

Winter's fists clenched. 'And where exactly did Gareth go to find the sheep?'

'I don't know that either! I...'

He spun round, abandoning her to return to his bike. Ivy wasn't here. His next stop had to be Dead Man's Hill. With his fear increasing, he ignored the woman who had altered her course of stuttering fear to one of rage.

'You bastard! Coming into my house and threatening me! I'll have the police on you! My son can do magic, you know. He'll hurt you for what you've just done! He'll turn your insides out!'

Winter revved the engine and took off without once glancing back.

***

He was still a long way from the cemetery and the hill behind it when he saw the lights. As far as he could tell, they were man-made and nothing to do with magic. All the same, he continued to gun the engine. What the hell was Ivy thinking? What was really going on? Winter pressed down on the accelerator. He'd ask questions later.

The moment he reached the entrance to the graveyard, he flung down the bike. Its wheels were still spinning when he took off in the direction of the lights. There were shouts and screams, each one sending a bloodcurdling chill down his spine. Then he saw Ivy, suspended in the air above a small group of people, her face contorted in an expression of pain and horror.

No.

Winter ran forward, his hands raised. In quick succession he threw out every single protection rune he could think of. Each one bounced uselessly off Ivy's body. Her mouth opened as if in a scream and her body began to shake violently.

Winter sped past a kid, who was pulling himself up from the ground with a dazed expression, and headed directly to her. Her eyes moved to him and for the briefest moment she seemed to relax. Her lips formed three unmistakable words that made his heart stop. Then the life seemed to go out of her, like someone had flipped a switch.

He was less than a foot away when she dropped like a stone. Winter held out his arms and caught her just before she hit the ground. There was an odd, beatific smile on her face.

For one brief moment, her eyelids fluttered open and his hope flared. 'Benjamin?' she asked. Less than a second later, her body went limp and her eyes closed.

Doing his best to quash his panic, Winter laid her down gently. He couldn't feel a pulse. He dipped his head closer to her mouth. No breath. Shit. With his mouth dry, Winter began compressions, pounding on her chest. 'Call a fucking ambulance!' He breathed into her mouth. Then he continued compressions again.

'Let me help.' A youngish man with a Scottish brogue knelt down next to him.

Winter didn't stop what he was doing but raised his eyes for long enough to scan the man's face. 'Name?' he barked.

'G ... G ... Gareth.'

Winter gave Ivy another breath. Then he took half a beat to draw a rune and send the man flying backwards.

The kid let out a cry and ran towards him. 'Gareth! What did that bastard do to you?'

Winter paid them no further attention.

'Adeptus! I know first aid. We can work together.' Barry, Ivy's erstwhile producer, fell heavily to his knees and took over the compressions. All the while, Ivy's skin turned paler and paler and she didn't move once.

***

The smell of antiseptic clung to everything but it couldn't conceal the underlying stench of sickness and despair. Winter paced up and down the corridor, his shoes squeaking. Every time a door opened, he held his breath. It was never for him. There was still no news about Ivy.

He lowered his head and stared at his feet. He still didn't understand what had happened. Why had she gone out there alone?

'Adeptus Exemptus Winter?'

He sprang to his feet, only belatedly realising that it was Amy, the runner from *Enchantment*.

'Hi.' He slumped down again.

'Have you heard anything?'

He didn't trust his voice. He simply shook his head and sighed.

She thrust something in his direction. 'She dropped this after she...' Amy scratched her head awkwardly. 'You know. She was reading it out when it all happened.'

Slowly, as if moving through sludge, Winter took the scroll. He stared at the words, then at the tiny insignia at the bottom. The Order. Ivy had got this from the Order. As he tried to make sense of it, another door opened. It wasn't a doctor.

'Has anyone told you how she is?'

Winter looked up at the Ipsissimus. 'No.'

Amy swallowed. 'I should go. When she wakes up, tell her I'm thinking of her.' She scooted away down the corridor and out of sight.

'I'll talk to them,' the Ipsissimus declared. 'Someone must know what's happening.'

Winter stood up. 'You're right.' His voice was flat. He held up the scroll. 'Someone must know.'

The Ipsissimus looked at it then at Winter. He let out a long breath and took the scroll from him. 'Well,' he said heavily, 'I suppose the truth was going to come out sooner or later.'

'You gave this to her.'

The Ipsissimus inclined his head. 'I did.' Winter waited for more. The Ipsissimus sighed and sat down. 'Necromancy is a tricky beast, Raphael. You know that. If it's not halted in the early stages, the consequences are devastating. We needed a powerful witch on hand to stop the magic from taking hold. Your Ivy didn't hesitate.'

Winter didn't look at him. 'You should have come to me.'

'You are needed in the Order.'

A muscle throbbed in Winter's jaw. '*You* could have done it.'

'I would have if I could. Ivy understood the reasons why I didn't. Believe me, if I could have taken her place and been assured that the Order would remain standing and sane, then I would have.'

Winter gritted his teeth. 'She wasn't in the Order. We are trained for this, we accept this is our job. She was not part of that. You made her sacrifice herself. You used an innocent to fight your battle. And now she's ... she's...' He couldn't finish the sentence.

'Ivy Wilde was fully aware of the consequences.' The Ipsissimus was silent for a moment. 'She didn't tell you because she wanted to save you from having to do it yourself.'

Winter turned his head to look at him. 'She said that?'

'She didn't have to.'

Winter waited for several beats until he was confident he had his rage under enough control. Then he stood up. 'You treated her like cannon fodder. You used her. You didn't even have the courtesy to tell me what was going on or to give me the opportunity to take her place.' He shook his head. 'I cannot be part of an organisation that treats people like that.'

A furrow crossed the Ipsissimus's brow. 'Adeptus Exemptus Winter, I sincerely hope you're not about to do anything foolish. I'd like to remind you that we now have a young boy in our custody who is going to need our help. Ivy could have saved herself and instead she chose to save him. She even suggested that he go to you for help. We need you in Arcane Branch. *She* needs you in Arcane Branch.'

'No,' Winter said simply, 'she doesn't.' He lifted up his chin and looked the Ipsissimus in the eye. 'I hereby rescind my position and resign from the Hallowed Order of Magical Enlightenment with immediate effect.'

'You can't do that.'

Winter shrugged. 'I just did.' His voice hardened. 'Now get out. You don't belong here.'

'Take some time to think about this. Don't rush into anything. I understand that right now you're feeling raw but—'

'You don't understand anything. And I'm not going to repeat myself. Leave this place.'

The Ipsissimus got to his feet. He smoothed down his robes and nodded. 'Very well. When you change your mind, come and find me.'

'I won't change my mind.' Winter's tone brooked no argument.

The Ipsissimus waited a beat, as if he still expected a sudden change of heart. When none was forthcoming, he turned round and left.

Winter collapsed back into the chair. This was all his fault. He'd brought Ivy here. If he'd been paying more attention, he would have known what was going on. He was a damned fool.

Yet another door opened. This time Winter didn't even bother looking up.

'Are you here for Ms Wilde?' a voice enquired.

Winter's head snapped up. The doctor, wearing a white coat and a serious expression, was addressing him. He swallowed. 'I am. Is she going to be alright?'

She smiled.

About the Author

After teaching English literature in the UK, Japan and Malaysia, Helen Harper left behind the world of education following the worldwide success of her Blood Destiny series of books. She is a professional member of the Alliance of Independent Authors and writes full time, thanking her lucky stars every day that's she lucky enough to do so!

Helen has always been a book lover, devouring science fiction and fantasy tales when she was a child growing up in Scotland.

She currently lives in Devon in the UK with far too many cats – not to mention the dragons, fairies, demons, wizards and vampires that seem to keep appearing from nowhere.

You can find out more by visiting Helen's website: **http://helen-harper.co.uk**

Lightning Source UK Ltd.
Milton Keynes UK
UKHW011841200921
390901UK00005B/1528